WE THREE

ONE AND ONE AND ONE MAKES THREE

Lara Zielinsky

Supposed Crimes LLC • Matthews, North Carolina

ISBN: 978-1-944591-58-8

www.supposedcrimes.com

This book is typeset in Goudy Old Style.

HE WAS HANDSOME...

ERIC had blond hair mixed with strands of brown. She didn't think he colored it, since his mustache was similar. It was also trimmed neatly, and he wore his suit comfortably, a clue that he was used to wearing good clothes. She had looked him over pretty thoroughly when she'd turned to his voice in the art gallery.

SHE WAS BREATHTAKING...

JESS caught her breath. There was no mistaking that face; even with the unmasked lines of her bow-like lips and the tawny tan of her Latina skin, she was unmistakable. This was Elena from Eric's photographs. Jess's pulse sped up as she regarded the brunette.

THEY BOTH WANTED HER...

"Jess," Eric said, "was just refreshing our drinks."

"He's an incredible photographer," Elena said. Jess was deeply affected by the woman's lightly accented tones. The woman's lips curled into a secret smile while she held Jess's gaze. "It isn't just the camera that gets so deep inside you," she added.

Elena's fingers drifted across the bar top. Tingles erupted up Jess's arm on contact and flowed into her chest. Stifling a moan, Jess rolled her bottom lip between her teeth.

"Perhaps I might still have a chance?" Elena said, her gaze staying on Jess. "Making out is hot, but sometimes I do love to *fuck*." The last word was so bare, spoken huskily. Seductive.

ALL SHE HAD TO DO WAS SAY YES.

ACKNOWLEDGEMENTS

Thanks go to many for helping me return to publishing stories. To the people at Supposed Crimes: Christy, you're the best for taking a chance on this different kind of story; Corrine, your editing has made my writing better and smoother. Thanks to all my beta readers at AO3, especially AJ Nordall whose enthusiasm, detailed feedback and comments convinced me I was onto something special with these characters. Thank you to all my fans for sticking around through the slow years. I'm grateful for the continued support from all of you.

For John and Lisa, the dream lives.

CHAPTER ONE

HOLDING A mai tai for Elena and a scotch and soda on the rocks for himself, Eric passed through Club Caliente's instructional room, designated for the month as the art photography gallery. He tried to act like he was ignorant of comments being made by people clustering around the displays, but he was nervous. Photography had been a hobby for years. More recently, though, he had begun focusing on more sensual and erotic subjects, and some of his pieces were on display tonight.

Couples gravitated toward the artistic or partial nudes and photos with boudoir settings. A few had recognized his primary subject: his wife, Elena, even if she was wearing a mask in all the images, or only visible from the throat down. He and Elena had been members at Caliente for five years and had sex with a wide variety of people.

He hesitated when he saw a single woman studying his photo display. She was alone, quiet, head tilted with clearly deep interest. She wore a slightly ill-fitting black suit—the shoulders a little too wide and the hem a little too long on her body. She had the jacket pulled back, which revealed a crisp white oxford dress shirt, also slightly mis-sized. The woman's blonde hair, which looked like it might be quite long, had been knotted and secured at the back of her head with a claw clip. It was messy, but indescribably enhanced her attractiveness.

His artist's eye was intrigued to find out how deep her attractiveness went.

The closer he drew to her, the more he thought maybe the suit was a loaner from an indulgent boyfriend, who liked the more androgynous appearance of a woman in men's clothing. But the next detail he noted suggested she was not on a date, but undoubtedly alone. She carried herself defensively, her hands in her pockets, her shoulders a little hunched, weaving a bit as if to keep her surroundings in perspective at all times.

Despite the music layered through the space from both the dance floor and the private club beyond the gallery walls, his footsteps echoed on the parquet. Her expression when she turned on him was that of a deer in headlights, but he kept moving forward. She wasn't just pretty; she was *breathtaking*. He had to meet her.

Her face was carved and thin, shaped by broad, arching brows. High, curved cheekbones swept down to where her jaw angled into a pointed chin. It was the most defined heart-shaped face he thought he had ever seen. She could have modeled for classically illustrated European fairy tales.

Her hair was pale gold, and her skin cream. Her lips were a natural pink, and unpainted, not even wearing a lip gloss. Crystal clear green eyes darted between his while she tried to discern his motives.

Eric cleared his throat and asked, "Do you like photography?" He nodded toward the photograph in front of her.

The blonde woman turned away without immediately answering. She returned to studying the photograph, and Eric's fascination with her grew. She was young, possibly only in her early twenties, but her gaze was so serious, he briefly wondered if she was also a photographer.

Finally she spoke. "They're... not what I expected. The... This one is so... romantic." Her tone was hesitant, as though she carefully considered each word before voicing it. Okay, so she wasn't a photographer, but she was deeply affected by the work.

Eric's body tightened in surprising anticipation, not necessarily of sex, but being turned on by the woman's intelligence; her body was merely a bonus. His grin was a bit exultant, but he let it come anyway. "Thank you. That photo is one of mine. I'm Eric."

She looked at a few nearby photographs and seemed to make a connection in her head. "Your model is very beautiful. Exotic."

Eric smiled again. "El is... well, she's... one of a kind."

The blonde gazed back at the photograph again. Her gaze traced Elena's body. His wife had posed on her left side, head against her upraised hand, eyes just a touch downward, enough so that she looked through her lashes at the camera. *Come here*, she seemed to say from slightly parted lips.

When he turned back to take in the blonde's reaction, he noticed the pulse in the blonde woman's throat throbbed, and her left hand opened wide and closed again slowly. *Oh*, he realized, *she's attracted to Elena*. That was a delightful discovery.

He spoke again. "I'm glad the photograph interests you. It's for sale, tonight's gallery is fundraising for the local domestic abuse center."

"Sale? I..." The blonde shook her head. "I... I couldn't buy it. It's just... really pretty."

Eric tried a soft-pitch line, hoping he wouldn't come off like a creeper. He'd at least like to know her name. "So are you. What's your name? Would you like to pose sometime?"

"Me? Posing?" The blonde again was surprised. "I'm not... Why would you waste film on me when... she is..."

"It's a lot of fun with the camera these days. No film. If we don't like it, it's just bytes to delete." Eric wished he had a card to give her. The more he looked at this woman, the more he wanted to photograph her. *Would she enjoy posing for him, or posing with Elena?*

Eric pleasantly stiffened at the images his mind conjured. He added, "You could meet Elena at least? She'd love to meet you."

"I could..." He read her expression, briefly distant, as though thinking it over. She looked at him more directly after a moment and seemed to be judging him. "How long has she been modeling for you?"

He reflected on his wife with a widening smile. "Just a couple years." He gestured to the photograph and recalled the session. "She planned out this whole shoot." Elena had played out a seductive scene while he snapped away, crossing the mattress with the sinewy grace of a cat, only to lay back, part her legs, and give him a perfect view of her fingers sliding in and out of herself. Above the frame of his camera, her eyes had darkened almost black, and she whispered "fuck me" repeatedly, until he turned off the auto-snap and buried his face between her thighs to lick up all that creamy and luscious cum.

He came back from his vision to find the blonde studying him curiously. "I got very lucky."

"Seems like you did." The blonde's thoughts were so clearly telegraphed that Eric was unsurprised by her words when they did come: "I would like to meet El... Elena."

"She's here tonight," Eric said easily. "We came for the opening of the gallery."

"So that's why you have two drinks," the blonde said, and her gaze drifted downward from his.

He blinked and chuckled upon looking to his own hands, indeed still holding drinks. The ice in his scotch was mostly melted. *Wow, he'd been talking a long time.* "I'm going to have to get these replaced."

"I can do that for you."

"Oh, no, actually, could I buy you a drink?"

"No drinking for me, I'm tending the bar. Well, I'm Gus's backup, anyway," she said.

Eric smiled wider; he'd learned something. "Hey, all right, so you work for the club. That's interesting. What's your name?"

"I... my name's Jess."

Eric smiled. "Very nice to meet you, Jess."

Jess moved quickly, trying not to put her head down—she wasn't bulling her way through a crowd. She glanced back once to see Eric still following her. The man was quite handsome, blond hair mixed with strands of brown. She didn't think he colored it, since his mustache was similar. It was also trimmed neatly, and he wore his suit comfortably, a clue that he was used to wearing good clothes. She had looked him over thoroughly when she'd turned to his voice in the art gallery.

Though aware his words were an attempt to pick her up, Jess hadn't felt awkward. He had a polite manner. He hadn't come off as shallow or desperate. This Elena, his model, seemed to be a real person, and he was quite taken with her. Jess thought this made him nothing more than he appeared: a photographer with genuine interest in her posing for him. Though she wouldn't be averse to other more intimate activities, either.

He might make a nice nightcap after last call and she closed the bar. If the nightcap could include his model, Jess thought she'd really enjoy that. The sensuality and hunger in the model's dark brown eyes had been pulling Jess in and making her feel a need for contact ever since she first laid eyes on the photographs. She was very open to the idea of sex without strings.

Then Eric had gotten that distant memory-filled look when he talked about his model. The way it seemed, from both the words and the photographs, he really knew the brunette, not only as sexy flesh, but as a person.

Such a man didn't seem like he'd treat women like objects in bed, and Jess's imaginings went from just sexy times with Elena to including Eric.

When she had stepped behind the bar, Jess took the glasses from Eric's hands. "Have you and Elena come to the club often?" She was dumping the glasses out, waiting for his response, when she realized she hadn't asked him what the drinks were. Her question came out over his own response to her first one:

"What were you drinking?"

"Elena and I have been members for about five years."

Eric chuckled, the sound throaty and bemused. "Elena had a mai tai. Mine's scotch and soda on the rocks." He leaned on the bar. Jess felt warmed by his interested study of her work.

"Here you are!"

Jess looked up at the female voice just as a woman reached the bar. She caught her breath. The face was familiar, even with the unmasked lines of her bowlike lips and the tawny tan of her Latina skin, she was unmistakable: *Elena*, Eric's model. Jess's pulse sped up as she regarded the brunette. Dazed, she placed the two completed drinks on the bar top.

"Of course," the brunette said, continuing to speak to Eric, but she was looking directly at Jess. "You're chatting up a beautiful woman."

Elena leaned one elbow on the bar, and glanced from Jess to Eric now, her smile bright. The angle of her arm tipped Jess to the fact that she and Elena were of similar height. "Introduce us?" Elena's tone held invitation.

"Jess," Eric said, "was just refreshing our drinks."

"He's an incredible photographer," Elena said. Jess was deeply affected by the woman's lightly accented tone. The full bow lips curled into a secret smile as she held Jess's gaze. "It isn't just the camera that gets so deep inside you," Elena said.

Elena's fingers drifted across the bar top. Tingles erupted up Jess's arm on contact and flowed into her chest. Stifling a moan, Jess rolled her bottom lip between her teeth. "Perhaps I might still have a chance?" Elena said, her gaze staying on Jess. "Making out is hot, but sometimes I do love to fuck." The last word was so bare, spoken huskily. Seductive.

More tingles—Elena's fingers still stroked Jess's—flooded into Jess's groin. She shifted and dislodged Elena's touch.

"I—yeah." Jess's body was in pleasant chaos. She had seen a cat playing with catnip once, a long time ago. Her body felt like that now—writhing, wanting to wrap herself around something or someone. Too warm. Drunk. "Me too."

Elena's smile came closer, her brown gaze continuing to hold Jess captive. When the brunette lifted her body partially over the bar and leaned forward, Jess got a brief view down the deep V of Elena's cinnamon-red cocktail dress of modest breasts cupped in black lace. Then soft lips drifted against Jess's cheek and she could only close her eyes to absorb the pure sensuality of the contact.

"Thank you," Elena murmured against the shell of Jess's ear, "for the drinks."

Jess's heart hammered in her chest. Elena slid back off the bar, brown gaze finally dipping away and releasing Jess. The brunette smiled warmly at her but then pulled Eric away from the bar. Watching them go, Jess saw Elena take the mai tai from Eric. The straw disappeared between dark lips, and half the liquid in the glass disappeared in a single pull as if the brunette had been parched.

Throat suddenly dry, Jess reached for a water glass. Unfortunately the glass she grabbed held soda water, bitter and flat. She wrinkled her nose and spat it back, then dumped the glass's contents in the disposal.

When she looked up again, a balding patron had approached and held out an empty glass. "Horse's neck, please."

Jess smiled and poured the ingredients together. Done, she nudged the glass toward him on the bar top and quoted him the price for a single-spirit mixed drink. She collected his cash and separated the couple dollars tip to her own pocket while he walked away.

The remainder of the evening passed uneventfully for Jess. She filled drink requests, cashed out tabs, and politely deflected passes. Nearing last call, Jess spotted the photographer, Eric, again. He and his brunette model, Elena, were walking with another couple.

Elena walked holding the hand of a bald thick-bodied Hispanic male who appeared to be around fifty years old. A willow-thin blonde woman held Eric's arm. From the crow's feet and tight throat, Jess guessed the woman's age to be also around fifty.

The foursome exited through a doorway at the far end of the gallery room. A small placard posted on the wall beside the door announced the group's destination: *Playrooms.*

She recalled then that both Eric and Elena had flirted with her. The opportunity to get together with Eric and Elena was slipping away. She wished briefly for another break, so she could find them and let them know she was interested.

"It's almost last call."

Jess turned to see Gus walking toward the bar. An older man, with a closely trimmed salt-and-pepper beard and mustache, Gustav, or simply Gus, was the club's head bartender. He had been circulating since midnight, checking the supplies at various water and refreshment stations and accounting in the stockroom, which had left her alone as the primary bartender for most of the last two hours.

She smiled at him, not pausing in wiping down the bar top with a clean damp rag. "Receipts have been good," she said. "I even made some tips."

"Beautiful woman bartenders always makes men tipsy." He was smiling, and his tone was teasing. He quickly crouched to account the bar's open bottles. "Any trouble?"

Jess shook her head. She had watered down very few drinks. The men who came by had been polite, usually buying drinks for themselves and someone else. The few who bought single drinks were chatty, usually enough for her to tell whether they had too much to drink. But they were all complimentary of her, not crass in their flirting, or rude. "No, no trouble. Everyone's being very nice. They probably don't want to scare the 'new girl' away."

"Did you enjoy your break earlier tonight?"

Jess nodded. "I felt a little underdressed, but I enjoyed the gallery art."

"The photography?" Gus asked, standing again, seemingly satisfied. Jess worked next to him, efficiently clearing traps and setting glassware, mixing cups, and jiggers into a bussing basin for transport to the club kitchen for full cleaning.

"Yeah, I always thought a crowd like this would prefer—" She paused, searching for the right word. She finally settled on the most basic description. "—porn."

Gus pulled a towel from his shoulder and started to wipe down the bar. She went on, sharing her surprise.

""But it was really... nice. Sexy. Very erotic, but really...

romantic. I met one of the photographers." Jess lifted the now full dish basin and stepped back from the bar. After locking the bar's cabinets, Gus followed her to the club's kitchen, holding open the service door for her.

"One of the swingers here?"

"Yeah, I guess. He and his model were through a few times."

"His model? Not his wife?"

"They didn't wear rings," Jess said.

"Not everyone does," Gus replied.

"I didn't know that."

"Genevieve and I wore our rings as necklaces," he said, pulling out the chain from under the collar of his button-up shirt.

"Genevieve? I didn't know you were married."

"Gen and I were married more than forty-five years."

Jess winced. She was soon to turn twenty-five. She thought of Eric and Elena, who had looked to be in their thirties, and the couple in their fifties whom the two had obviously gone to play with. "So you were swingers to make your marriage more fun?"

"At first it was about that. This was the late 1970s. Free love was all the rage."

"Is swinging just wife swapping? Singles don't swing, right?" She tried to recall if she had seen any single people heading for the playrooms.

"Single men are often discouraged by the entry pricing. Like here, most places it's very high. Attendance policies at clubs are strict for singles, too, but I've seen some single men and women pay entry to clubs as a 'couple' and then spend most of the night playing with others. And single women are very popular with the couples."

"Do you still... play?" she asked.

"No. Why? Are you looking for a date?" He grinned.

She shook her head. "No," she said, "just wondering." Methodically she dried glasses before putting each one away into the cabinet above the stove. "Did you enjoy watching your wife play with other men?"

"We swapped with other couples, yes, but she was more interested in unicorns."

Curious at the term, Jess lost focus and accidentally clinked one glass against another when putting it away. Closing that cabinet, she glanced over her shoulder at Gus. "Unicorns?"

"A single female playing on her own, often bisexual. Very rare, hard to catch. Just like the mythical unicorn."

"Oh." Jess felt her thoughts spinning. A tingle in her stomach whispered what she wanted to do with all the new information. Resolutely, though, she bit her lip and finished her job.

In the early hours of the morning, after Gus escorted her to her assigned hotel room as a club employee, Jess carefully hung the borrowed suit and shirt to air. She washed her bra and socks in the sink, spreading the socks out to dry on the room's air control unit, and hung the bra on the showerhead. Finally, she dug out her tank top and boy shorts and crawled onto the single bed after slipping them on. She twisted and turned until the sheets wrapped around her legs. Her eyes drifted closed with the cool feel of the ceiling fan's breeze on her face and chest. She wondered if Elena was a unicorn. She wondered how formally attached Elena and Eric were. She wondered if she could have sex with one of them, or both of them. She wondered if she could be a unicorn, too.

One-night stands with men or women littered Jess's past. But it was always one at a time. She remembered having an argument once that being *attracted* to both men and women did *not* equate to needing orgies or threesomes. The idea had simply never turned her on.

However, the memories of interacting with Eric and Elena had Jess vividly imagining scenarios where all three of them were satisfyingly entangled. She put her hands between her thighs and sifted through ideas as she teased her own folds.

Eric was a quiet personality, maybe even introverted. The artist within was clearly a primary aspect of his personality. He'd been thoughtful when they talked; interested in her, but also, just as clearly, interested in what she had to say. Physically, too, he was her type—not beanpole lean nor overly chunky. He was a little more mannered than most of the men she'd slept with, and older than most of them, too.

Then Jess turned her mind to the whirlwind of Elena. The Latina had a bold, extroverted personality, enticing to Jess like a moth to a flame. Jess had particularly been drawn by the woman's Spanish accent. It shouldn't have been unique; Miami had a million Spanish-influenced accents that Jess had heard in just a few days. But there was a smooth deliberate enunciation to Elena's Spanish-accented English, which Jess imagined would be great delivering hot, sexy words. Or, *god... instructions.*

Coming hard on her own fingers at the thought, Jess knew if Eric or Elena came to the club again, she would make it clear she was interested in more than a photo shoot.

Elena pulled the cocktail dress off of her arms and down her front. She made a long study of her body in the full-length mirror of the master bedroom. *Thirty-five*, she thought, judging the soft plane of her stomach curving down into her pelvis, and the sleek muscles of her runners' thighs. *Not bad.*

She heard the shower shut off and then the sounds of Eric moving aside the curtain and stepping out of the bathtub. Elena smiled at her reflection and started to peel out of her lacy bra and stockings.

Still running warm after the night's activities, Elena relived their night at the club. It had been a while, since Eric's work schedule had become erratic. Carl was a satisfying fuck, reasonably good at foreplay, and he lasted long enough that Elena had managed two nice orgasms before he pulled out and she sucked him off. They'd lain back together on the king-size mattress in the semiprivate playroom. Mutually stroking and considering another go, they watched Betty suck Eric while he tongued her in a 69. They continued to watch as he fucked Betty—reverse cowgirl—to a screamer. Elena had been drawn to Betty's nipples twisting in Eric's fingers, but she was uninterested in more sex at the time.

Now, however, she was ready for Round Two.

Bending over and rolling her stockings off her toes, her garter still on, Elena felt Eric's slightly damp and warm hands spread over her exposed ass. She knew her vulva was easily visible between her legs, and Eric's sliding fingers massaged lower and lower until they dipped between her labia. She leaned forward, spreading out on the bed, and shifted her feet outward to open herself more. Eric's one finger became two.

Her pussy throbbed. Eric added a third finger, then the thumb of his other hand curved underneath and stroked her clit. She demanded "more" with a moan.

"Flirting with that blonde bartender and fucking Carl wasn't enough tonight, huh?" he murmured. He leaned between her thighs and his soft cock rubbed between her ass cheeks.

She shook her head. "Finger me," she said.

"Did you like watching Betty suck my cock?" Eric asked. "Did you imagine teaching the bartender how I like it done?"

An image of Jess flashed through Elena's mind's eye. The woman was shedding her suit and unbuttoning her shirt. A vision.

Would Jess have just handful-sized tits or bountiful boobs? Elena had seen women in suits with both when they were uncovered; some liked to hide in androgyny with cloth wraps, but some flaunted the lines between male and female by wearing men's clothes but keeping a feminine styling with lace and frills. Jess's suit had been neither. And a bit too big on her. So Elena couldn't decide which type Jess might be. But the images were making her stomach quiver and her pussy clench.

"Fuck me," Elena demanded breathlessly.

Eric now had three fingers pumping inside her. His thumb stroked just at the sides of her labia. "I think Jess could be interested," he murmured.

Elena gasped and groaned. Eric knew how much she used her imagination in sex and was still priming her. "Did you like seeing Betty rocking on my cock? Would you want to see me make Jess's breasts bounce like that? Or would you demand to fuck her first?"

Elena felt her passion rocket higher. *Damn.* Eric was hitting all her buttons now.

"Fuck, yes," she said, breathing hard. Her heart rapidly pounded; she moaned. Her imagination was fully charged. The memory of sweat glistening on Betty's skin made her nostrils flare as if she was filling her lungs once again with the scents of sex and sweat. Then the older blonde's face contorting in orgasmic pleasure morphed into Jess's face.

Eric now had four fingers in Elena, and the sound and feel of the heel of his palm slapping her mound fed her desire even more.

"Loved the way she moved," Elena said breathlessly. "Wanted to see her breasts so bad."

"Would you want to suck them?" he asked.

She licked her lips and squeezed her inner muscles on Eric's fingers. "Mmm-hmm." When his fingers left her, she whimpered, incoherent and needy.

Eric replaced his fingers with his cock. Elena pushed up on her palms and straightened her arms. She pushed back with her hips and his penetrations deepened.

"Fuck," she growled. "Fuck me."

Wrapping his arms around her waist, Eric's forearms pressed up under her breasts. His hips slapped into her ass with each drive of his cock. Deeply and repeatedly, he slammed his full length into her pulsing pussy.

"Eric," she breathed, mind spiraling on a sea of sensations.

"El." His moans joined hers. Then they both were coming. With staccato grunts, Eric held Elena still. Her muscles squeezed him, and his cock released his balls' load.

Grinding back, Elena demanded more.

Eric continued moving in her, even while his cock softened. The irregular motion sent aftershocks through her quivering body. When the frantic feelings waned, her limbs became limp and her body heavy. Eric picked up Elena and settled her into the middle of the bed. She curled up, inhaling and exhaling when her overheated body came in contact with the cool cotton sheets.

Eric slid on the bed and spooned her before pulling the bedsheet over them both.

Before sleep completely took her brain offline, Elena wondered when they might go back to the club and gauge Jess's level of interest in spending some sexy time together.

CHAPTER TWO

ERIC STRODE in quickly to the lobby of Club Caliente and spotted his friend Hector Melendez behind the registration desk. Hector and his wife, Maya, were the owners of the members-only adult sex club.

"Hey, Hector," Eric called.

Hector looked up from the papers he was shuffling and stood immediately, walking quickly out and around the doors and counter. "Ay, *mi amigo!* Your pictures are a hit!"

"So your message said," Eric replied briefly, to contain his excitement. He was supposed to be a mature adult, not an adolescent full of himself.

He was a few inches taller than Hector, so he kept a step or two back so neither of them had to awkwardly crane to look eye to eye. "It will be a good donation for the shelter, I hope."

"The buyer pay double for two prints, since I tell him they are one of a kind. This is your half." The club owner brandished a small wad of cash.

Eric looked at the folded bills Hector pressed into his hand. The outermost one was a hundred-dollar bill. Unfolding them, his eyes widened more and more as he added up the amounts in his head... "Six hundred dollars?"

"He purchased two."

Eric blinked. He tried to recall everyone he had talked to on

Saturday night about his photo prints. "Which two?"

"I have them in the office. He gave me other money to ship them."

Eric eagerly followed Hector behind the registration counter to the hotel's business office. There, on the desk, were two of his canvas-printed photos. He was not surprised by the buyer's first choice, not really. Elena had posed on the beach, but he had added layers in Photoshop to make it appear as if she were reclining not on warm Miami Beach sand, but inside a giant clamshell. He'd named the photograph *My Latin Venus*.

The other photo print was a more pedestrian piece of erotic photography, and largely untouched. Elena sat in the middle of rumpled sheets he'd arranged on the floor of their home playroom. Her legs were spread, her elbows rested atop her bent knees. Her hands were folded underneath her chin, supporting her very direct look at the camera. Her expression was intense, as if daring the viewer to look away from her eyes to the dark hairs curling around her sex, or the hanging mounds of her unencumbered breasts. But Elena was smiling, too, as if knowing the temptation not to ravish her was probably too much. It was an arousing portrait of a woman who knew very well how attractive she was.

Eric looked again at the wad of bills in his hand. He could buy a few more art photography add-ins for Photoshop. "I should treat El to a night out," Eric said.

"So, good?" Hector asked.

"Incredible," Eric confirmed. He tucked the bills into his pocket. "And I definitely need a drink."

"Hotel's bar is already open," Hector said. "We have a new bartender on days. She overlaps with Gus for the afterwork crowds."

Eric perked up. He immediately remembered Jess, and the blonde's polite receptiveness to his flirting. "Are you talking about Jess?"

"Yes. You met?"

"Saturday night at the opening."

"She does not seem your type," Hector said.

"I enjoy many types of women, my friend," Eric replied. "You know that."

"Ay, *mi amigo*, I do." Hector and his wife had been playmates of Eric's and Elena's frequently over the years. But, a couple years ago, Hector and Maya had gotten into BDSM play. From time to time, though, Hector scheduled a BDSM for Beginners seminar in one of the playrooms converted to a "dungeon." After one class, Eric and Elena had realized they simply did not enjoy it enough to seek it out.

Hector's words drew Eric's mind back. "Jess keeps to herself."

Eric had already guessed as much. "Well, I'm gonna get that drink. Then I have to get going. I have a hop to Falmouth tonight."

"You be safe up there," Hector said before sitting back down at his desk. Eric walked back out to the lobby and across it to the hotel bar.

Jess listened with half attention to the pair of businessmen having draft beers at the end of the bar. This area of Miami was such a hub for convention activity, she had already overheard enough to learn that both men were "looking for some action" before the end of some insurance conference. She had also discovered one had a wife and a two-year-old son. He was also a swinger of some experience and talked about having a "hall pass" from his wife, and money already set aside for playtime. The man with the Coors Light was single, however, and had lamented the pricing when he'd asked at the desk: "But single women get in damn near free."

"What do you have in bottles back there?"

Looking up from wiping the counter, Jess was immediately caught by blue eyes; she didn't hesitate to smile, immediately recognizing Eric. His good looks and his offer to shoot her had not been far from her mind over the last four days. "Hi," she said. "You want a beer, or something stronger?" She recalled he'd had scotch when at the nightclub.

"Just a beer. I have to fly tonight." Eric slid onto the stool in front of her.

Jess nodded and listed off the top dozen beers most men seemed to prefer. Eric chose a Shock Top. She retrieved the bottle, popped the cap, and presented it. "Anything else?"

"You got fries or chips?" he asked.

"Nachos with queso," she replied.

"I'll take an order of nachos, then." His smile was warm, and then quickly hidden behind the bottle as he lifted it to his mouth.

When she slid the nacho order in front of him, he looked down at it then back up at her. "Share with me?" he asked, then lifted a nacho with a tidy bit of melted cheese and held it out in invitation.

Jess took it from his fingers with her own. "I shouldn't," she said, but she did, enjoying the easiness of Eric's smile.

"It's just one chip," he said easily, taking another from the plate for himself. For a moment there was only the sounds of crunching while they both chewed. Finally, Eric cleared his mouth with another swallow from his beer. "It's Jess, right?"

Jess nodded, fishing for her water bottle under the bar's counter. When her mouth was clear, she dipped her head again. "You're Eric. Photographer."

"In my spare time," he answered. His smile disappeared behind his bottle again. "Speaking of, given any thought to my suggestion? My days off this week are Monday and Tuesday, so I am looking to shoot something." He finished his chips off quickly after a glance at his wristwatch. "Oops. I'll need my check."

While printing his check, Jess thought about how to respond. Now that the invitation had been repeated, she hesitated. Monday was a day off for her. She wondered if Eric knew that or had simply guessed because she worked late weekend hours, she was probably off on a weekday at some point.

Bringing the printout to him, she asked obliquely, "You're not shooting Elena?" He probably realized she was fishing for information about the brunette. Gus had pointed out how much people in this lifestyle appreciated clear communication. She wasn't comfortable being completely blunt, but she hoped Eric would understand her question's dual layers: *Yes, I'm interested in doing this with you—I'm also interested in Elena.*

"Elena is also free Monday," Eric replied. He pulled a cardboard coaster from a nearby stack and flipped it over to the unprinted back. "Call," he said, scribbling a number. "We'll set things up." He set the pen down across the coaster and stood. After swallowing the last of his beer, he smiled warmly at her and said, "I gotta fly."

It took two, almost three days before Jess made the call, though she had decided, yes, to seize the opportunity several times. The first time happened at 3:00 a.m. after closing the bar, which was decidedly *not* a good time to call. Then she decided when on a lunch break, not really noon and not dinnertime, but she didn't want to be calling when Eric was working. She definitely did not call that time after imagining Elena and Eric between her legs, then her between theirs. She'd fingered herself to orgasm instead in the middle of her bed, as dawn barely seeped in between the window blinds.

It was just about 7:00 p.m. on Friday night. Jess wasn't due to start her shift in the bar until 8:00. Now, she thought, was the perfect time. She'd snagged a wrap with meats and cheeses from the kitchen and warmed it in her in-room microwave. She was showered and dressed, so she wouldn't entertain thoughts of jilling off to the sound of Eric's voice on the other end. She lifted the coaster close and input the numbers into her cell phone. She had not wanted to make the call from the hotel's line so, so, with her tips that first week, she'd purchased a refurbished one and set up a cash-card account plan.

Jess listened to the line ring, heart thrumming.

"Hello, you've reached the Tan—"

Inhaling sharply at the sound of the female voice, Jess pulled the phone from her ear and ended the call with a hard poke. She tossed her cell phone onto the bed and jumped up, turning in the small space to stare at the device. *Elena!*

Before she could process further, her cell phone sounded, indicating an incoming call. Jess saw it was the same number she had called.

You want this, you idiot! She's calling back. Be honest. You were going to tell Eric yes. So tell her you want to meet up.

Jess exhaled and then fortified herself with a steadying inhale. She lifted the phone, pressing the green button as she did. "Hello?"

"I just had a call from this number?" Elena sounded puzzled.

"Hi. I... yeah. I... you probably don't... remember... me." Jess paused in her stuttering, inhaled and exhaled, and willed herself to be braver. "I'm... the bartender from Caliente? I... my name's Jessica?"

"Jessica?" Elena hesitated. "Oh, Jess. Hi."

Jess' heart rate slowed marginally as she absorbed the other woman's light and pleased tone. She tried not to sound like an idiot. "I... uh, Eric came by the bar earlier this week."

"Did he leave something?"

"No, well, yes. He left me this number. Said I should call to set up... a shoot. Maybe? I guess? Yes," Jess finished, trying to sound more certain. "I'd like to do it."

Elena's hum came through the line, and slipped down Jess's ear, into her throat, her chest, and then curled, like a warm baby rabbit fidgeting to get comfy, in the pit of her stomach.

"When?" Elena finally spoke.

Just as had happened on Saturday night, Jess was unable to immediately respond, luxuriating in the sound.

But talking on a phone was not the same as talking with a person at a bar. When the silence went too long, Elena's voice came tentatively on the line. "Jess? Are you still there?"

Blinking, Jess answered quickly, "Eric said something about being off Monday and Tuesday. I'm off—" She hesitated before adding eagerly "both days," and chose one. "Monday," she finished.

Elena's reply set off entirely new flutters in Jess's body. "Monday will be wonderful. He can pick you up on his way from the airport."

"Oh." Jess had been expecting an address, planning to figure out the Miami public transit to get to some photography studio in the city. "What... anything in particular I should... wear?" she finished weakly.

"That suit you wore Saturday night will be wonderful. Anything else I can loan you. Eric'll have to shower and change when he gets home, too."

"Oh." Jess saw her opening. "Maybe I should come separately... later, then?"

"Oh no, we are all coming together," Elena said, and her tone was equal parts laughter and seduction. The warm flicker of attraction Jess had felt to the brunette from Saturday night flared to hot life. "It's a date. Monday. Expect Eric around two. He'll ask for you at the desk."

"Okay." Afterward the line was quiet, and Jess held her breath.

"I look forward to seeing you again, Jess," Elena finished. Another moment of silence followed then, and before Jess could find words, she heard the line close.

The phone tumbled to the bed from Jess's numb hand. *Holy shit*, she thought, falling backward against the bed. *I have a date. A hot* date, if Elena's tone was anything to go on. She replayed the conversation over again, closing her eyes and breathing deeply.

An alarm startled her, signaling that Jess needed to report for her shift. Her legs were shaking when she pushed to her feet. She wondered idly, but with an excitement she hadn't felt in years, if she would be able to walk after Monday's activities. If just talking with Elena left her shaking, what would she do when—and she knew now with certainty it was when, not if—they had sex?

Elena ended the call when Jess did not reply. She bit her lip, trying to interpret Jess's few words and barely audible reactions. She had heard the other woman's breath catch several times, and the stumbles when she was speaking. She had thought the blonde experienced with flirting, since she'd been so easy with Eric, but now she wondered if Jess was too naive to really know what she wanted, despite being clearly swayed by Elena's flirting. It wouldn't be the first time Elena had miscalculated a prospective partner's experience.

The shower shut off, pulling Elena from her thoughts. Eric emerged from the master bath into their bedroom, his towel tucked around his waist and his chest hairs still matted and damp. He looked at her still holding the landline's wireless handset in her hand. She answered his unspoken question with one of her own: "You gave Jess our number?"

"She finally called." Eric smiled.

"I don't think she thought the number you gave was to the house. She hung up when I started speaking."

"Did she call back?"

Elena shook her head. "I called the number back." She looked down at the handset again then up at Eric. "Are you sure this is a good idea?"

"She's obviously new at this," Eric agreed. "But we're all just going to have some fun. She agreed to a photo shoot. So that's what we'll do."

Elena groaned. "I think I just complicated things."

"How?" He sat next to her and she couldn't help but inhale his clean scent, and felt it steady her.

"I told her you'd pick her up at the club, ask for her at the desk. When she suggested she come later..." Elena's voice trailed away, and she felt her cheeks warm. "I said 'we'd all come together'."

Eric laughed. "My seductress." He wrapped his arm around her shoulder and kissed her head. "You just keep being you, sweetheart. Jess is gonna have fun, and I'm pretty sure she's capable of making her own calls to stop. Go."

"Or go slow," Elena finished, her voice chorusing with his, as they completed their mantra together. As the words faded away, Elena smiled, once more feeling hopeful. "Monday can't come soon enough," she added.

"For Jess either, I'm sure," Eric said, again kissing her temple.

She leaned into his chest, resting her palm there and feeling his steady heartbeat. "What should I set up while you're away?"

"Weather's expected to be nice. Not too hot, and not raining. Why not plan a few nibbles around the pool?" She shot him a glance, and he smirked. "Hey, I can't help my mind wandering to some pretty nice pictures with her and you."

"You'd be shooting outside. So you won't need the lighting kits, unless we go until after sundown." He nodded. Elena continued, "Maybe I could put a float or two in the pool." She considered the state of the furnishings on the stone patio around the in-ground pool. "I'll run the pool cleaner. I should also clean the lounges with some Clorox, and buy new tanning lotion." She shook her head. "No, sunblock would be better. She is blonde and light-skinned."

"Should I make sure she brings a swimsuit?" Eric asked.

"You might tell her we have a pool. She is expecting some clothing changes for the photos. I told her to come in that suit from Saturday night. I also said I had things she could change into."

"You do like the way a good-looking woman wears a suit," Eric remarked.

Elena could not deny it. She had first seen Jess across the room talking with Eric as she mixed the drinks. The first thing Elena had noticed, after her blonde hair, had been the crisp white shirt collar and the soft shoulder lines of the black suit jacket. She'd drunk in the woman's appearance as she neared. Leaning close to change her drink order had also been when Elena first inhaled the woman's scent; "slightly sweaty, all-natural woman" was her favorite perfume.

CHAPTER THREE

THOUGH SHE had asked what to wear to the shoot, and been told to wear her work clothes, Jess studied her paltry selection of strewn on the made bed in her hotel room for something appropriate. What she had though was two pairs of extremely worn jeans, holes in the knees and tattered hems from wearing them in bare feet. Her few shirts were tees and tanks of varying stretched condition. Her only button-down was a long-sleeve men's-style large she'd pilfered from a previous bedmate. She did not want to be wearing *that*, she thought. Even slightly rumpled from her shift the night before, the suit and its accompanying button-down white shirt were the best choices for a professional photo shoot.

Semiprofessional, she corrected. Eric had pointed out that photography was only his hobby. Jess had gathered from the brief interaction at the bar that he had some other job that frequently took him out of town. Elena, too, had pointed out he would be picking Jess up "on his way back from the airport."

The hotel's bedside phone rang. Pushing her hair back from her face—she hadn't decided on up or down yet—Jess grabbed the handset. "Hello?"

Mr. Melendez said, "Eric Tanner is here. Says he's meeting you?"

"Yes," Jess answered quickly. "I'll be out front in a minute."

"Of course."

Jess looked at herself critically again and grabbed a hair clip. Several cursory pulls of a comb and she wrapped the hair in and around the clip. With her hair out of it, she thought her thin face looked a little rounder, and her cheeks a little less hollow. She met her own gaze in the mirror and noticed the wideness of her pupils, from being in the dim lighting of the hotel room. Foregoing sunglasses, she blinked into the afternoon sunlight and then walked quickly along the corridor and open-air walkways to the front of the club.

Her boss was nowhere to be found when she entered the lobby, though she didn't look very hard. Mr. Melendez made her uneasy. Gus had negotiated her shift to bartending. Originally, she had been assigned room-cleaning duties, but the club needed hands and she could mix drinks, so he'd allowed her to move to the bar service, which Jess now appreciated.

Gaze moving around the lobby, she found where Eric had settled in a chair, holding open a copy of the local paper. His body and attention were angled away from her, so she walked quietly up and looked over his shoulder. The page held comics. That made her smile, reinforcing that Eric was far from old and stuffy. She might have had to rethink her attraction to him if he'd been reading the business section.

He looked up and caught her gaze. "Hi."

"Hi," Jess said. "Do you have a favorite?"

"Classic *Peanuts*," he answered. "Yours?"

Jess had no idea. She had been through so many cities that, even though she read local papers, looking at want ads, she'd seen many different comic strips. She glanced over his shoulder and randomly selected one that looked colorful and funny. "That one."

"Interesting," Eric said. Then he put down the paper and stood up. "You ready to go have some fun? Oh, she told me to tell you we have a pool. And she's preparing some lunch."

Jess hesitated. "Are we still taking photos?"

"I hope so." Eric added, "But there's no reason we can't eat, or have a swim?"

Jess shook her head. "Where exactly are we going?"

"My equipment's all at the house."

"So, the number you gave me was...?"

"My house, yes." Eric held the door for her as they started out to the parking lot. He blocked her way, and his expression was serious. Jess relaxed further with every word he spoke.

"Look, if you're not into something, you say no. At any time. I can go home now and leave you here. But honestly, I'd like to get to know you more. Elena would, too."

"You picked me up in a bar," Jess pointed out.

"Technically it was a photo gallery, and yes, I think you're very sexy," Eric pointed out. "I know you also are into Elena. So, I thought I'd bring you together. See what magic happens."

Jess asked, "What do you get out of this?"

"A new friend, and maybe a few pretty pictures," he answered. "Nothing more is expected." After a moment, he checked again. "So? You okay?"

Jess looked back at the hotel lobby, then to the parking lot. She knew almost no one in Miami outside her job, and almost no women; Maya, Hector's wife, was head of the housekeeping staff and didn't have anything to do with the bar, so they'd barely spoken two words.

Could this begin something new for her? For the first time in years, Jess could honestly say, "I made some friends, went out, and had some fun," and not have to make up a story to cover the fact she'd gone to some random bar and picked up a drunken one-night stand to scratch her itch. Even though this one had started out the same way, she realized, there was something different about Eric and Elena.

She also knew that going off with someone to their home could put her in an iffy situation. When she met Eric's eyes again, she saw he was calm; she didn't sense anything more than honesty from his waiting posture. "Will you tell me more about you and Elena while we drive?"

Eric's smile widened and he nodded. "I can absolutely do that." He stepped off the curb and led Jess to an ocean-green convertible coupe. "Weather is perfect for the top down."

Jess slid into the passenger seat while he held open the door for her.

"Most of the time El drives it. I usually use public transit, or she drops me off at the airport. But I only had a sixteen-hour run. She told me to drive myself to the airport in it, so I'd be able to pick you up today."

"El lives with you, then?"

Eric started up the engine, and then paused as, apparently, he finished processing her words. "Um, you know that Elena and I are married, right?"

"I thought she was your model."

"She is. We've also been married for six years."

"So, you *are* what Gus called 'unicorn hunters'."

Eric laughed. "Are you a unicorn? You seem pretty real to me."

Jess shrugged. "Meeting you on Saturday, I enjoyed myself. You seem really interesting. And Elena..." Her voice trailed off as she again thought about the feelings simple near-contact with the dark-haired woman brought. She felt her cheeks heat a little. "I did get hot thinking about you, and Elena... and me, well, doing something." She cleared her throat. "I sort of figured that's where this was going."

"We can go there. And, for the record, I *was* flirting with you on Saturday. El's just much more direct than I am." Eric let out a noise that sounded like indulgent laughter, and that, more than even his words earlier, made Jess relax.

"So, Elena wants us to have sex?"

"Yes. She's really hot for you." A note in Eric's voice suggested he was somewhat in awe of his wife's attraction to Jess.

"Does she pick up women often?" Jess felt emotion knot her throat. *Wow*, she thought when unexpected moisture welled in her eyes. "She was... intense. And, on the phone. She is... direct."

"Too much?" Eric asked.

Because it was clear now that Eric wanted thoughtful, truthful answers, Jess considered seriously how to put her many emotions succinctly. She started with an honest admission. "I've had one-night stands. I have had sex with, well, quite a few people. But I've never done this... a threesome before. I want to experience new things... I feel... excited." She breathed out and felt a giddy twitch in her stomach. "So, no, not too much."

Eric smiled. "She'll be glad to know that, so be sure to tell her."

Jess looked down at her hands in her lap and saw her work clothes again. "How explicit are the photos?" she asked.

"Anything you like. Since you say you've never done anything like this, I'm interested in what you would want. Boudoir is a very intimate style of photography, so we can start with just making you look good enough to eat."

"Elena said I could wear this," Jess said, gesturing to her work suit.

"I know. She told me. She's got a thing for women who wear suits as well as you do."

"It's not even mine," Jess said, fingering the lapel now. "I got it from Gus, the lead bartender, for my first night. I only have jeans. Maya helped me by sewing a few strategic tucks into it."

"It's obviously yours now. Gus certainly couldn't wear it again," Eric said. "I agree with El," he added. At a stoplight, he turned his head and his blue eyes steadied her. "You do look good in it."

She nodded, accepting the compliment.

The car made a turn and bumped over a road separation. Jess looked out the side window and realized they had entered a suburban neighborhood. Spanish and Caribbean styles dominated the choices in structure and décor. As well, there were the ubiquitous bars on most windows and doors. Gardens of tropical flowers filled many front lawns, and those that weren't filled with flowers had been artfully bricked. From what she could see, rear yards were privacy fenced, and contained screened enclosures for pools.

Eric pulled up a driveway that curled around the side of a one-story house with a mud-red Spanish tile roof. The tan stucco had dark brown faux sills under each window, and the roof was lined with dark brown aluminum gutters. Neat, narrow beds of annuals lined the curved brick walkway leading to the front stoop. Instead of bars on the street-facing windows and door, each window had white hurricane drop-shutters. The front door was dark brown, and next to it was a picture window, also edged in a dark brown ridge of stucco. The curtains were closed. The driveway circled to the east side of the house around a tall and wide but neatly trimmed bush.

When the car engine had been turned off, Jess stepped out onto the driveway in front of a closed roll-up garage door. Next to her, the backyard was hidden from sight by white eight-foot-high PVC fencing. She looked up and down its length and saw no gate.

"No side entrance increases our privacy," Eric said.

"Oh. Yeah. Of course." Jess shook herself. "You have a very nice home."

He gestured for her to come with him. "Wait'll you see the inside. I've done a lot of the remodeling myself. And Elena loves decorating."

Jess walked around the back of the car, meeting Eric at the end of the walk that led back around to the front. She hadn't realized until that moment that part of her trepidation was from being treated as a "secret" in some way. Eric was taking her in through the front door.

The walk passed between gardens of flowers, and the front

door was "guarded" by a pair of twin palms only a bit taller than the house's roof. The fronds formed an arch, shading the front stoop. Jess waited behind Eric while he unlocked the door and stepped across the threshold. He then held it open for her to enter.

"Welcome to Casa Tanner," he said.

Jess looked around the entry area while scuffing her boots on the entry rug. She saw Eric take his shoes off and line them up with others in the corner. Sitting on a tiny bench by the door, she followed his example and removed her boots. She curled her toes in her socks, out of sight under the legs of the pants, and fretted about the hole she knew she had in one heel. She was debating if she should take off her socks when she heard footsteps.

"Hi."

Jess looked up to see Elena walking toward them wearing an hourglass summer dress. The white fabric had geometric patches of overlapping colors. The brunette wore no stockings or shoes. When Jess's gaze lifted again to meet Elena's eyes, the brunette continued, "I'm glad you came." Elena's cheeks reddened at the same time Jess caught the double entendre. Quickly apologetic, Elena held out her hand and restated, "I mean, Jess, it's really nice to see you. Again."

Jess stood from the bench. Without her boots, Jess and Elena were very close in height, and their gazes continued to hold. She took Elena's offered hand, and the slenderness and smoothness of it was almost as intoxicating to Jess's sense of touch as the woman's voice was to her ears. She resisted closing her eyes. Instead she turned when she felt Eric moving close past her. She stepped forward to make room for him, and Elena's fingers skimmed her wrist and their bodies brushed before Elena stepped back.

Breaking the intensity of the moment, Eric said, "I'm going to get a beer. You want something?" Jess blinked and found him standing in the archway deeper inside the house. "Jess?"

"I... Actually, I'm not really a beer drinker," Jess said.

"Wine? Water?" Elena suggested.

"Water, please."

Elena's hand slipped away. Jess followed the couple into the kitchen of their home, feeling her nerves settle.

"You haven't been here long?" Eric asked. "What brought you to Florida?"

"Looking for something new," Jess said. "Gus calls me a free spirit, but really, I'm a drifter. I've sort of grown into the rootless life."

"You're not very old," Elena said.

"If you're fishing, I'm twenty-five. I gather both of you are in your thirties?"

"I'm thirty-eight," Eric concurred. "I graduated from high school in Dubuque, and then enlisted in the Air Force to become a pilot."

"Are you in the reserves?" Jess asked.

"Retired. I'm a commercial pilot for Diligent Air."

"Oh, now the 'gotta fly' makes sense." Jess laughed, and the sound made Elena smile. "What about you? Where have you modeled?"

"I don't actually model. Except in Eric's pictures. We find the photo shoots, like the swinging, add spice to our sex life. I used to work as a flight attendant."

"That's how we met, actually," Eric said. "At a layover party."

"What's a layover party?"

"When flight crews fly long-distance routes and stay overnight in a city, some of us get together. The more domestic ones plan sightseeing if it's someplace cool." He crushed his now empty beer can, walked over to a low cabinet in the kitchen, pulled out something, and tossed it in. "More often, though, we crowd into one big hotel suite and have sex," Eric finished as he turned back. He smiled at both her and Jess. "I'm gonna shower. Then, I believe, we have a picnic on the deck?"

Elena nodded. "Just some finger foods. I thought we'd all prefer to eat light." When Eric left, Elena moved forward after him. Now she was close enough to Jess, she again smelled the woman's scent. "You want to take a dip in the pool, Jess?" she asked, covering her inhale.

"I didn't expect to go swimming," Jess said.

"You can borrow one of my suits, if you want." Jess shook her head. Elena nodded. "Okay. Let me know if you change your mind." She was pleased when Jess followed her out the sliding doors to the pool.

Elena went to the pool's clean trap and emptied it into the garden. "Have a seat," she suggested when she turned.

Jess's hands had gone into her pants pockets as she looked around at the deck chairs, lounges, and the deck box. "It's really nice," Jess said.

"Thanks." To encourage Jess to sit and return to the relaxed connection she experienced back in the kitchen, Elena moved to the deck chair closest to where the blonde stood and sat down. Jess's gaze traced her stretched-out legs. Elena gestured. "Here."

Finally, Jess sat on the edge of a lounge chair and looked at the water. "Nice," Jess said again.

"You sure you don't want to get wet?" Jess's eyes widened. This time, instead of covering her double entendre, Elena silently cheered. The woman's mind was so obviously on naked thoughts. Elena decided, *nothing ventured, nothing gained.* Quietly she said, "The privacy fence allows for my skinny-dipping habit."

Clear green eyes locked on her face, hungry and searching. Elena felt Jess's desire as a suddenly palpable touch. With a need to connect, Elena reached out to Jess's hand gripping the side of the lounge chair.

Suddenly they were both standing, and Jess had turned Elena's grip around to pull their bodies together herself. Swimming in Jess's green gaze, Elena's blood pounded in her ears. She licked her lips. Jess's mouth pressed over hers, heat and hunger, and wet and soft, and *oh fuck*, Elena moaned. She gripped Jess's hand harder and felt the slight sting of nails. She inhaled Jess's scent and opened her mouth to fully experience the taste of her.

They weren't wrestling, but Jess appeared to want the same thing as Elena: to get as close as possible. She pulled her hand from Jess's grip and grasped the lapels of the woman's suit jacket. She stumbled; Jess moved back, and Elena followed.

Abruptly, both women were falling. Elena jerked when her body hit the water. Her dress was lightweight cotton, but when soaked it felt heavier. Her hair matted to her head but thankfully did not block her eyes.

Elena splashed until she righted herself and spotted the ladder, swimming over to it. Jess was a stroke behind, but the woman's work suit had half fallen off her shoulders, not letting her arms have full range of motion. "Take your jacket off," Elena said.

Treading water, Jess worked her arms out of the jacket, tossing it onto the deck. Then Jess pulled herself out of the pool using the ladder. Crouched by the handrail, picking up the jacket, Jess had her chest level with Elena's gaze. The soaked shirt had plastered to her skin and her bra was clearly visible beneath it.

"I'm sorry," Elena said. "I'll have your suit dry-cleaned."

"Looks like I'll be borrowing some clothes, anyway," Jess said as she looked down at herself.

"I thought I was the only one getting wet." Eric's voice made both women turn. He stood in the open doorway of the sliding door in cargo-style tan shorts and a Hawaiian print button-up shirt. His hair was damp, but he'd combed it.

The cool breeze chilled and tightened Elena's nipples against her soaked dress. Eric said, "Why don't you and Jess find dry clothes." He walked up to them, and Elena was relieved to see Jess only dip her head instead of looking embarrassed or protesting. "I'll set up."

It was then Elena noticed he had one of his smaller digital cameras in his hands. Had he snapped pictures of them? She met his eyes, and he gave a twist of his lips and a wink.

Carrying Jess's suit jacket, Elena went to the deck box and removed two towels from the plastic bin inside. "Are you okay?" Jess shivered. Elena started to put the towel around Jess's shoulders, but the woman's lowered eyes gave her pause. She put the towel in her hand instead. "Wrap this around you."

Jess did, but then she removed her pants from underneath the tucked-in towel. "I'll drip less water on your floor," she said. Her gaze was back to being direct, and Elena wasn't sure how Jess felt about their sudden soaking.

But she took the pants from the blonde's hand and then wrapped them and the jacket in another towel. She gave the bundle to Eric.

"I'll deliver these to the laundry."

"They should be dry-cleaned," Elena said.

"Yeah, but they can hang out there for a bit," Eric said. "Now, both of you go change."

His hand on her shoulder warmed and steadied her. She looked at Jess. Whatever was happening, it was at least good Jess was still here and not demanding to leave.

She smiled and got a small smile in return that softened the knot trying to form in her stomach. "C'mon, I'll show you to the guest bathroom."

Dressed in a pair of Elena's dark blue deck shorts and a borrowed Caribbean dashiki, which hid the fact that she had taken off her bra because it had also been soaked through, Jess reached for a napkin after finishing another meat-and-cheese-laden cracker and wiped her mouth. Next to her, Elena smiled and then stood. As the brunette walked around behind her, Jess felt a simple touch slide over one shoulder blade toward the middle of her spine.

Someone else might not have noticed it, but Jess was peculiar about touch; she hadn't had much of it in her life that was simple connective contact. She was more familiar with purely sexual touch. Elena's touch was something in between. She was clearly intensely physically attracted to Jess, but also restraining herself from showing it.

Jess was sure Elena didn't think she'd noticed. The touches were light, and always in passing as the brunette moved behind her, retrieving this or that item from the far end of the table. Eric sat across from Jess, and his eyes followed his wife each time she got up. When a sensation like static electricity discharge first slid down Jess's spine, from her nape to the small of her back, she'd recognized it for what it was: awareness of Elena.

As for Jess, yes, she was extremely attracted to Elena. The other woman's every word or deed seemed to carry more than one intention; she couldn't help being attracted to that complexity. Jess found Elena hot as hell, and the fall in the pool had done nothing to dampen her arousal.

If anything, the fall in the pool had simply told her that, yes, sex *would* happen. Elena had apologized profusely every time she came to the guest bathroom door. Recalling the feeling of Elena's body against hers in those brief seconds before hitting the water made Jess's nipples tingle, and her clit twitched against her borrowed clothes, the stimulation making her squirm on the bench.

Elena's fingers briefly tangled in the ends of her hair when Jess moved. After finger-combing through it after the shower, Jess had decided to let her hair dry loose across her shoulders and back. Pulling her fingers away, Elena's face held apology as she resumed her seat. Jess simply finished the cheese wedge she had been chewing.

"Everything is so good," Jess said and licked the tips of her fingers. For a moment, Jess thought about other flavors she could have. Her cheeks warmed. Neither Eric nor Elena had indicated that they wanted to move on to sex yet.

In fact, they both seemed to simply be enjoying eating and talking. Eric had explained more about his work as a pilot, and Elena had explained why she left the airline. They seemed to simply want her to get to know them.

It was a novel idea—to have friends, to be friends with those you would have sex with. Anonymous and shallow had been her style for so long, Jess could only remember the name of one person she'd had sex with in the last seven years. That was unavoidable; she'd had to write it on several documents after he'd vanished.

Now it seemed Jess not only had two friendships starting, but she would have proof of it, too. Eric had promised her several prints from today and had been snapping pictures of her and Elena ever since they walked back out to the pool area. He'd gotten Elena to laugh and pose a couple times in a baby blue terrycloth jumper that was closed—mostly—by Velcro up the front. A small opening at the woman's throat highlighted her dainty collarbones, and the curves of her breasts showed when she leaned forward over her food.

Jess watched Eric across the table, looking through the collection of shots on his camera's preview screen now. He still nibbled, but in between he meticulously cleaned his fingers on Wet-Naps. She was drawn repeatedly to the smooth ruffling of his mustache against the cracker's surface. Then she would be drawn to his fingers moving against the camera screen. Obviously, he was saving some photos and discarding others. He'd said that was one of the reasons he liked digital photography. She was curious what the camera had captured. She and Elena had been bringing out the trays of fingers foods from the kitchen so often, Jess seldom saw Eric snapping the pictures.

While putting various cracker stacks on her plate before she sat down to eat, she had purposefully posed once. Eric had called to her to turn around, so he could capture her hair in motion. She did, tossing her hair, and spreading her hand across her hip as she had seen Elena do.

He'd complimented her on her loose hair then. She'd revealed her quandary before he'd picked her up, of whether to wear it up or down. Taking the camera down from his eye, he said, "Next time I'd like to start with it like this."

She'd glowed at that. The idea of a next time pleased her. She looked from Eric to Elena. She shifted closer to the brunette, who sensed the motion and looked up.

It wasn't awkward at that moment, when Jess gazed into deep brown eyes. Elena swallowed what she had been chewing and smiled. Jess smiled back. Motion caught her attention from the corner of her eye and she turned her head to see Eric moving the camera away from his face. He'd taken another photo, this time of the two of them.

"May I see them?" she asked. "Before you make prints?"

"Of course," Eric agreed. "We can call tonight 'dinner and a show'."

Elena said, "There's a multimedia big-screen TV in our living room. He hooks the camera right up to it."

"We'll have to go inside soon," Eric said as he wiped crumbs from his mustache. He was looking off at the sky behind Jess and Elena with a critical eye. "Afternoon rains look to be moving in."

Jess stood and stepped back from the bench seat and started collecting plates and condiments. Elena went to the end of the table and stacked other things onto trays, while Eric gathered his tripod and a lens bag which they hadn't actually used. Jess felt briefly sad about the missed opportunity for more outdoor shots.

Eric reached Jess, following Elena, before they entered the house. He leaned forward and spoke. "How're you doing?"

Jess looked over her shoulder and found his eyes smiling at her. "I'm having a really good time," she replied honestly.

"Good," he said. "C'mon, let's look at some pictures." He moved around her, his hand brushing her back.

Jess leaned into his touch. There had been boys in the group homes, older "brothers" at foster homes, and men who she'd joined in hotel rooms for quickie sex. Eric wasn't like any of them. She knew he was attracted to her and wanted to have sex with her. He had said as much. But he wasn't urgent or pushy; he seemed content to be sociable. Being the recipient of the attention of a mature man was a new and novel feeling. Jess smiled at him and followed Eric inside the house.

In the kitchen, Elena said, "I have banana pudding for dessert."

Jess declined, adding, "Maybe later."

Elena offered another bottle of water instead, which Jess accepted, though for the moment she didn't open the bottle. Eric held up a wine bottle from a rack just outside the kitchen. "Chocolate wine," he said.

When Jess and Elena both nodded, Eric served three shot glasses from the bottle. Handing one to each of them, he tapped, and toasted, "Here's to some very lovely shots already."

After downing his drink, Eric said, "You ladies follow when you're ready. I'll go connect the camera."

Elena lifted the chocolate wine bottle. "Another?" she asked.

Jess let the brunette cup her shot glass and her hand as she filled it, enjoying the warm contact of their fingers.

"Another toast?" Elena suggested.

"To what?" Jess asked.

"New friends."

Jess echoed the toast and clinked her glass with Elena's.

Then she followed Elena's example and downed the second shot in a single gulp. The sweet chocolate and smooth texture hit her tongue and then the alcohol buzzed her brain. She inhaled. Elena was smiling when she put down the shot glasses and refilled them a third time.

Elena led Jess out of the kitchen. The living room was awash in white leather. A love seat, chaise, and padded footstool faced a faux fireplace. A half dozen four-by-six framed pictures had been set on a shelf above it. The wall above held a flatscreen TV. Eric had set his camera on the mantel and connected a cable dangling down from the back of the screen.

Elena gestured for Jess to sit, and she chose one side of the love seat. Eric perched on the footstool while manipulating a couple different remotes, occasionally reaching up and pressing a button on his camera.

Jess looked from Eric to Elena and sipped her shot of chocolate wine. *Make a move if you want something*, Jess's mind whispered. She shifted and suggested, "There's a spot here." She was glad she had spoken up when Elena accepted the invitation and settled beside her.

Eric hadn't cleared his camera's card before the afternoon, and the first several shots reminded Jess why she had accepted Eric's invitation. Elena in various stages of undress filled the huge screen shot after shot. The dark-haired seductress was in full view. Her tawny skin contrasted with a crisp white top. In each successive shot the fabric parted further and further, until her breasts were on full display. No tan lines, Jess noted. Clearly Elena didn't just skinny-dip, but did a little nude sunbathing, too. Then her gaze began to take in the rest of the woman's body. Light played across generous hips, and shadows hid the treasure between her thighs. Arousal rising, Jess licked her lips.

Elena shifted, and Jess felt the woman's leg move against hers. Jess cast a side glance and saw Elena putting her shot glass to her lips, color deepening on her cheeks. The woman downed the rest of her chocolate wine in a single shot. The move suggested she was bolstering herself to take some action. Jess waited, her breath caught in anticipation.

She moved her hand from the leather to Elena's thigh. The

terrycloth of Elena's jumper had ridden up, and Jess's fingers brushed warm skin stretched over tight muscle.

"Okay, here we are." Eric's voice broke the silence. "Today's photos."

Jess looked back up at the screen; Elena's fingers laced with hers as day-bright photos faded in and out onscreen. Each photo showed long enough for Jess to study many details. She was again awed by Eric's skill. Elena's gaze, seldom direct at the camera, was filled with self-awareness and desire. It wasn't until Jess's first picture appeared that she realized, in many of the pictures Eric had taken, Elena had been looking at her.

In this photo, Jess was emerging from the house wearing the borrowed dashiki and shorts. She had turned to close the sliding glass door behind her. She glanced at him, remembering his request at the table during the meal for her to pose. He was "an ass man" through and through. She laughed lightly. When she felt her fingers squeezed, she turned her head to see that Elena was smiling at her.

Being purely objective, Jess could admit she did look good. She hadn't worn properly fitting clothes in so long, she'd forgotten her own figure wasn't boyish. Add her hair down, and Jess was able to understand why Elena now held her hand and Eric smiled indulgently at the two of them sitting together on the love seat. If she needed any more proof that he and Elena wanted her sexually, here it was.

In the next photo, Jess had noticed the camera. She had put on a pose, fingers in her mouth, pulling them out one by one as she sucked off the sauce from a carrot dipped in ranch dressing. She'd always thought her hands, work-rough as they were, not her best feature, but there, displayed against her lips, she thought maybe they weren't too bad. Her nails were clean, short, and smooth. The tendons showing in relief suggested they were strong hands. On the leather between their bodies, Elena's fingers caressed hers, and she decided she would buy some lotion.

The photoshow continued. Eric had captured many pictures over the trio's two hours spent outside. She remembered posing for some, and watching Elena pose for others. Still more, though, were random captures when she and Elena were not looking.

Finally, the one that Eric had captured as Elena and Jess's gazes met appeared onscreen. It wasn't the last, but even after it faded from sight and was replaced, the image remained in Jess's mind.

That look they shared was, she knew, the same before the kiss that had sent them stumbling into the pool. The heat between her and Elena was as physical as the woman's hand now in hers.

On the love seat now, Jess turned her head; Elena leaned toward her. "May I?"

Jess nodded. Elena's lips gently touched and shifted on hers. Jess felt no fervor, just warm communion. When the kiss ended, Jess followed Elena's gaze to Eric, who was frowning.

"My camera's still connected to the damn TV," he grumbled.

They laughed, so did Eric.

Jess finally finished her shot of the chocolate wine. When the pictures had finished, Eric removed the camera from the cable. Watching his fingers move nimbly, she wondered what was next. Her thoughts were scattered by the alcohol, and she'd started to lean into Elena's shoulder. The terrycloth of Elena's jumper made her cheek tingle. She brushed at the sensation, even as Eric moved closer, his camera once again snapping away.

She frowned. He stopped clicking, lowered the camera, and asked, "Is this all right?"

"Mmm, fine," she murmured. "Feeling good."

"Maybe too good," Elena said. "I think you're falling asleep."

Jess tried to push herself upright to deny that she was tired. She was enjoying the ebb and flow of emotions. Everything was excitingly new. Yet at the same time blissful comfort stole into her limbs.

Eric put down the camera and reached for her hand. Without hesitation, Jess grasped it. She came to her feet, swayed a little, and smiled at him. He smiled back. She looked back over her shoulder to see that Elena, too, was getting up. The brunette moved her hands to the small of Jess's back. Eric kissed her forehead. Jess sighed. She reached behind her and drew Elena's hands onto her hips, then covered the quivering in her stomach. Full lips touched the back of her neck; she breathed deeply.

"Bed sounds like a good idea," she said, and a brief image of the three of them tumbling onto sheets poured adrenaline into her veins that argued with the exhaustion. "Don't want to go," she added. Stepping back, she looked from one to the other sincerely. "I've had a really good time."

"There's nothing stopping us from doing it again," Eric said. "I'll drive you back to the club."

"I'll bring your clothes by tomorrow," Elena said as she followed Jess, leaning on Eric, to the front door. "After they're dry-cleaned."

Jess leaned away from Eric and kissed Elena again. "I'm really glad I came," she said.

The brunette's gaze turned dark and seductive and her lips twitched. "Not yet," Elena said.

Feeling loose and good, Jess laughed. "Okay. Not yet."

Eric picked his keys up from a tray by the door. Jess stepped out first. When he stood in the open doorway, Elena caught Eric's arm above the wrist, and their gazes intersected silently before she kissed him. "Take care of her," Elena said.

"Of course," he replied.

Elena stood in the doorway after Jess and Eric had started down the walk, back to the side of the house and the car. "Good night, Jess."

Jess let Eric's hand go and hurried back up to the doorway. She held Elena's hand. "Tomorrow?" she said.

"Would you like to have lunch?" Elena suggested.

"Yes," Jess answered. Then she searched Elena's gaze, the invitation, she hoped, crystal clear. The brunette cupped Jess's face in both hands and held her in place while her lips pressed searchingly over Jess's. When Jess's lips parted, seeking small breaths, the tip of Elena's tongue made Jess's head spin for reasons that had absolutely nothing to do with the alcohol she had consumed.

"Yes," Elena echoed.

On wobbly legs, Jess hurried back to Eric's side. Tomorrow couldn't come soon enough.

Just barely after sunset, twilight gave the area a soft glow when Eric pulled up to the front of the Caliente property. For autumn in Florida, that meant it was only a little after eight in the evening. Jess sat for a moment in the seat of the convertible before moving. It was obvious to Eric that she was reluctant to let things end. He reached past the gearshift with care. When his hand touched hers, she didn't startle. She smiled at him. He smiled in return.

"I really had a good time," Jess said again. She seemed at a loss for words. "The ride cleared my head, you know. We could..." Her voice trailed off.

Eric brushed his thumb around the back of her hand and remembered watching Elena's hand tucked around Jess's just the same way. Jess looked down with him to their linked hands, and then she was leaning toward him.

She brushed his bottom lip with both of hers in a featherlight kiss. He smiled into the contact. Letting her lead, he was pleasantly delighted when she moved to his upper lip and stirred the hairs of his mustache. "I do want to see how this feels. On me," she said quietly. Pulling back, she openly stated, "I hope today wasn't a disappointment."

Eric smiled a little tightly only because her words had tightened part of him that was going to make him seem less than gentlemanly if he didn't hold himself with a firm rein. "No disappointment. I'm just calculating how soon we might spend time together again."

"I'm working every night," she said.

"And I'm flying every day. But," he added, "you'll see Elena tomorrow when she brings your clothes."

Jess rolled her bottom lip between her teeth. "I'm not working tomorrow."

Eric wondered, and hoped a little, that the lip-pull meant what he thought it meant for Elena. He'd witnessed their kiss in the doorway, and before on the love seat, and though they didn't know, before that he had seen the cause of their fall into the pool. He smiled and lifted his hand entwined with Jess's, pressed a kiss to her fingers and then let her go. "You two should do something together. I know Elena enjoyed today a lot."

The blonde's head tilted a little, then she shook her head. "This is all so new to me."

"Good new?" he asked. She'd said on the drive out that the idea of the three of them excited her. *Did she still feel that way?*

She smiled. "Yes." She stepped from the car and he was treated to a rear view of black T-shirt and spandex shorts. She turned to close the door and caught his study of her. "Tell Elena she can take her clothes back tomorrow." She had lowered her voice and leveled her gaze at him as she spoke.

Eric's blood immediately pounded his cock hard; he shifted on the seat to get comfortable. The look in Jess's eyes told him that she was hoping to have Elena take the clothes off her. He inhaled and shook his head, pleased by her initiative. "Damn, and me without my camera," he said.

Jess's smile was full of smirk—*god*, he thought, he loved when a woman discovered her power. The blonde still had a long way to go; she hadn't grabbed his face, or even Elena's, to claim kisses from them tonight.

But he had no doubt at some point, if they could keep seeing her, she would.

The night that happened would be a night to remember.

CHAPTER FOUR

ELENA HAD never been in the section of the Caliente that served as employee quarters. Many clubs had employee living areas because the hours were long and often odd. Those without outside connections often lived on-property somewhere. Though they owned and also worked at the hotel, Hector and Maya had a large suite in the main part of the hotel because they regularly entertained. This wasn't exactly an "under the stairs" servants' wing, but it was simple, and she could hear the industrial-sized air conditioners cycling just outside. Abruptly, though, she went from plain walls to the start of a mural where an intersecting corridor opened. A plaque on the wall next to the corridor opening stated Employees Only.

Continuing to walk, Elena passed three rooms, two on the right and one on the left, checking the numbers on each. Finally, she stopped in front of room 19, which Hector had said was assigned to Jess. Elena shifted the dry-cleaning bag from one shoulder to the other and knocked.

No sound immediately came from the space beyond the door. A few seconds passed in silence, then the door opened, and Jess stood in the doorway in a pair of girl boxers and a tank top. She smiled at Elena.

"Hi," Elena said. "I hope I'm not too early." When Hector had called from the desk to tell Jess that Elena had arrived, she hadn't had a chance to talk to her. After only a short exchange, Hector had hung up and gruffly given Elena directions.

"I haven't dressed yet," Jess said. "Just finished my shower when Hector called."

Elena noticed that Jess's hair was down, and mostly dry. It was an easy leap of logic that the blonde had spent her time using a hair dryer. It was also delightful to see Jess so at ease around her, walking around in almost nothing as she decided what to wear.

It was a torment, too. The handfuls of Jess's breasts were currently unrestrained by a bra. The girl boxers only rested down an inch on her thighs, showing off hard-muscled legs that made Elena lick her lips. Jess turned to a small single stack of drawers and gave Elena a view to remember as she bent over to pull out clothes. Eric was right; Jess's ass was amazing.

When Jess turned around, Elena noticed the clothing in the woman's hands was the dashiki and deck shorts she had been loaned at the house. "I asked Maya to wash them, so they're clean."

Elena stepped forward and held out the dry-cleaning bag. "I had your suit cleaned."

As they made the exchange, Elena realized she had a slight height advantage in her wedge sandals because Jess was barefoot. When Jess turned to put the suit in the closet, Elena asked, "What would you like to do for lunch?"

When Jess turned, Elena saw that her green eyes had darkened, the pupils wide. Elena bit her lip, anticipation quivering in her belly as she held hope.

"I was hoping you'd like to do *me* for lunch," Jess said.

"That," she breathed, "sounds perfect." She stepped forward. Either unconsciously or not, Jess's thighs parted around her leg, and her own knee pressed slightly against Jess's heated center as the space between them disappeared.

Elena indulged herself in the taste and feel of Jess's throat, lips moving there between pulling kisses from the blonde's lips.

"I was really disappointed that I couldn't finish our day properly yesterday," Jess said while grasping Elena's shoulders to hold herself upright.

"Eric is fond of the saying 'good things come to those who wait,'" Elena said. She, however, was delighted to not be waiting for the blonde any longer, and apparently the feeling was mutual. Lean but soft hands grasped Elena's thighs and massaged them before moving underneath and pushing up the hem of her summer dress.

When Elena felt the backs of her legs impact the bed, she pulled Jess with her and fell onto it. She rolled until she was half on Jess, a leg suggestively pinning the blonde while she did a little skin exploration of her own. Under the tank top Elena found softly defined muscles, which tightened and rippled under her touch. She pulled it up to get at the woman's skin. With Jess's shoulders pinned to the bed it wasn't coming off, but Elena was determined to feast on those breasts, which had been tantalizing her dreams.

Following the silent encouragement of fingers in her hair and soft moans of her name, Elena shifted and repositioned her knee. Then rocking herself against Jess, she grasped a breast and sucked its turgid nipple between her teeth. Moans turned to mewling pleas, and it was only as a distant sound that she began to hear rapping against a surface. Almost absurdly delighted by the idea, Elena thought that their rocking was causing the headboard to hit the wall.

But then Jess growled—*damn, that was sexy as hell*—and moved away from Elena. She started to protest, only to finally recognize the rapping sound for what it was: someone rather insistently knocking on the door. "I'm gonna...," Jess grumbled, the threat unspoken but clear from her rough tone.

Backing off the bed and standing, Elena watched Jess roll from the bed herself and stumble once before reaching the door. The knocking hadn't stopped.

"What do you—" Jess demanded at the same time she opened the door. "—want?" she finished weakly. Though Elena couldn't see who was at the door, she had a reasonably good guess that it meant their midday tryst was at an end. "Mr. Melendez?" The blonde's tone was meek—there was a story behind that, Elena realized.

"I need you to open the bar. Gus is not yet returned from his errands. The bar must be opened," Hector finished with emphasis.

"But I haven't—"

"You can make drinks, serve drinks, make the customers happy to spend their money. Open the bar."

Jess nodded her head. "I'll be there in five minutes," she promised. She quickly pushed the door closed.

The blonde turned, her mind so focused on her employer's request that she startled when she saw Elena. The pain and distress evident in green eyes, though, made any hurt Elena felt at being forgotten vanish instantly.

"I gotta go," Jess said.

"I heard," Elena replied.

Jess hurried to the closet where she had just hung up the dry-cleaned suit. When she pulled it from the bag, the paper bag tore. Elena heard Jess exhale, obviously attempting to calm down. Silently, Elena collected her things: the borrowed and now returned clothes, and her purse and shoes from where she'd dropped and kicked them as soon as the possibility of being in Jess's arms had been presented.

Jess put on the white shirt first, leaving it unbuttoned while she stepped into the pants. When she straightened, closing the pants around her waist, Elena was again assailed by the reality of Jess's beauty. The gold of her hair, the white of the shirt, the pink of her nipples through the white tank top, the deep black of the pants.

"You need your bra," Elena said as Jess started to button up the shirt.

"I can get away without it," she said, and finished.

"Jess..." Elena had no idea what to say.

"I gotta go," Jess said. She scooped up her shoes and slid them on bare feet. "The bar's at the front. I can... I can at least walk you out that far."

Elena said nothing and followed Jess. On the walk to the front of the hotel, Jess kept a step ahead. Elena witnessed a resolute transformation from sexy woman to working stiff in the way Jess gradually straightened her posture and took faster strides. The final touch came when Jess used a fat claw clip to pin up her hair.

Unfortunately, Elena felt that "damn, that's makes you even sexier" would not be a welcome comment right now.

Jess stepped behind the bar and moved quickly to the register. A fully electronic POS, it had no cash drawer. She expected that Hector had left her to retrieve it from the hotel safe and would be arriving soon. By then, she knew, she had better have the bar itself set up to take and fill orders.

She began searching under the counter for the various drink-mixing items and pressed the button on the ice maker to start replenishing the supply. Once she had straightened again, a motion to her right and across the bar caught her attention.

Elena was settling onto a barstool. The woman laid her purse on the counter next to her.

"You should go," Jess said. She didn't want the brunette bored, their time together cut short. She was already frustrated by it and knew she wouldn't be pleasant company.

"I'd like a drink," Elena replied. "I missed my lunch, and so did you." The brunette smiled. The knots in Jess's stomach loosened slightly. She couldn't quite smile yet, but if Elena continued to stick around, it might not be so bad.

"What would you like?"

"Rum and Coke. Light, please. I also need to see what's on the menu?"

"Eric had nachos the other day."

"I'm not a fan," Elena said simply. "What about a wrap or salad?"

Jess nodded while mixing the requested rum and Coke. "I can send to the kitchen for a salad. What dressing would you like?" Dropping a straw into the tall glass, Jess slid Elena's requested drink across the bar.

"Vinaigrette, please." Elena's fingers caught hers briefly as she took the drink. "Thank you."

Jess met brown eyes that held sincere emotion. "Thank *you*," she stressed. "I'm sorry about our lunch."

"I know. It can't be helped. Just means I have more time to plan a perfect seduction," Elena said, and Jess bit her lip at the woman's secret smirk. "I think Eric and I will visit the club Saturday night. Are you working?"

"I'm scheduled, yes. I don't know what Mr. Melendez will do with a lot of overtime hours. Unless Gus gets back quickly, this could be a long shift."

The door to the bar area opened and Jess looked up to see Mr. Melendez striding in, carrying a locked cash drawer. He said nothing about her standing with Elena and talking. But she didn't really give him a chance. She immediately crossed to the end of the bar and followed him to the POS, where he unlocked the release and set it in the register.

"It has $186.47 to the penny. I'll expect a reconciliation receipt at the end of your shift."

Jess forced down the heat in her face. "Yes, sir. Of course."

He straightened, handed her the money tray's key, then looked toward Elena. "Entertaining in your room?"

"She's a friend. We were planning to go out to lunch," Jess said. The details hadn't been worked out, but she was sure she didn't want to tell him Elena was someone she hoped would become a frequent and intimate part of her off-work life. The realization that she had a friend, that they would go out socially, not just as fuck-buddies, made Jess blink and bite her lip as she restrained her giddiness from going on full, embarrassing display.

Mr. Melendez left, but not until after silently studying Elena for a long moment. He seemed to come to some conclusion before turning on his heel and heading back to the front desk.

As her boss left, a man in suit and tie came in and immediately approached the bar.

"What can I get for you, sir?" she asked the customer.

He dropped his briefcase on the floor by his barstool. "Miller Lite. Draft if you have it."

Jess glanced at the draft taps and saw that they did have the requested brand. "I'll be right back with it. That'll be three dollars, please."

"Open a tab," he said, sliding a card across the bar.

"Yes, sir." Jess entered the information and opened the man's tab on the POS. A quick pass at the draft taps and she slid his beer efficiently to him.

Elena moved away from the bar, taking her salad with her when Jess started getting a steady stream of customers. She sipped her soda slowly, wanting to linger as long as possible without drawing attention. The men who entered over the course of the afternoon all wore variations of business attire, from salesman chic to office-casual shirtsleeves. A few wore polos and Dockers.

Why they would come to the bar of an adult hotel in the middle of the day when there were plenty of others near the convention area wasn't really a surprise. Many men tried to pick up women when away from home on business. She'd left the airlines because of the constant pickup lines, never quite able to let them roll off. The resentment had built faster once she was married. She'd wrestled with that after she and Eric officially started swinging. How could she appreciate flirting and pickup lines in one area of her life, and get rigidly pissed about it in another?

Elena enjoyed flirting. A lot. But she felt underlying aggression and assumptions from men when she was outside the clubs that was simply not used by men and couples when she and Eric were swinging. Talking it over with him, Elena had concluded that part of the reason was also her mental separators between "worktime" and "playtime." She didn't generally like one to mix with the other. Reconciling her attraction to Eric and participating in the layover parties had been awkward for a very long time.

Thinking that it would help her get over her anxieties, Elena resigned from Diligent Air. But a year later, she and Eric had not swung with any more DA employees. Not even Britt, the first woman Elena had shared sex with Eric with. She still saw the other woman occasionally, but there was never sex, or even an offer of sex.

She exhaled. The abrupt ending of their intimate relationship with Britt had hurt quite a bit at the time, and still had the ability to derail Elena if she dwelled on it too deeply.

Deep into her thoughts, Elena startled when a shadow fell across her corner table. She looked up to see Jess. "Want another?" the blonde asked.

Elena looked down to see that she had finished her drink, the glass held tightly in her hands. "Please." She relinquished the glass. There was a soft squeeze in her chest when Jess's fingers brushed hers in the exchange. Jess also collected the empty salad dish.

The blonde smiled at her. "Be right back with your refill," she said.

The bar was quite busy again during the next hour; Jess filled, and refilled, many drinks. Soon another hotel staff member had been called to bring food orders from the kitchen.

Though her second drink was finished, Elena didn't leave. Her gaze continued to follow Jess. The unease of working the bar alone had vanished, and a confident efficiency had replaced it.

Elena began to wonder when Gus would return. According to Hector he had been on errands. This was supposed to be Jess's day off.

"This seat taken?" Elena looked up to see a dark-haired man gesture at the seat across from her, his business jacket on his arm and his tie loosened.

"This is a party of one," Elena said.

"We could make it a party of two. Much more fun that way, don't you think?"

Elena leaned back a little, surveying him with her best "not interested" expression. Usually the silent scrutiny was enough for most men to know she was not amenable to being picked up. This one, however, blithely sat down. Elena immediately straightened. "No," she enunciated.

He waved over the woman who had just brought food to another table. "Beer for me, and a refill for her." Elena saw the woman's name tag read "Delia."

"I'm not—" Both Elena and Delia's responses began the same. Elena started to her feet.

"Sit down, sweetheart. I got this," he directed to Elena. He turned back to Delia. "Now, run along, and bring my order."

If he'd snapped his fingers, his manner couldn't have been more high-handed. Elena gathered her purse and started to move around and leave the table.

He turned in his chair and put his leg out. Long enough that she couldn't walk around it, his legs were high enough that she couldn't step over them either. Elena was effectively trapped in the corner. There was no way out. Well, that was if she didn't want to make a scene.

A glance at the tables to the left and right, and Elena saw no one looking her way. There would be no rescue through public pressures.

"Miss, there was a problem with your card." *Card?* Elena looked from Mr. Self-important to see Jess approaching with a credit card and receipt in hand. She hadn't given one yet. Her confusion showed on her face. "You need to come with me."

Oh. Almost immediately, relief flooded through Elena's frame. Jess was rescuing her in the most businesslike way possible. "Yes, of course."

Jess looked pointedly at the man's legs. Hunching his shoulders, he pulled his legs in, unblocking Elena, who immediately stepped out of the corner and walked away next to Jess. She was shaking so badly that the heel of her wedge landed wrong and she started to fall. Jess's hand quickly caught her elbow and steadied her.

"Thank you," Elena said.

"I didn't know you were still here until Delia came and told me 'a man is hitting on the lady.' I hadn't served any female customers, but then I looked over where she pointed. Why are you still here?"

"I was finishing my salad."

"You did that earlier. I brought your second drink to that table."

"I haven't paid my tab yet," Elena said.

"Okay. So, you should, and then I think you should go."

Elena hesitated. A man tapped his card on the bar nearby. "I'll be with you in a moment, sir," Jess said. Then she looked back at Elena. "Go home."

"Really?" Elena asked.

"I'm sure you have things you can do. It doesn't look like I'm going to get away. Will I still see you Saturday?" Jess asked while she ran Elena's check and collected her credit card.

"Your number's in Eric's phone."

Jess wrote numbers on the back of the receipt Elena would keep.

"Now you have my number. Call me?" Jess asked.

Elena smiled. "I will."

CHAPTER FIVE

"I DON'T think the situation really calls for intervention," Eric said. Across the bar table, the man he was answering put an arm around his wife's shoulders. "We shouldn't be messing in other countries' business just because they do something we don't like."

"Man, that's social justice, and we're the leaders of the Free World."

"Not lately," Eric said. He saw Elena shift in the seat next to him, finishing her drink. He mentally calculated it was her second. He was still on his first whiskey and soda. "You know what? I think it's time to table politics. Shall we take our ladies to the dance floor and show them off? El?" he finished, brushing her shoulder with his hand.

"Hmm?" She swallowed and lifted her gaze to meet his directly.

As they stood, Eric leaned against her to whisper his concern in her ear. "Are you all right? You've been quiet."

"Fine." And that tone, Eric knew, was a sign that something was on her mind, big-time. She'd tell him if she needed his thoughts, he reminded himself. Elena didn't like to be pushed until she'd figured out a lot of what was bothering her by herself. But she could be distracted. So he took her to the dance floor section where extra tables were set up during the day, but now was lit by the pulsing light assembly hanging from the ceiling. Bodies rocked to the rhythm, drinks and dates in hand.

The front bar was the public entry to the club; the interior was members only. As he pulled Elena into his arms on the dance floor, he nodded to Carlos, who stood next to a set of black-painted double doors with neon script lettering: Members Only. You had to pass through the doors, showing your member card, and then walk the gallery. Finally, down another corridor past changing rooms and restrooms, were the playrooms.

Hector had told Eric once that the strict separation was necessary "for legal reasons." Eric preferred it. Having a place where people acted "normal" rather than just "trolled for sex partners" elevated this place from other on-premise clubs in the city that were converted from stripper clubs, or old Triple-X theaters. There'd been a time for those in his life, when he, too, had been a single male trolling for sex partners. But when he and Elena had started to come to Caliente, there'd been no looking back. This was their swinger home. He hugged Elena to him. Her body fit perfectly against his, and he nuzzled her hair.

Her breath hitched, and he pulled back to study her. "Hey," he said. The song changed to a faster beat, though not louder, a benefit of being a combination bar and dance floor. The bartenders and waitstaff still could get your order. Eric smiled to encourage Elena's smile. She did smile—but he could see that it was a bit forced. There was a furrow in her brow, and her lips were thinned, pressed together, and pulled up only at the corners. "You didn't tell me how your lunch date with Jess went," he gambled.

Elena didn't answer immediately; instead her lips pursed. *Ah,* Eric thought, *something went wrong on their date.*

"We didn't get to have lunch together, or really anything. She was called up to work a shift."

Oh. *Oh,* Eric thought. That explains everything. Almost. "Were you interrupted?" Elena nodded. *Shit.* "Was it bad?"

"Awkward. I stayed around here, had a couple drinks, a salad. But... there was no more... I know she would have come back if she could have."

"So Jess is another you, huh?" Eric knew it was painful for Elena, but he admitted to himself he found it a bit amusing.

"She apologized. She wanted to see me again. I know we already said we'd come out tonight, but..." Elena glanced toward the bar, where Eric saw Jess working, rapidly filling drink orders, standing next to a male bartender. "I don't know how to start again. The mood changed so fast," she said.

Elena's distraction tonight was now fully explained. She'd been trying to watch Jess, to gauge when she could possibly approach her again. It occurred to Eric that he hadn't seen Jess leave the bar once all night. Their drink orders had been taken and delivered by a redheaded waitress wearing fishnet stockings, a skintight black skirt, and a pink button-up that strained to contain her ample cleavage. He knew Saturdays were probably the busiest night of the week here, but surely the blonde should've had a break at some point, like she had the night of the gallery opening?

"The bar's last call is 2:00 a.m. We can stick around until things close up and she's off the clock. Then maybe we can talk with her? She had such a good time with us at the house on Monday. I can't imagine she's not still interested in spending time together." He led Elena back to the table. "You like to keep work and play separate. It's not really hard to imagine she does the same."

Elena's eyes gleamed a little then; he'd returned some of her hope. "Yeah."

"I'm sure it was just a misunderstanding. But being off-balance after an interruption doesn't make it easy at the time to see all that."

Her smile was more genuine this time. "I guess you're right."

Eric gave his chest an exaggerated pat. "Of course I am." She did laugh, as he wanted, and Eric mentally patted himself again for knowing her so well.

Eric set a plan in motion a few minutes later. While Elena danced with the couple they'd been talking with earlier, he asked the redheaded waitress for two drinks: a mai tai and a scotch and soda. He requested that Jess make them, insisting, "She knows how we like them." He also requested his tab be closed out.

When the waitress returned with the drinks and the bill, Eric used the pen to write a short note that he wrapped inside the bills for Jess's tip, separate from the redhead's. "You see that Jess gets this," he said, pressing the rolled bills into Delia's hand.

"Yes, sir," she said. As Eric watched, she did exactly as he requested and delivered the roll of bills hiding the note to Jess's hand. The redhead whispered something when Jess made a comment. Jess looked out from the bar, obviously seeking him out. He met her gaze across the distance and nodded. She said something to the other bartender and stepped back from the bar, before unfurling the bills and finding the note.

A moment later, just as Elena was returning to the table, Jess's nose crinkled with her smile as she read Eric's note. She lifted her head and her gaze found him quickly. She flashed the note up briefly and raised her brow. He nodded back and covered his thumbs-up by hugging Elena as she sat down.

Jess worried her teeth against her bottom lip as the minutes continued ticking well past closing time. It was nearly 3:30 a.m., last call had been two, and the bar had stopped all service at three. Gus had already left to deliver the cashbox to Hector and the club's safe. She had yet to finish all the closing tasks; a drain was stuck and seemed glued shut from something that shouldn't have been sent down the system. She had just popped off the drain cover with determination when she heard footsteps.

"Gus, thank god you're back. This damn drain is stuck," she huffed, not looking up.

"I could take a look," a male voice that did not belong to Gus answered.

"Eric!" Jess straightened and looked toward the sound, and then stopped, uncertain. Elena stood next to him. "Elena," she added, feeling the distance intensely, even as she drank in the woman like she was dying of thirst. "I didn't expect... I'm sorry... Tuesday, I..." She weakly rounded her shoulders, not knowing what to say but desperate to repair what had become an important connection in such a short time.

Elena walked forward. Jess looked down when Elena grasped her hands and removed the screwdriver. Then Elena clasped her fingers and lifted them.

"I forgot that I disliked when work and play crossed paths," Elena said. "I owe you an apology for making you think you were wrong. I was... bothered... and hot, from our play. I got annoyed we had to stop. That's what you saw."

"I was frustrated, too." Jess shook her head.

"Do-over?" Elena asked, and Jess was so eager to make amends that her relieved "yes!" started over the end of the brunette's words. Elena asked, "When do you work next?"

"The mimosa brunch tomorrow for people staying tonight."

Jess saw Elena share a look with Eric. "Would you mind if we stayed the night?"

"Here? But why? You... your house?"

"We'd like to spend some private time with you."

"Really?" Eric cleared his throat in response to Jess's surprise, and she hurried to explain "The note. I know what you wrote, but... you mean it?" Eric hummed agreeably.

She looked at both of them curiously. "What will you do for clothes?"

Eric sounded like Lucifer himself—seductive and erotic—when he responded. "They'll air while we're having a fuck-ton of sex."

Jess's cheeks warmed. Damn, she wanted that, so much. Eric's playfulness was beyond anything she had previously experienced. "I guess there's only one question left."

"Our room, or yours?" Elena asked.

"Well, okay, maybe not. My room has, as you know, just a single."

"We've checked into one with a king-size bed," Eric said.

"You already checked in?"

"We were hoping you'd say yes," Eric said.

"And if I had said no?" Jess asked.

His blue eyes were included in his smile then. "The smile earlier tonight after you read my note said yes. Was I wrong about that?"

Jess felt Elena's hand grasping hers. She looked from Eric to Elena and then back to Eric, squeezing Elena's hand. "You weren't wrong." She couldn't believe she really was getting another chance at this. At spending time with these wonderful people.

"Good." Eric stepped forward and cupped Jess's cheek, kissing it so softly that tingles traveled down to her belly. "Room 233."

"As soon as I'm done here," Jess promised.

Elena had vacillated between undressing and putting on a hotel robe or remaining clothed so that Jess wouldn't feel pressured the minute she walked in the door, but she wanted this to be an enjoyable encounter for all of them.

Eric, bless his Libra balance, had taken off his shirt and removed his socks and shoes. Currently he reclined in just his pants against the pillows piled against the headboard and flipped through the cable channels with the remote.

He'd offered to "take the edge off" for her with a quick shower fuck, but she had declined. She looked at the desk next to the dresser that supported the flatscreen television, and where he had laid out his camera equipment. "We can start easy, relax and play," he said.

Elena finally sat down on a chair beside the bed and removed her heels. As if that had been a signal, a knock came at the door.

Eric moved to his feet and went to the door. Looking into the peephole, he threw Elena a thumbs-up before stepping back and opening the door.

"Hi, Jess," he said. From Elena's position she couldn't see the blonde, but Eric leaned out, and then Jess was coming into the room.

Jess was still in her work attire, her white shirt rumpled, and the pants brushing against the carpet because her shoes were in her hand.

"I can take those." Eric took Jess's shoes and placed them by the door, next to his own.

Elena stood. Both barefoot, they were a similar height. She met green eyes and held out a single hand. "We don't have to start where we left off," she said. "Eric brought his camera, so we could have fun shooting photos. No sex."

"Photos still sound fun," Jess said. "But I definitely want the sex, too." Then Elena was treated to fingers tenderly cupping her cheeks and guiding her mouth to Jess's. Then Jess traced Elena's lips with the tip of her tongue and caused molten quicksilver desire to pool in Elena's belly.

"You've tasted me," Jess said against Elena's ear. "This time I get to taste you." Elena's nipples tightened more with each succeeding syllable in the woman's husky tone.

Elena sat on the edge of the bed and watched Jess kneel at her feet. Jess slid her hands up under the dress's hem and unpinned the garters from her silk stockings. Elena looked up to see Eric sitting in the chair she had been in earlier. He was relaxed and watching Jess touch her. Jess rolled the stockings down and off Elena's legs.

Then Jess spoke. "Eric, unzip your wife so I can suck her breasts." Elena looked at Eric, a little surprised. While they had discussed all three of them doing this, Elena had thought it might remain just her and Jess at first while Jess became accustomed to the idea.

Eric slid onto the bed behind Elena and held her in his warm, steady hands. He kissed her nape, shoulder blades, and back, while he gradually pushed the dress off her body. Jess leaned forward and kissed the front of Elena's throat, under her jaw. Elena lifted her chin and her head lolled back against Eric's chest. He kissed her ear and whispered, "Open your eyes, darling. We're going to fuck you."

Elena opened her eyes and her gaze intersected Jess's,

swimming in the green. When Jess's mouth moved lower, Elena leaned back fully onto Eric's knees and welcomed the blonde's weight partially atop her. The woman's knee pressed up between Elena's thighs and her insides heated and melted. Jess kissed her mouth and palmed her breasts, and Elena stopped thinking about anything beyond this moment, or the next one immediately following, becoming totally consumed by the sensations of now.

She cupped Jess's head when the woman's lips pressed and circled on her breasts. When Jess latched on to a tight nipple, Elena inhaled at the suddenness of it. Then she sighed as pent-up need was finally fulfilled. "Yesssssss," she breathed, tangling her fingers in blonde hair. She heard Eric's throaty chuckle behind and above her.

The blonde's mouth was never still nor quiet. Jess hummed around Elena's nipples, then she brushed the very edges of her teeth against Elena's areolas. Electrifying arousal flew along Elena's nerves. She squirmed and lifted her hips. She picked up Jess's head once, twice, and then again, each time taking a kiss. The blonde returned to her breasts after each time, and Elena was frustratingly close to coming, even though she didn't want to. Not yet, anyway. Looking ahead to more time together, Elena wanted to savor every moment. Her mouth watered at her mind's suggestion, and she held Jess's head and throatily said, "Let me undress you."

When Jess lifted up, Elena again could open her eyes, and she saw the blonde look up past Elena's shoulders to Eric behind her. Eric's movements suggested he was pointing out something to the blonde. Jess's sudden smile became wide-eyed and eager comprehension, and she backed off the bed. Elena's gaze followed her to the play bag on the desk. When Jess turned back, she held two sealed dental dams.

Elena leaned forward and tugged the tails of the white shirt out of the waistband of her black pants. She parted the white shirt slowly, button by button. Pushing aside the cloth, her palms grazed satin skin. She pressed her lips into the slopes of Jess's soft stomach. Jess was fit but not hard-bodied, and the woman's stomach made Elena eager to simply rest her head there and be surrounded by her scent. She inhaled and exhaled. Next, Elena parted the catch and zipper of Jess's pants and slid them down bare legs. Below a wiry thin patch of blonde-brown hair, Elena found glistening pussy lips.

She called moisture to her mouth with determination. *Damn.* A rip sounded above Elena's head, and she reached up to find a fresh dental dam pressed into her hands.

Jess laid down on the bed on her back and parted her legs. Elena spread the dam, stroking, and hopefully stoking Jess's passions with her touch. From her moans, Elena gauged she was doing all right.

"I can't wait to see you come," she murmured, stroking with her thumb as she talked.

Jess lifted her head until their gazes met again. "Same here."

Elena looked back at Eric, who had returned to the chair. "Get over here, Mr. Tanner," she teased. "You deserve something too, for arranging this."

"Me? What did I do?"

"Tell me what was in that note you included in Jess's tip?"

"A tip for Jess," he replied simply and obtusely. She shook her head and chuckled.

Jess answered instead. "It said, 'Will you come to help Elena smile again?'" She chuckled, and added, "He spelled 'come' as c-u-m." After a moment, she asked, "Is it working?"

Elena looked from Jess to Eric, then back to Jess. She smiled, fingertips moving over the dam, and held green eyes as Jess's breath caught. The smile widened further before it disappeared between Jess's thighs.

"This isn't work," she teased, feasting her gaze on the beautiful wet cunt before her. "It's play."

When she finished speaking, Elena plied her tongue over Jess's sex, pushing and tapping and massaging open Jess's labia beneath the dam with her fingers. Then, with Jess's fingers gripping her hair, Elena sucked the blonde's burgeoning clit between her lips.

Eric's hand was on Elena's back as she made Jess's panting become moans, then whispered pleas, and, finally, cries of peaking pleasure.

She'd fingered other women to orgasm as their husbands watched, and she'd even been face-deep in another woman's cunt as the woman's husband fucked her from behind, licking both balls and pussy. What she hadn't enjoyed in quite some time, not since she was with Britt and Eric at the layover parties, was a woman who hadn't had their own man to fuck them. She, too, had been single then. This experience was different, and Elena felt a shell of ennui cracking from her senses. She hadn't even been aware something had been choking within her.

Her heart hammered in her chest and she reached back with one hand, feeling for Eric's hips—he'd stripped out of his pants—and silently pulled him against her ass. *Fuck me*, she thought.

Reading her mind it seemed, Eric slid his fingers inside her pussy, which immediately became warmed and wet from Elena's arousal. When Eric's cock replaced his fingers, Elena's moans vibrated against Jess's clit. Jess was pushed over another edge, and Elena felt the dam slip when it was coated in Jess's fluids. She pressed it more firmly against the woman's heated flesh with her fingers and continued licking Jess through another writhing peak, and then another. Finally, Jess's fingers were nudging, not clutching, and Elena let up. She rested her chin on the top of Jess's mound, meeting glazed green eyes.

Her smile widened impossibly further when she saw Jess's lopsided, exhausted smile.

"Give me a minute to recover," Jess said. "So I can hold you while Eric fucks you."

Elena crawled up Jess's body and tossed the dental dam to the side. Eric slid his cock into her again, and Jess held her while he pushed in slow and strong. Her head laid on Jess's chest, and her belly was dampened by the light remains of Jess's fluids. She listened to the woman's heartbeat gradually slowing.

Her pussy milked Eric's cock, and her orgasm, when it came, left her muscles quivering, until Jess's arms engulfed her. She felt a light pressure on the top of her head and knew the blonde had kissed her hair.

Elena closed her eyes, swept along by the waves of peaceful sensations.

Chapter Six

Jess uncurled from Elena gingerly. The brunette remained sleeping, she thought, studying the relaxed, smiling lips. Her gaze lingered on a lock of dark hair that was showing varying shades of brown against the woman's cheek. She had moved her scrutiny to the slightly fluttering lashes and was wondering what Elena might be dreaming, when she felt Eric's gaze on her from Elena's other side.

By silent accord, both she and Eric rose to their feet. At the end of the bed, Jess searched through the pile of discarded clothes for the ones that were hers. Eric grasped her shoulder. She stilled and looked up, not sure what to expect, and not really sure how to act with this man who had mostly just watched her with his wife. Is that how this was supposed to work? Wasn't she supposed to have sex with both of them?

He seemed not to have cared about that. "Thank you." His lips brushed her ear and kept his whisper from waking his wife. "I know she really enjoyed tonight."

Jess sat down to pull on her pants. It was weird not to feel anxious to leave after the sex, only knowing she had to, but if she didn't... "Seeing her pleasure, causing her pleasure, is pretty addictive," Jess agreed.

"Same here." Elena's voice reached them from the bed. Surprised, Jess saw Elena lifting her head from the pillow. "Not sleeping...," Elena said. "Trying to figure out how I can convince you to stay longer."

"I need to go to my room," Jess said.

"Why?" Jess had to admit the question was reasonable. "There's still a couple hours. Set an alarm so you go in time for your shift," Elena said. Clearly trying to entice Jess, Elena sat up, letting the sheet drop from her breasts, and lifted her head on a bent arm.

"Tempting," Jess teased. After Jess had recovered and Elena had been fucked thoroughly by Eric, Jess had licked and sucked Elena to another orgasm with Eric's help.

"Is it working?" Elena asked.

Jess caught Eric's smirk even as she walked over to Elena and pressed the brunette down on the mattress with hands to her shoulders, followed by a kiss that made Elena moan. "This isn't work," she said. The phrase was already becoming something of a mantra between she and Elena. "It's very serious play."

Elena cupped her cheek, and Jess met soft, deep brown eyes. "I want more playtime," she said.

Jess nodded her agreement. A broad hand landed on her shoulder and she looked up to see Eric smiling at her. "I'd really like that," she told Elena and Eric honestly.

Eric held open his arms, and Jess surprised herself when she stood, fit her body against his, and grabbed the belt loops of his pants. She pressed her face into his shoulder while he put his arms around her back. This had been an incredible couple of hours, opening her eyes to many sensations she was still processing—like people who still wanted her around.

"You brought Elena's smile back," he said. "So, we'll get together another time? With better planning?"

"If this lacked planning, I can't imagine what he might actually do with real advance planning time," Elena said, sounding less erotic and more awed. "He sent you the note, *and*," she added to Eric, "you reserved this room during that conversation with Maya before you went off to DP her with Hector, didn't you?"

Eric shrugged. "With more time to plan, I'd have more condoms." Then he tilted his head toward her, his gaze soft. "This was for you, El."

Jess looked at him in surprise; she hadn't thought that not having condoms handy might be the reason Eric didn't really touch her. She now understood why he had backed off quickly when his cock brushed her thigh. He was being a responsible sex partner.

"You should thank him properly," Jess said to Elena. "And you," she added to Eric, "I'll thank later. When you have those condoms." Jess patted Eric's bare chest, tugging the hairs there with her fingers. Like his mustache, the hairs tickled and made her think how his chest would feel against her skin.

Eric smiled and kissed her temple. Jess bent down and kissed Elena one final time. "I really need to go."

In the kitchens and ready for her shift, Jess stood at a counter eating a cold bagel with cream cheese, taken not from the trays set to go out to the brunch buffet but from the supply still bagged in the back of the industrial refrigerator. Carter, the head chef, was finishing filling the warming trays with sausages, bacon, and pan-fried country ham. The sous chef, Jim, was pulling four trays of muffins from the ovens, where they had been warmed to remove the chill from refrigerated storage. Carmen filled fruit baskets and sent them out with waitstaff coming and going in a steady stream of activity.

Jess had already helped when she arrived, taking a box of jellies and distributing them evenly to the centerpieces of each of the deck tables and other serving areas out around the pool where the brunch was being set up. Maya had shooed Jess back into the kitchen when she overheard that Jess hadn't eaten yet when talking with Gus.

The cream-cheese-covered bagel was a luxurious breakfast compared to many mornings when she'd survived on ninety-nine-cent coffee she could refill in her travel mug, thanks to competing convenience store promotions. But this was the start of something new: stability. Tomorrow was her first real payday in almost three months of odd-jobbing it. And she had been making tips, cash enough, she thought, to buy a couple real pairs of slacks and shirts suitable for work. Maybe, she added to herself giddily, she'd buy a proper date dress.

Walking out to the bar to begin her shift, she saw Eric and Elena emerge with other hotel guests. Both wore only towels around their waists, Eric's chest hair a bright blond in the sunlight and Elena's breasts a golden brown. They took turns rinsing under the showerhead by the hot tub before sliding into the water with another couple, also nude. Many of the guests this morning were comfortably naked, or nearly so. She saw flaccid cocks and pierced nipples on many guests. Tattoos too, and the artistry ranged from erotic to silly. This being Jess's first weekend at the club, she had to stop herself staring several times. She frequently shook her head and dropped her eyes back to her work.

"Is a beautiful morning," Gus said as they worked side by side, mixing the mimosas and Bloody Mary drinks, most popular with the brunch crowd. "Nice view while we work, eh?"

She nodded, then asked, "Is it like this every weekend?"

"Yes."

Jess looked across the deck to where Eric helped Elena step from the hot tub. The water glistened on both their bodies. They took their towels over to a table, smoothing them over the cushions before sitting down. "Do you mind if I take a tray out to the tables?" she asked Gus.

"Go ahead. I'm sure they're thirsty." He made no mention of who "they" were, but Jess didn't question it. She arranged a tray of three mimosas, three Bloody Marys, several fruit cups and muffins, then moved out to the tables. She told those who asked that her "order" was meant for a specific table, so as not to lose any items. When she reached the Tanners' table she paused a moment, listening to Elena speak. Then, as she sensed a break in the flow, she caught their attention. "Can I offer anyone drinks? Muffins?"

The couple with the Tanners immediately claimed two of the Bloody Marys. Both Elena and Eric took mimosas. She placed all the muffins on the table, and Elena claimed one of the fruit cups. "Anything else?" Jess moved the other cups to the table too, before straightening again.

"No." Jess studied the woman with platinum hair who had answered. Under the table, whether she knew Jess noticed or not, she was stroking Eric's cock.

"I'm Jess," she said, formally introducing herself and forcing her gaze to look over everyone at the table in turn, instead of only Eric and Elena. "I'm bartending this morning. Let me know if you need anything."

"Do you handle room service orders?" the man asked. From his tone, Jess guessed he wasn't asking her if she delivered drinks, but rather, if she delivered personal services.

Eric moved the woman's hand off him and shook his head at the other man. "Caliente doesn't have that service, George."

"Thought I saw her this morning," he said under his breath. Jess tucked the empty tray under her elbow and walked back to the bar.

Later that morning, Jess received a text message on her phone. It had buzzed in her pocket and she'd been antsy until she could check it on her break. She'd not returned to the Tanner's table since bringing the tray, but she had noticed the Tanners left George and his wife behind only a short time later. Finally, she stepped out to use the bathroom and read it: *Call when we can get together again.*

CHAPTER SEVEN

ELENA TOOK Eric to the airport before dawn on Monday. She smoothed a bit of hair behind his ear when she kissed him as they stood in the loading and unloading zone to say goodbye. They looked like any other couple, until he put on his captain's cap.

"You'll need to go to Tito's for a cut when you get back from this shift," she said. She touched his hair again, seeing it peeking out from under the cap, and ran her fingers through the ends of the strands. Eric had gotten an exclusion for his mustache, but the airline was very particular about a "professional look" for their pilots. So even though Elena liked his hair a bit on the shaggy side, she liked Eric in uniform even better. There would be no flouting the rules and possibly losing his job.

"You, on the other hand, always look perfectly," he said. He brushed his lips against her ear as he added, "Perfectly fuckable," which made her cheeks warm. Pulling back, he kissed her lips and pulled her against him, lifting up so that she felt his cock, slightly thickened, against her belly. "I had a great time this weekend."

"Me too," she said. "See you tonight, flyboy."

"Let me know what Jess says to our message."

"I will."

Back home, Elena switched into black running shorts, black sports bra, and a neon pink tank top. Tying her feet into her cross-trainers, she put her cell phone in her armband and connected a

Bluetooth earpiece. Her personal Pandora playlist began through her exercise tracking app, and she completed three different stretches during the first two songs. She planned a long run, determined to run off some of the weekend's caloric indulgences while also sorting her thoughts. Out to Atlantic Avenue beach park and back, almost twelve miles, ought to do it.

Jess's first paycheck presented her with a bit of a problem. She had no checking account to cash it. Hector had already suggested she set up one, but the banks all wanted direct deposit commitments—which she imagined is why Hector wanted her to have one; it saved the club overhead. But Jess had lived cash-only for so long, the idea of not having it left her wondering how she'd be able to manage her expenses.

She accompanied Gus to his bank where a nice customer service rep had told her about their account services. When she was asked for her address to receive the card in the mail, Gus had jumped in with a post office box. They could get mail at the club, he said, but some people knew that section of town had no apartments or houses. "You can receive things at my box for now, set your own up later."

"I don't expect to get much mail," she said.

"I don't, either," Gus said. "I ain't got bills, living at the club. And I ain't got family, 'cept Genevieve."

The similarities in their situations made Jess feel less awkward. "All right."

"We still gonna go shopping?" he asked. Gus walked with her away from the cashier where she had cashed her paycheck, depositing all but the hundred and change he'd recommended, since she had her tips.

"I need at least a second pair of pants for work, and shirts."

"We can hit up Dickie's for the work clothes," he said. "You need anything else?"

"You can't drive all over the city ferrying me, don't you have things to do?" Jess protested.

"If I don't drive you, you'd have to get a bus. And you'd waste some of your money and a lot of time—the transit isn't very efficient. Besides, this will be the most fun I've had in months."

"Gus," she said, climbing into the passenger seat of his rusty sedan. "This is crazy. But thank you."

"You're welcome." He grinned, put the car in gear, and

continued to act as chauffeur and friend until eleven, when they both had to return to the club and get ready to open the bar for the business crowd. Jess wore her new Dickie's slacks and a gray-green shirt that properly fit her. She had even managed to acquire a pair of boots with nonslip soles without using all her money.

Sipping coffee from Diligent Airlines' complimentary setup by the door, Eric settled into a padded seat at a table in the crew lounge. He looked out at the planes coming and going off the runways and smiled, thinking he was damn lucky to be doing something he loved so much. It was a direct contrast to Carl from the club, who always complained about the politics of his job as associate comptroller of Miami-Dade. The new fellow, George, hadn't been much better, a salesman from Paducah, Kentucky, in town for an industrial plumbing event. The women he'd spent time with this weekend were far better. Even when she was doubting herself, Elena was incredible. Carl's wife, Betty, had talked about her garden and flirtatiously turned it around to talk about how she loved to be "tended." George's wife, Stacy, if he recalled correctly, had been very quiet socially, though she was enthusiastic when it came to having sex. Because of the encounters, Eric had used up his last two condoms in the play bag. So he hadn't been able to have penetrative sex with Jess.

He'd definitely wanted to. When he'd touched her, he found her soft and warm, and her ass, as he had said from the beginning, was amazing. Watching Elena play with Jess's breasts, he'd wanted to as well. But he didn't want to start something he couldn't finish properly. Despite the restraint, the way they had been together had been pretty damn wonderful. He'd gotten to see Jess's face when El drove her over into orgasm with her mouth. He'd gotten to see her smile when Elena came on his cock a few minutes later.

He really hoped that Jess contacted Elena to meet up again.

Reluctantly Eric turned his mind from the weekend's activities and toward the forthcoming flight day, while he awaited the rest of today's assigned flight crew. Megan, his head flight attendant, walked in next, rolling her small flight bag behind her. She was perfectly coiffed, red-colored hair swept up in a bun and her airline logo cap already secured with bobby pins. She smiled when she saw him and moved quickly to his side.

He stood and greeted her with a professional handshake, though, honestly, they were too well acquainted for distant pleasantries. Over the two years they'd worked together, they'd had sex probably three dozen times. "Good morning, Meg," he said.

She hugged him and kissed his cheek. "Morning, stud. I'm looking for a lunch buddy," she suggested, using their public code for "fuck-buddy" requests.

"Can't. Our flights today are a direct to St. Louis, then a one-stop through Atlanta back to Miami. We're back in Miami by six." He found he only briefly regretted the lack of layover time even though he always enjoyed sex with Meg.

Meg pouted. "Not even a quick bite, huh?" He shook his head. "You'll let me know if you change your mind?" she questioned, before walking back over to the coffee she'd previously passed.

He answered, "Of course." The flight board dinged, signaling the arrival of another plane to the terminals. He looked at the details. "We're up," he said. "Time to go check out our wings for the day."

Within minutes, Eric and Meg were walking down a boarding tunnel and shaking hands with the pilot coming off the night shift. "Javier," he greeted. The Cuban with the salt-and-pepper hair removed his cap, tucked it under his arm, and shook Eric's hand. Meg continued on into the plane.

"They're reloading her," Javier said. "Here's the full checklist, but you should keep an eye on the starboard flap sensor. I went down and eyeballed it, but it kept blinking that numbers two and three were stuck up."

"Any drag?" Eric asked.

"Not that I could tell." Javier had a very experienced touch. If the flaps were really stuck up, like the sensors indicated, even a little, Eric knew the man would have noticed the drag on the control stick.

"Good." Taking the checklist, Eric decided if the flap sensor was still indicating a "stuck up" situation, when he got to the hub in St. Louis, he'd file for a technician review and get a different plane swapped in for the return flight. It might cause a delay, but a stuck flap, while seemingly small, could make for rough landings. From the flight weather service, he knew that heavy crosswinds were expected today over Atlanta.

He waved Javier off then stepped inside the fuselage himself. Turning left, he entered the cockpit. Another man, rail-thin with midnight-black closely cropped hair under a Diligent Airlines cap, already worked between his flight board and checking items on a preflight checklist.

"Test the starboard flaps," he told Jorge as he sat down and clipped the checklist in place by his seat.

"Will do, cap."

It was a few minutes of comfortable working silence while he and Jorge went through the preflight lists. When the cockpit door opened, he glanced over his shoulder. Meg leaned forward. "You fellas need anything in here before Vicky and I tell them they can send on the passengers?"

"Nothing."

"No, thanks." Eric's and Jorge's responses overlapped.

"Given any more thought to lunch in St. Louis, Eric?" Meg asked.

Eric shook his head. Missing Megan's pout, he put on his headset and tapped into the tower. "This is Diligent Air flight 2302," he stated. "Requesting runway instructions. We're loading passengers now and headed to St. Louis."

"DA flight 2302," the tower replied. "As soon as you clear the terminal, take taxiway 4N to runway 14L. You're behind Delta 6578."

He looked at his radar board and saw the various flight numbers moving around on the ground and in the air. "Copy that, tower." Hearing the commotion of passengers boarding behind him, Eric smiled. He checked the data on the weather for the flight out. Once Meg reported all passengers had boarded and she'd closed the doors, Jorge checked the fuselage seal sensors and reported "airtight." Eric reversed the engines and backed the plane slowly from the gate.

Once on the taxiway behind Delta's Boeing 767 flight 6578, Eric opened the inflight comms and spoke with his passengers.

"Welcome aboard Diligent Air flight 2302, a direct morning service flight to St. Louis. The weather here in Miami is a beautiful, balmy eighty-two degrees. STL reports clear conditions on the other end for our arrival around 8:22 a.m. local time, where the temps will start out in the sixties and climb to around seventy-six high for today. We are expecting clear weather on our route over the Gulf Coast of Florida and into the heartland over the Mississippi delta, so it should be a smooth flight. We are third in line for our runway and should be taking off in about seven minutes. During taxiing, takeoff, and landing, for your safety, please remain seated with your seatbelts on. Once the seatbelt signs are turned off, we will be cruising at 27,000 feet, and should complete our flight in just under two hours." He added, "Now, please listen as our flight attendants brief you on our safety and emergency procedures. Again, I'm Captain Eric Tanner. My crew and I thank you for flying Diligent Air. Enjoy the flight."

Running along Atlantic Beach Road, Elena's ears filled with the crashing sounds of the surf. The white noise blanked her mind efficiently and let the Latin jazz music carry her away. Several miles back she'd felt the rhythm of her legs' movements become automatic. Her breathing was deep, but not labored. Her heart rate had been in the optimal zone when she'd checked that too at a crosswalk.

A horn sounded and she looked up, surprised to realize she had reached Government Cut, a channel used by ships in and out of Miami. The ferry from the island was just pulling out from its berth, with a few cars parked and secured to its decks as those who worked, instead of played, on the island made their way over to start their workday.

She thought about the privileged lives of many who lived on the island, and the travel of the cruisers on the ships. Vacations, resorts, travel. She'd been raised in Cuban Miami and grew up envious of all the people going into the ports, the airports, the resorts, and the exclusive clubs. She had wanted to travel from very early. Bilingual in English and Spanish, she was eager to tap that talent and work somehow in the tourism industry, but she'd gotten seasick the few times she'd been on the water. Everyone said "the big boats" were different, but she hadn't wanted to test that theory after embarrassing herself on a small party boat, celebrating their upcoming graduation with her privileged white boyfriend and his family. She groaned at the memory. Two days later, the morning of graduation, he had broken up with her. Apparently a "she might be pregnant" rumor had circulated from the incident. She had laughed it off, but it became a "scary prospect" to his parents. Not because they were too young. Instead it was "the girl was pretty enough to sleep with," but Dane's father had refused to allow marriage to "a Hispanic who probably wasn't even legal."

She still found people like Dane's father, people who saw her heritage in her face, her skin, her hair, and shunned her for it. But South Florida wasn't as bad as some places she had been on layovers as a flight attendant. It didn't matter she spoke perfect English; she had an accent. In their eyes, that made her "less."

She had heard the same tone from George about Jess just before Eric coolly rebuked him. They'd left the man and his wife at the table before either she or Eric called him out for his assumptions.

Back in the room, they'd immediately realized George must have seen Jess coming from their room. Once he realized she worked at the hotel, he'd decided she was also an available perk. Packing to leave, she and Eric had both voiced concern that their actions had put an unfair shadow over the younger woman. Walking to the front to check out, they had resolved, in the future, to connect with Jess only outside the club. So, Eric texted the invitation to call.

Elena sat down on a bench at the beach park, fully immersed in her feelings and thoughts surrounding Jess.

She felt a need to do something when it came to the blonde. She remembered the freeing feeling that overcame her when she was fingering and licking Jess to orgasm. She'd needed Eric to fuck her then, in part to feel her connection to him, but also, she realized, it had been to stay tethered to reality. The edges of her vision had gone hazy, and she'd felt so light. Once she'd orgasmed, the floating feeling had lessened, but the wonder and pleasure of experiencing that freedom had remained.

Her phone vibrated against her bicep. She took it out of the armband and studied the screen. The alert, just disappearing, indicated a new email. The subject read: *Re: business proposal.*

Eric threw his flight bag onto the back seat when he reached the car, and then took the car keys from Elena. After they were settled, Eric driving and Elena in the passenger seat, he leaned across the gear shift and kissed her.

"How was your day?" he asked when they were clear of the worst of the merging lanes.

"I got a message," Elena said, and she sounded excited.

So Eric asked the logical question, "From Jess?"

"Oh. No. I haven't heard from her. This was something else." Elena frowned, pursed her lips, and then continued, "I've been thinking of other ways to earn income."

"I thought we were fine with just my paycheck?"

Elena shook her head. "I didn't mean... How's this? I've been considering some different things to do with my time."

Somewhat facetiously, but because the young woman was easily brought to mind, Eric suggested, "Get Jess to come over and you can do her."

Elena swatted his arm. "I'm serious," she laughed.

"So'm I." At a stoplight, Eric was treated to a look of consternation, so he dropped the more playful line of discussion. "Okay. So, you're looking for ways to spend your time. Hobby? I can teach you photography."

She shook her head. "I can take pictures. But the hours in front of a computer don't interest me. I wanna be out, moving, talking to people."

"What about volunteering or community organizing?"

"I am so not soccer mom material. And I'm not really calm when it comes to politics."

Eric knew that. He could treat such things as mental exercises, and even with a sort of emotional distance, but Elena had strong opinions. He'd more often be bailing her out of jail if she got into activism. "Okay. So, what exactly do you have in mind?"

"Organizing travel tours."

He smiled, thinking immediately it was perfect. "Tons of companies in the Miami area need agents. And you're bilingual. You'll find someplace you can really shine."

"I could, but..." Elena's hesitation made Eric look over at her at the stoplight. "Actually... I was thinking of starting a company," she said, her expression earnest.

"What about all those companies? That's some heavy competition." Eric guided the car into the driveway and stepped out to look at her over the car roof as she got out.

Her smile was bright, and her earnestness had become eagerness as she followed him into the house. "Not if I specialize in adults-only, club-centered guided tours."

"Adult travel tours. We've seen those, too."

"Not as many and not around here," she pointed out.

"Where would you want to go?" He was trying to be on board, but Elena had gotten out of the airlines and stopped traveling.

"Swinger and sex clubs overseas." She ticked off regions on her fingers. "Latin America, the Caribbean, and the Spanish Riviera." He nodded. "Remember how much fun we had in Costa Rica, Mexico, and Puerto Rico?" she added.

Giving it some honest thought, Eric sat down at the kitchen island and let his mind wander over the memories.

During Elena's last two years with Diligent Airlines, the company had run a "first-class travel club" promotion with vacation rewards for frequent fliers. In the first year only 142 people in total qualified for all three of the destinations out of 1.4 million customers on the airline annually. It was only double that the next year. When DA's execs hadn't seen the desired return on their investment, the entire program was dropped. The miniscule number of winners had still been flown, at a loss to the company, to the pre-reserved resorts.

Flight crews had been given rooms in the hotel blocks, since there were so many empty, and were told to submit site reviews and suggestions for further programs. While having a place to lay their heads had been nice, the amenities were too sedate and family-centered at the booked hotels. So Eric and Elena had gone into the surrounding cities. Thankful for international data plans, they'd visited a swingers' dating club website, and found far more interesting places and adult activities to spend their time and energy on. Their feedback to the company had been about the food and the bars and clubs, but they had seriously gotten their swing on at the more private clubs.

Exploring all this new territory had been like energy shots to Elena. She'd dived eagerly into each experience. Her language skills had helped them out of a couple hinky situations, and that had given her even more confidence.

Mexico, as they had told Jess, had been the site of Eric's first anal fisting at Elena's hands, thanks to a beautiful Jalisco silver tequila. In Costa Rica, Elena had her first all-woman orgy. Club members in Puerto Rico had introduced Elena to a swing, which was why they now had one set up at home.

"Your mind went exactly where mine did when I first had the idea."

Eric came out of his thoughts to find Elena pushing a beer toward him across the island's faux marble surface. She smiled knowingly.

He took a large swallow from his glass, then said, "Those were incredible trips."

"Exactly. But I didn't want to go into anything without checking out a few things. I got an email back today saying I don't need a license as a travel agent. I can register with a professional organization to build legitimacy, have a profile, and point of contact DBA."

"What about the U.S. State Department? Travelers need visas, passports, entry and exit declarations."

"That's all the responsibility of the traveler, but a website with the links, summarizing the information and documentation needed is a good idea. I can research and write all that up."

"How will you plan packages?"

"Emailing, phone calls. Once I build an itinerary and get some dates, I can advertise and collect deposits—fully refundable in case the trip doesn't make numbers. I'd then negotiate final rates on the transportation, flights, hotels, and clubs."

He was beginning to share Elena's enthusiasm. "Is there any profit margin?"

"Even to start, we would make enough to go on the trips ourselves without using personal money."

The idea had merit, and he liked the idea they'd have mini "vacations" leading these tours. "How long are the trips?"

Again she showed she'd been doing research. "The tours that get the most commitments seem to last five or seven days. Two weeks is long, and the numbers drop off significantly."

"Five or seven days is still a long time. I can't get that long a vacation off of DA's flight rotations without consequences. And multiple times a year?"

Elena lifted her wine cooler bottle to her lips, but when her throat only moved once in a small swallow, he knew she was thinking, not drinking.

"It's a neat idea," he said. "Though it sounds like a lot to take on."

"Okay," she said, putting down the bottle. "I'll keep working on it."

"How about...?" He considered how things might work. "Since you don't need licensing to be an agent, why not start by joining an established travel agency or tour operation?" He brought up the more secure idea again. "I can help you with the resume."

"I can look," Elena said, her tone flat. Eric covered his frown by lifting his beer bottle to his mouth.

"Miami's a major multicultural hub. There have to be a lot of businesses arranging international tours, and even if they're not strictly adult, that might be something you can build toward. I know there are travel offices in the airport commerce center. We could commute together again."

Elena turned away and dropped her empty wine cooler bottle

in the pull-out cabinet designated for recyclables. With her back still to him, she asked, "Are you hungry? I can start dinner."

"Sure. I'll shower," Eric said. He stood up and left his beer, which was not quite empty, on the island.

Watching Elena move around, collecting food items, spices, and a skillet, Eric knew he had caused his wife's sagged shoulders, but didn't know what to say to fix it. When the skillet landed loudly on the stove's glass cooktop, he winced; Elena didn't react.

Eric said, "I love you," before he went to the master bedroom. He laid out the pieces of his uniform on the bed before entering the bathroom. Turning on the water, Eric thought, *El will be okay after some space.*

The dinner table was quiet; Elena knew it was her fault. She hadn't considered that Eric wouldn't support the idea of her starting a business. Or that he might assume he would always travel with her. He flew all over the U.S. without her. Surely she could do four or five days on a tour without him?

She also didn't want to work by someone else's rules; she wanted to make her own. She'd been working for others since she was sixteen, ever since her first job as a McD's cashier. She'd been interested in management, but never got promoted beyond shift lead so she'd moved to waitressing. Then the chance to travel as a flight attendant had grabbed her imagination and she'd not looked back—until now.

"I'd really like to try," she said. She decided she'd bring up the idea of traveling by herself on the tours later, get him used to the idea of her being an independent businesswoman first.

"I know, and I'm sorry I reacted badly," Eric said. "I didn't... could we try house parties first?"

"We've attended a few of those," she said softly. "This is more about traveling."

"Yeah, but we can open it beyond just our known friends. Let them bring in people they know. We can buzz all the clubs in the Southeast. It would widen contacts. Then you can look overseas."

"This isn't about having more varied sex, Eric. I like our circle of friends, but I want to travel, and I want to do it on my own schedule." She hesitated, then added, "And not just when you're free."

Eric nodded, but it was clear he didn't yet understand. Elena sighed and suggested a way to start small. "Okay. House parties to start? To get my name out there and grow my reputation. I'd like to create something more than 'come to our place for sex', though. We can have themed dinner parties, or movie nights."

"What about pool parties and barbecues? In the warmer months," Eric added. "For the cooler months, how about strip poker nights?"

Elena nodded, agreeing to the idea. "I can makeover the playroom for different themes. Get people interested in the idea of experiencing different cultures?"

There was a buzz on the kitchen counter. Eric looked up. "It's your phone, I think," he said.

Elena slid her chair out from the table, hurrying to collect the phone. It wasn't a call, but a text.

"It's Jess. Texting on a break from work, but she says hi." She leaned a hip against the counter and held the phone in both hands, ready to respond.

"Say hey for me."

Hey, Elena tapped back. *Hector still being a dick?*

Jess's reply was simple: *No.*

What's on your mind? she asked.

You, came Jess's reply, and Elena blushed. *Miss you.*

Miss you too.

Eric came to Elena's shoulder. "Oh, hey, invite her over."

Elena typed, *Wanna visit? When are you free?*

Y! was the reply; simple, excited. Elena smiled. *I'll be off Wednesdays from now on. Too slow here to need two handling bar.*

'K. Pick u up at 2?

I can borrow Gus's car.

Elena frowned. *Sure?*

"George, remember," Eric said. "That's why we decided to only meet her offsite?"

Elena nodded. She entered a new text: *OK.* She added their home address.

Saved, Jess replied. *Jeans good?*

Eric's hands were on Elena's waist when she typed, *Perfect.*

CHAPTER EIGHT

GETTING OUT of Gus's beater, Jess looked around at the neighboring houses as she walked to the Tanners' front door. The houses on the cul-de-sac had SUVs and strictly maintained lawns—not surprising as there was a lawn crew trimming bushes one house down. The two children being shepherded inside another house by their skort-clad mother wore green-and-gray soccer uniforms.

After her shopping trip, Jess felt only slightly out of place. Her jeans were new, and so was the tangerine button shirt, but they were plain denim and cotton Walmart store stock, not designer brands. At least today she wasn't wearing her "work" clothes.

Jess found a front door buzzer button and pushed it, then crossed her hands in front of her to wait. The exposure of waiting on the front stoop made it feel like time was moving slowly. After she'd felt her palms start to sweat, she reached again for the buzzer.

The door flew inward as her finger's press made the buzzer sound again. She heard it both outside and from inside the house, behind Elena, now standing in the doorway.

"Hi," Jess said, but she was startled to silence. Elena was dressed in shorts and a tank top, wearing a full-length dark blue apron that was spattered in gray. "What are you doing?" she asked.

"Eric and I started spackling so we could paint."

"Did I mistake the time?" Jess asked. "I thought you said two?"

"I did. C'mon in." She stepped back and gestured with her

hands. She held a plaster-knife in one hand. "Eric's still downstairs. I had come up to use the bathroom when I heard the door."

"You sure I shouldn't just go? Come back another time?"

"Nah, we can shower then have dinner." Elena waved her forward toward a door that was propped open. She moved it further open with her hip.

"You have a basement?" Jess asked. "How?"

"It's limestone and concrete, super watertight," Elena said. "Incredibly rare this far south."

"I bet. Don't you have a canal just out back?"

"Yes. The pool's in a limestone-concrete shell, too. Eric and I were lucky to find this place."

"What'd you want a basement for anyway?" Jess asked.

"Eric wanted a 'man cave'." Elena smiled. "But I convinced him we should have a playroom," she said. "C'mon."

Jess followed Elena down the steps into an area lit by pools of light coming from strategically hung car-repair lamps. The space was probably only about two hundred square feet, and deeper than it was wide, though not by much. The gray walls had obviously been scraped down and spackled to smooth them. Since Jess had been her own handywoman more than once, she recognized the signs of a room about to be painted pretty easily. Drop cloths covered the floors, their edges touching the walls, and painter's tape had been used to protect all the edges in sight.

Eric stood at a saw table in the middle of all this, looking up through a pair of thick dust-covered goggles. He wore a tank top, and his arms were covered in sawdust. As soon as he saw them, he ripped off the goggles, used a cloth hanging from the belt at his waist to clean his hands, and came quickly over to Jess and Elena.

"Hey!" he said enthusiastically. "Good to see you!" He looked at Elena. "Guess we lost track of time."

"You don't have to stop on my account," Jess said.

"Yes, we do." Eric rubbed his stomach. "We'd planned to stop for lunch and clean up before you got here."

"Care to join us?" Elena asked.

"For lunch?"

"For the shower," Eric said.

Jess knew she could enjoy that, but... "Why don't you explain what you're doing here?"

He pulled out a chair, roughly dusted it off with his rag and offered it to her. "We're remodeling. El's got this idea for creating adult travel tours. I suggested we start with house parties."

"Isn't all this your photo studio?" She noticed the umbrella reflectors, and a canvas obviously used as a backdrop had been laid over a stand. She recognized some other items from Eric's photos of Elena. There was a mattress in one corner with rumpled red sheets, and a footlocker next to it.

"Technically it's the playroom, but since it wasn't being used a lot, yeah, I do a lot of my shooting here. It can be redressed a lot of ways."

"We're building a riser," Elena explained. "I'm assembling the ruffle," she added, pointing to a pile of cloth next to another chair.

"You need help? I can cut a straight line, follow directions, and use tools." Jess brightened at the idea of being involved in something creative.

Eric rubbed his mustache, then scratched because he'd transferred some of the sawdust onto his cheek. "We can finish this another time. But now, I have a better idea."

Elena was laughing. Neither she nor Eric had cleaned up, and now Jess's skin held a light dusting of "artfully applied" sawdust, according to Eric.

The blonde was stripped down to her bra and boy shorts. Around her hips she wore one of Eric's tool belts, and she had a hammer in her right hand. She leaned on a brace already built for the riser and posed as if hammering in a nail. Elena had provided a cloth scrap from the ruffle as a hair tie. The result was a woman who looked playful, strong, and erotic.

Eric had fetched his camera and set it up on a tripod, then arranged the umbrella reflectors to brighten the space more completely. The hanging car lamps still provided the light, but now the focus of the space was Jess. Eric had finally gotten the blonde to pose for him.

Sitting aside on the chair, Elena simply watched as Eric cajoled, teased, and encouraged Jess into various poses that highlighted her many stunning qualities and put her at ease.

"It's Tool Time with the Tanners," Eric called out. "Welcome to our stage the newest cast member, Jess Davies."

Jess's color had heightened in her cheeks, and the finest sheen of sweat had appeared on her face since they had started. A strongly muscled arm flexed, raised and then lowered, again mimicking using the hammer against the riser's nails.

"What are we building today, Jess?" Eric asked.

"A bed, Eric," she said, then her gaze leveled, and Elena, behind Eric, was treated to the heat of arousal in green eyes. "For fucking."

Continuing to click away, Eric laughed; Elena felt her blood thrum with excitement, and her own cheeks and throat heated.

"Why don't you show off some of your techniques," Eric said. He was still chuckling. "There are a few things you can use in the chest."

Jess walked over to the footlocker. When she bent over, she twitched her ass—that perfect ass. Elena found herself suddenly in the path of direct green eyes when Jess asked, "Come help me out here?"

Moving forward, Elena knew what things Jess could find in that chest. She stood beside Jess while the woman moved items this way and that, but she didn't care about the contents. She was enthralled by the excitement in Jess's face. Suddenly the blonde straightened up. Jess now had a knob-head vibrator in hand. "Batteries?" she asked.

Swallowing, Elena nodded. "They're fresh." Eric had her use it in one of their most recent shooting sessions.

Jess thumbed on the control and the soft buzzing reached out and rippled over Elena's senses.

"I think I've found just the thing," Jess said, turning now fully to the camera and running her fingertips over the vibrating tip.

Elena sucked moisture into her mouth; when she didn't hear Eric say anything either, she turned her head to see him giving Jess a thumbs-up, eyes tucked behind his camera.

Finally he spoke. "Whenever you're ready."

Elena asked, "Would you like a hand with that?"

She caught Jess's smile just before the woman's lips brushed hers. "I thought you'd never ask."

Jess laid on the mattress and moved across the sheets, rolling on palms, shoulders, and hips, enjoying the smooth cotton against her skin. Used to rough sheets in even rougher beds, she was simply enjoying the softness. Her imagination went to the hedonistic and she closed her eyes. She blocked out the camera clicks and focused instead on Elena's touch as she helped her. A tangle of her hair under her shoulder was instantly fixed by Elena. "There."

She laughed to cover up the awkwardness, and warm laughter

answered from both her companions. Elena adjusted a pillow under her shoulders as Jess parted her legs at the knees, and then brought her feet together. Though her sex was covered, she was going to make her actions clearly visible to Elena, who had sat back and was no longer touching her.

She lightly touched the vibrator to the muscles of her stomach, making them jump and tighten. Watching her own motions, Jess slowly moved the vibrator head over her shorts and down toward her vulva. The sensations made her clit twitch and her pussy pulse.

Elena slid one of her hands up Jess's calf then thigh, and soon Elena had stretched out next to Jess. Her fingers moved over Jess's stomach, adding to the pleasant tingles from the twitching muscles. Finally, Elena's hand joined Jess's on the vibrator.

Elena's mouth moved over Jess's shoulder, up onto her neck, then on her throat under her ear. Tingles elicited moans. Jess leaned her head back to grant the brunette more access and felt the faintest brushes of the woman's hair against her skin as her mouth impressed more delight upon Jess's skin.

With a gentle tug, Elena claimed control of the vibrator, and then the speed of it pulsing against Jess's vulva increased. Her moans became husky groans, then turned to pleading when the vibrations began causing that perfect chain reaction that she knew would lead to a mind-blowing orgasm, the kind she hadn't had in many years. She leaned back on one arm, and with the other wrapped around Elena's, she blindly sought out the woman's mouth, a needed anchor when the demand for release started to throb in her body.

Throatily, she demanded, "Fuck. Fuck me. Now."

Elena slid over her, above her, and, while the vibrator head was cupped in her palm and pressed against Jess's throbbing clit, Elena's fingertips pressed inside Jess's desperately clenching cunt.

Jess's mouth fell open, the sounds muffled when Elena's mouth covered hers and her tongue dipped inside and matched the dance of her fingers. Jess's orgasm wasn't starbursts but a throbbing, which built slowly and filled Jess from belly to toes and up to her head. She sucked on Elena's tongue and made random sounds, from expletives, to praises and cries as her nerves continued sharing the pleasures they experienced. Suddenly she crashed over the edge, once, then again, and again.

Finally she could make no more sounds, her mouth dry. She panted and grasped Elena's forearm, attempting to still the woman's motions in her sex, wanting more but feeling she couldn't possibly. "Oh. Uh. Okay," she said. "Okay. I... fuck." She sighed out the last word until it was only a breath of sound. "I... wow. That was..." She shook her head, blinked, and cleared her vision, finding Elena smiling, brown eyes gazing down into her own.

"Incredible," Elena breathed, and she kissed Jess tenderly, her fingers moving away, but damp and gentle against Jess's quivering belly.

Jess could think of nothing to say, so she nodded. Husky laughter warmed Jess's ear as Elena rolled partly off Jess's body but didn't end contact entirely. Her leg draped across one of Jess's, and her breasts—Jess hadn't recalled Elena stripping out of her clothes, but she was not complaining—pressed against Jess's upper arm.

The vibrator had been turned off and put aside somewhere, though she couldn't be sure where. She only knew she couldn't hear it, feel it, or see it anymore. She turned her head slightly, which brought her chin nestling into Elena's throat. She felt slightly chilled as sweat evaporated from her skin, and she tasted and smelled the telltale saltiness on Elena's skin too, telling her that the brunette had also exerted herself.

Jess couldn't recall the last time she had felt so calm and satisfied. Faintly she felt Elena's pulse under her lips and let the steady rhythm of it lull her senses until her eyes were closed. Something was draped over her and Elena and blocked the cool air from chilling their overheated skin further. A single word softly reached her ears: "gorgeous."

Eric had begun the photo session with the intention of capturing every moment of Jess and Elena's interactions. But when Elena had pulled off her pants and top and moved against Jess, Eric had seen his wife's gaze drink in Jess's reactions to her touch. He had stopped clicking and moved away from the camera, enthralled.

Settling to a chair, he had been unable to stop watching, but he knew something rich with emotion was building between the two women. He wasn't jealous. Elena wasn't forgetting him—she'd glanced over her shoulder once, needing to include him, and smiled before tangling her tongue with Jess's as he saw her fingers disappear inside the blonde's body.

He heard clearly, whether Jess did or not, Elena's whispered admirations, the pleasure she voiced at how responsive the young woman's body was to her touch, the desire Elena expressed at wanting to see Jess's orgasm.

But this was not a display for Eric. This was a sexual communication solely between Elena and Jess. His playful camera work may have instigated it, but the women were capably carrying it through to the finish without him.

When the room was quiet again, he saw Elena shiver, and the way she pressed against Jess told him she was cold. He grabbed the pushed-aside sheet and pulled it up over their figures.

His own movement told him how stiff and hard he had gotten. When he sat back down he rubbed himself through his shorts, easing the tension a tiny bit. But he didn't want to disrespect what he had seen by "beating off."

The quiet of the room became total. His breathing rasped in his ears. He realized that Elena and Jess had closed their eyes, their own breathing calm and quiet. He exhaled and lifted one leg up onto his other thigh to relieve the tightness around his cock from his shorts. Gingerly he opened his zipper and grasped himself. He squeezed around the head and balls, offering his cock both relief and more torture. He did it again and closed his eyes, this time to block out other stimuli, namely the women resting on the mattress nearby.

"You got a wrapper for that tool, handyman?"

Eric's eyes opened to find Jess watching him, her hand resting on Elena's bare breast. She had rolled onto her side. He cleared his throat. "Chest," he answered.

"Get it," she said.

He started to push to his feet, cock still out of his pants, then hesitated. "You sure?"

"You watched Elena fuck me."

"I turned off the camera," he admitted.

"No pictures?"

He shook his head. "It..." He trailed off. "Didn't want to share that."

"Eric." Now came Elena's voice, out from next to Jess's shoulder. "Stop being the perfect gentleman. Come over here and fuck the women."

He joined them on the mattress, but not before grabbing two condoms from the chest. His cockhead was engulfed by Elena's mouth almost as soon as he sat down. She moved her throat expertly, knowing just how his cock would respond to the vibration, while she unpinned the button and finally yanked his shorts off his hips. Removing his underwear was a bit trickier; he really was sticking as straight out as he tended to get, his cock curved to the left near the tip. He was definitely ready to pound something, though not literally nails.

While Elena attended to his cock, Jess rolled until she had pressed her breasts to his chest and was thoroughly kissing him. She didn't use her tongue, but she seemed to enjoy nipping, a teasing will she, won't she, and he joined the game, chasing her mouth when it left his, until he reached behind her head and asked again if this was okay. She nodded; he kissed her.

Elena unrolled the condom down his shaft; the pressure of the action made his head a little hazy. He sat up, and Jess touched his cock for the first time purposefully with her hand as she moved across his legs. He bit his lip, the pinch of pain distracting him from coming prematurely.

Holding her up under her thighs when she straddled him, he looked up into Jess's face, then across her shoulder into Elena's eyes. Jess's hand pressed down between their bodies and her fingers wrapped around the base of his cock. Using her own thigh muscles to control her descent, Jess lowered herself onto his erection.

She experimentally squeezed and rocked her hips. A hum and smile lightened her eyes. He held still and let her control what she wanted.

Eric loved being in a woman's body. Jess was no different, not really. But she held his gaze while her inner muscles pulled at him. He put one hand back to steady himself and kept the other on her thigh. "Stay" was on his lips, but he fought it down, instead offering up a moan of pleasure.

Elena's hand joined his on Jess's thigh. They felt the flexion in the blonde's muscles together and it made him groan, how much pleasure he and Elena were experiencing with this young woman. His restraint and the desire to let Jess set the pace slipped. He jerked his hips upward and pushed down on her thigh. She began to move up and down faster.

Fuck. Just like that, he was gone. Lying back, he grabbed both Jess's thighs tightly and pulled her down, even while he forced his hips up, pumping his cock in her heat. He looked up at her body above him. She was arched back against Elena's chest. His wife was kissing Jess's throat, and Eric had an idea what had changed Jess's pace. But he didn't care. *Damn*, he was gonna blow. He fought off the urge and concentrated on slowing his movements, dragging his cock against the clenching walls of the tight pussy surrounding it. He felt the ridges inside of her and reveled in the gasps and sounds falling from her lips.

Elena's legs straddled his behind Jess, her hands moved up from Jess's thighs. He saw his wife's hands squeeze Jess's breasts and felt a corresponding squeeze from Jess's pussy on his cock.

His and Jess's voices mingled, the sounds growing more and more incoherent. Eric finally felt a ripple starting from the base of his balls and pushing up the length of his cock. Jess's body constricted, and he felt the erratic twitching of his cockhead releasing his load.

Lifting up slowly, Jess's inner muscles milked his length while he gripped tightly on the base of the condom, partly to be sure it didn't slip, but also to slow his spurts, and the inevitable softening that followed. He watched himself emerge from within her, and saw her fluids glistening on the condom. The sight made him lick his lips.

Fingers slipped down a soft abdomen. Eric enjoyed the differences of Jess and Elena's bodies. Jess's fingers parted herself around him, becoming covered with her own fluids.

Jess brushed her fingers to his lips. Her scent filled Eric's nostrils and his cock twitched, wanting to get back in the game now. Even though he knew he needed recovery time, there was a desire to slide back in and wait—surrounded by warm woman—to harden again.

It was a feeling he experienced with Elena; one of the reasons he'd married her. To be soft was to be vulnerable. That wasn't something he did easily. He knew rationally that he found women's bodies addictive, and Jess's was a particularly beautiful example of his type. Blonde, brunette, or redhead, he enjoyed women who were fit and yet soft.

That's why he loved swinging. He loved the feel of a woman in his hands, on his cock, and he enjoyed their sounds when he pleasured them, or he watched them being pleasured. Still, when Elena settled to Jess's other side and her brown gaze found his across Jess's shoulder, and her hand slipped into his on Jess's upraised hip between them, he felt something indefinable and compelling about sex with Jess.

He kissed strands of hair that lay across her cheek and felt the curve of her lips in a smile; she sighed in what he guessed to be satisfaction, and her fingers slid lazily through the hairs on his chest.

Against Jess's thigh, he squeezed Elena's fingers, showing her the smile that stretched his own lips.

Leaving the basement, Jess suggested they shower together. Soaping each other's bodies became a laughter-filled experience. Jess got an elbow to the head from Eric while they attended to Elena— Eric lathering her upper body and Jess lathering and kissing her lower. Eric's cock came to attention again when Elena soaped it while Jess teased his nipples, as Elena had suggested. A near fall set all their hearts racing, and Eric stepped first from the shower soon after.

"You ladies should finish here," he said. "I'll start dinner."

Content to continue, Elena soaped Jess while she lifted her arms and washed her own hair. The shampoo smelled of mint, and Jess felt her scalp tingling.

"You like that," Elena said. Her hands moved over Jess's ass when she stood and pressed their bodies together. The woman's legs were soft and firm against her own, and the swells of her breasts were pillowed against Jess's. She reached past Jess, and the water stopped pelting their heads and shoulders.

"I'm having so much fun," she said.

"Me too," Elena said. "I'm so glad Eric found you gawking at pictures of me." Elena's tone was light, teasing.

"I wasn't 'gawking'," Jess protested, though she totally knew she had been. "His photos were so different from the others." She lowered her hands from rinsing her hair and wrapped her arms around Elena's back. "But yes, I wanted to fuck his model so much."

"Now you have. What next?" Elena asked.

"Get her to fuck me again," Jess replied, showing a pleased, tooth-filled smile.

Laughing, Elena handed Jess a robe from the back of the door. "Food first."

Jess flipped her hair out from beneath the robe's collar. "What are you going to wear?" She followed Elena, who was still nude, into the master bedroom.

Elena pulled out a long, sheer piece of fabric from a drawer in a low dresser set under a mirror. "Sarong," she replied, wrapping it and tying it off around her hips, leaving her breasts bare.

"Do I get to watch Eric eat you for dinner?" Jess teased. "You're going to torture the man." She shook her head. "What am I saying? You're going to torture me. I love your breasts."

"I'm partial to yours, but thank you," Elena said. She walked back to Jess, cupped her cheek, and Jess followed the tiny strokes suggesting she bring her mouth down, and brought their lips together. Leisurely, she explored the woman's mouth. Jess felt Elena take her hand, and she was led from the bedroom back to the main part of the house.

Mouth-watering aromas greeted them in the kitchen. Sizzling reached their ears. Back in his shorts and now wearing a gray T-shirt, Eric stood at the stove. What smelled like chicken snapped in a skillet of popping oil in front of him while he used a spatula.

"I thought you might enjoy my world-famous strip chicken," Eric said.

"World-famous?" Jess asked dubiously, but she felt playful, too, leaning on the counter and watching him cook. Elena's hand rested on Jess's lower back and her head rested on Jess's shoulder.

Eric's blue eyes twinkled when he glanced over his shoulder at her and Elena. "Yep, I've had women the world over strip after I've cooked it for them."

Elena laughed. "So what do you do for women you've already fucked?" It was clear she was posing the question for Jess's benefit, since she looked from Jess to Eric while she spoke.

"Get hard as a post and ready to do it again."

Meeting Eric's eyes while he was smiling, Jess didn't doubt he was getting hard just talking to them. A tension in his eyes and a directness to his gaze promised he was serious.

He did want to fuck her again. A glance at Elena revealed the brunette wanted more sex, too. A history of one-night stands told her that this was likely only one night of fun, even if it was more varied and certainly more partners than she'd ever had.

Elena trailed her arm up Jess's and drew her from her thoughts. "It's time for a little sharing," the brunette said. "C'mon, help me put out the dishes."

Jess followed Elena to the dining table, and the buffet against one wall. Drawers opened, dishes came out, then silverware and cloth napkins. Copying Elena, Jess set two places on one side, while Elena set up one end.

Elena started, "I've always known I wanted intimacy with women and men." She retrieved stemware from a cabinet. "I got caught with my girlfriend by my mother when we were sixteen. She became super-restrictive, and I left home as fast as I could after high school."

"I was in a group home for orphans when I was sixteen," Jess replied with ease. "I hadn't known any adults who stepped up and acted like parents. The woman running this place was different. She seemed to care that I figure out how to be independent. I used to masturbate while imagining her saying, 'you should learn to do for yourself, Jess'. Man, she made me hot."

"Always been into the older woman, huh?" Eric chuckled.

Elena side-eyed him, but asked Jess, "When was your first time?"

"When still in the system, I only made out with boys. I was attracted to a few girls, but there wasn't really..." Jess trailed off.

"What stopped you?"

"I didn't want to get thrown out, or labeled deviant. One of the boys at the home was gay, he'd been thrown out of his last foster home when he was caught with a boyfriend. I didn't want to screw up any chance I could to find a family someday. So, no, I... pushed down those feelings."

Eric's arrival with their food disrupted the conversation briefly. Everyone settled into seats and passed around the bowls of food. In addition to the chicken, there was a casserole of green beans in a cream sauce and covered with french-fried onions. Eric had also put buttery rolls in the oven.

Jess hummed in pleasure at the variety of flavors. Chewing and swallowing, she cleared her palate with the white wine served with the meal. Then she said, "It's delicious."

"Glad you like it," Eric replied. "I learned to cook for myself in the Air Force. Most single guys never cooked for themselves—always hopping out to the bars, picking up chicks. 'Weekending' they called it. My sister and I were raised by a single mom. I wanted to be a good husband, not like the shithead who left our family. So I didn't play around while enlisted."

"You didn't...? Then how did you get into swinging?" Jess asked.

"The sex parties among the airline flight crews weren't swaps, since most of us weren't married. But they were group sex... fun, laid-back. You were expected to look and move around the room. I didn't, though, not at first. Britt was my 'steady' at these things. We fucked, but when we were done, I'd masturbate and just watch everyone else. Until I saw Elena."

"I came to one party, the new girl," Elena said, picking up the story. "Britt had invited me. I had a crush on her. I didn't know she had been with Eric. We were both on a bed, in the middle of having sex. I'd had too much to drink. I got brave and kissed her. She responded."

"I didn't know Britt was into women," Eric continued. "I got hard instantly and took Britt from behind while she continued kissing Elena."

"We all had a conversation afterward, kind of like the one we're having now," Elena said. "Britt said that she would love to have a private threesome with Eric and me." Elena chuckled.

"Did you?" Jess asked. Elena and Eric nodded. "Was it good?"

"No, it was terrible," Eric said. "Britt and Elena and I stumbled through. Slipped in fluids, too hard with the fingers, or wrong angles—every awkward moment possible. I was flaccid as a flounder most of the time."

That didn't sound like a positive start. Jess wondered, "That's terrible. How'd you end up married and swinging?"

"Elena wanted to try again." Eric shook his head, sounding amazed even retelling it now. "In my mind I'd given such a shitty performance, I was sure neither woman wanted anything to do with me. But Elena, well, she was determined. She realized I loved the show, the risqué-ness of it all, having sex with coworkers when we had all these nonfraternization rules. She ambushed me and took me right to the edge with a blowjob just before we left the hotel for a preflight check-in."

"I told him, 'keep it up, and you can fuck me when you land.'"

"I didn't keep it up, but I was like Pavlov's fucking dog. I saw Elena leaving the plane, and suddenly I was rock-solid again. She and Britt and I went to the crew lounge, and I fucked both women until I swear I was dry."

"You like a challenge," Jess said. "Spontaneity is my thing. Waiting to come here was the most planning I've done in years."

"I've mellowed a lot," Eric replied. "But I love spontaneity too. Getting to know different people is my favorite thing about the lifestyle."

Elena started collecting the plates. "Sex with both Britt and Eric was a revelation for me. Like I said, I knew I was attracted to both men and women. I'd just never considered the sheer amount of fun I could have with multiple partners."

"That explains the playing, so when did marriage enter the picture?"

"When the company found out Eric and I were having sex," Elena said.

"Just the two of you? Not others?"

Eric's face darkened visibly with real anger. "We were 'turned in' by someone who got jealous. Elena had turned down this aggressive little prick at a party. We found out he snapped pictures on his camera phone. He showed them to the execs."

Elena lightly touched his hand. He blew out a breath and most of the darkness receded.

"We got out of the reprimand," Eric continued, "I said we were engaged. That kept us both employed. Damn double standards would've had Elena fired for fraternization, but my job was never in jeopardy."

"After six months pretending to be engaged, Eric asked me for real," Elena said. "He promised nothing would change, he wasn't looking to tie me down. We loved seeing new places, flying was a high for both of us. So we did it."

Ice cream sundaes and a movie were the intended after-dinner activity. But the feature presentation was barely started when Jess leaned over and sucked a dropped dollop of melting ice cream from Elena's breast. For the blonde, Elena's skin was suddenly more interesting than the slow exposition of the urban rom-com. Another drip of ice cream fell from Elena's spoon, and Jess started exploring the mingled tastes of salty skin and sweet cream.

Eric brought out a sheet to cover the white rug, and the women laid out on their backs. Almost none of their ice cream was eaten after that without first being dripped, dribbled, or outright dropped on skin.

His cock hardened against their hips while he crouched over and sucked ice cream from their breasts. Elena moved underneath him on her back, between his knees. She licked and sucked him while he chased drips down Jess's breasts and licked her belly.

On some level, he was aware that Jess had moved her hand between Elena's thighs to finger his wife, mostly because occasionally Elena moaned, and her throat vibrated around his cock. He seldom lifted his head from the enjoyable pleasure of playing with Jess's clit while she writhed on his tongue in her belly button.

His cum dripped slowly from the tip. While Elena's deep throat was pleasurable, the feeling was not building him fast, toward an explosive finish. Eric was actually relieved she wanted slow, too. He wanted to last a few more times tonight.

Jess's exhalations became panting and intermittent sounds. She started pushing down on his head. "Please," she asked, clearly wanting his tongue to replace his thumb.

"How's this?" He wet his finger with his tongue and broadened the strokes of his thumb while increasing the pressure.

"Mmm, uhng, yessss." Her legs closed on his arm, and she humped his hand while he continued to move his fingertips. When she came, his hand was coated by her cum.

His cock was no longer in a hot mouth; Eric looked to see his wife had sat up. She kissed him and then lightly held his fingers. He raised an eyebrow. Pressing his fingers to his own lips, she said, "I already know she's tasty."

When Elena started to lick clean Eric's cock, Jess asked for a taste, and took it from Elena's lips when the brunette nodded. Eric sat up on the couch while Jess and Elena shared his partial erection like a candy stick between them. When he was fully hard again, Jess unrolled a condom on it.

"Can I lick you while he fucks you?" Jess asked, fingering Elena from behind while she lowered herself onto Eric, balancing herself on his shoulders.

Eric smirked at Elena. "She won't last five minutes," he told Jess. "You could really taste her if I take her ass," he said. "What do you say, El?"

"Then *you* won't last five minutes," Elena teased him. She stood up and turned around. Kissing Jess, she moved Jess's hand from her damp labia to Eric's cock. "Guide him in," she said.

Jess took Eric in her fingers. The condom's lubricant made him slide easily in her hand. She stroked his length and squeezed his girth when he dropped his head back against the couch cushion. Pleased how her touch affected him, Jess brought her other hand to Elena's belly and brushed her thumb down on the woman's clit hood. When Elena made a small sound, Jess asked, "Like that?"

"Want your mouth." Elena's voice was tight. She began moving up and down on Eric.

Jess obliged, leaning forward, continuing to apply her thumb, but she also licked at the woman's labia. She paused to inhale and appreciate the dark flushed flesh before diving in again and again.

Eric held Elena's arms, supplementing her balance. Her feet spread wider on the rug and she breathed deeply. Jess fluttered her tongue and drew more of Elena's musky flavor into her mouth.

Expressing her appreciation and pleasure, Jess hummed against the neatly trimmed hairs, and was rewarded when Elena moaned. Elena's hand moved into Jess's hair, stroking it. She decided the reaction was positive a moment before she heard the woman murmur, "Fuck, yes."

Jess sucked on the woman's clit and Elena's moans increased in frequency. When her chin bumped Eric's hard shaft, Jess backed up quickly and narrowly avoided Elena coming down on her head.

She couldn't help it; she laughed. Leaning back, she caught her breath and watched the way Elena's cunt lips stretched and grabbed Eric's cock. She'd had that thickness in herself earlier, but it looked even bigger now. And Elena's cunt seemed hungry. Jess licked her lips and brushed the woman's inner leg to signal she was coming back in. Eric's cock tasted wonderfully of Elena's fluids. Jess licked down his shaft and dabbled her tongue around his balls, lifting up the mix of their fluids pooled in the creases.

"Uh," Eric grunted. Taking that noise as a good cue, Jess continued rolling and sucking his nuts around her tongue. "Damn...," he breathed, sounding like he was struggling for control. "Goooooood." The sound elongated as he was swept by the sensations.

Elena rotated her ass and ground down on him. He grasped Elena's hips, and Jess noticed the strain in the tendons of his fingers, suggesting he was trying to hold his wife still and push his cock even deeper inside her.

Jess heard Elena's breathy demands. "Damn. Yeah. Fuck. Eric."

She leaned back and watched the couple working together toward orgasm. Both their faces were flushed, eyes closed. Elena shook a bit. Eric wrapped his arms around her, and Jess kissed the bare thigh quivering next to her. The brunette threshed fingers through Jess's hair, seeming to center herself as much as make a connection with Jess.

In the silence, Elena asked, "You okay?" The brunette's eyes, though glazed, searched Jess's.

"Yeah, I... I'm good. That was... a new experience," she finally decided. "You okay?"

"Yes." Elena stood, and Eric slid free. Elena's juices made the condom glisten, and Jess could see the condom tip had filled with Eric's cum. He squeezed the base and sat up, using the motion to clean up his cock as he removed the condom. "I didn't think you'd be able to get that hard again," Elena said to him. "What happened?"

"Jess sucked my balls." Eric tossed the used condom into the trash can. "Damn, you have a magic tongue."

Jess smiled broadly. "Glad you liked it." She sat comfortably on the sheet, enjoying its softness against her skin. She wrapped her hands around her upraised knees and looked up at Elena, who was now standing. Elena held out her hands to help Jess up. Instead, Jess tugged to suggest the brunette sit down.

Obligingly, Elena knelt and put her own hands on Jess's knees, then she leaned forward between her legs and kissed her lips. "C'mon, you should get back in the robe. You're chilled."

"I feel pretty hot," Jess teased, but she did rise to her feet. "I made an experienced swinger couple come all over themselves," she added, reveling in the cockiness she felt.

Eric held his arms open. Jess took the cue and squeezed into his chest. His body was all warm, firm muscles. An enjoyable sense of security filled her. The light hairs on his chest held his scent and she brushed her nose through them.

"I'm glad you enjoyed yourself," he said.

While still hugging Eric, Jess felt Elena press naked against her back, hands moving on her hips and her breasts. Her trimmed bush pressed into Jess's back and ass. Elena gave her body a brief grind, and Jess lifted her head, meeting brown eyes over her shoulder.

"So am I," Elena said.

"It's time to go, I guess," Jess said.

Elena kissed her temple. "Yeah." Jess pouted, not seriously, but still, Elena nibbled her protruding bottom lip. Mirroring Elena's smile, Jess pressed their temples together. Elena asked, "Are you free next week?"

Jess had hoped, but still she was surprised. "Yeah?"

Eric's hand warmly pressed against her lower belly and drew her attention to him. "Yeah."

She didn't have to think twice. A second time with these wonderful people? "I'd like that," she agreed.

CHAPTER NINE

ON WEDNESDAY, a week later, Jess checked herself in her hotel room mirror. Clean jeans, check. Boots shined, check. Jess put on the cotton button-up. Radically she'd bought sunset orange, instead of her usual muted suitable-anywhere blue or white. She smoothed down the collar and argued with herself about leaving one or two buttons open at her throat, trying it one way then the other before finally deciding at two.

She was interrupted by a knock. Gathering up her new bag, she declared her preparation finished then went to her door. Opening it, she smiled at Gus, who held out a key.

"I'm headed up to open the bar now," he said. "Do you still need the car?"

"I'll likely be out late, is that okay?"

"You havin' a good time with your friends?" he asked.

"Yeah," Jess replied, smiling as she thought about Elena and Eric waiting for her. They were all planning to use a new addition to the playroom.

Gus pressed the key into her palm, bringing her back from her pleasant thoughts. He said, "I'm glad. Jus' be safe."

"We always are," she replied.

Walking out toward the front of the hotel with Gus, Jess kissed his cheek before he turned into the bar.

"Jess, where are you going?" Hector asked.

"I'm going out with a friend," Jess said.

"Who?"

"Someone I met," Jess said. "We're hanging out, working out," she suggested.

"What gym?" Jess wondered why Hector cared; it wasn't like she was expected back for a late shift at the bar.

Gus interjected, "I won't need any help today or tonight. We barely made receipts last week." Hector grumbled something Jess didn't understand. Gus nudged her back. "Go on, Jess."

"I decide that," Hector replied. But he was looking at Gus, not Jess.

"My cell's on," Jess said quickly, sensing a rising heat between the two men.

"Go on, Jess, you deserve the break," Gus said again. "Hector, I need the cash drawer." Jess realized Gus was being thoughtful, maybe a little protective. Of her. The thought of someone looking out for her filled her with awe.

Still processing the rare support and shouldering her bag, Jess watched the men go toward the office together. Gus led the way. Hector glanced back over his shoulder at her, frowned, but then followed Gus without saying anything more to her.

Jess pushed through the glass doors and left the Caliente.

Elena looked at the playroom's addition: a sex swing. Though it had been temporarily mounted before, she and Eric had finally decided on a permanent spot and secured the assembly to solid ceiling beams. She'd mounted hospital-style curtain tracks to make a "room" around it, with maroon theater curtains. When the curtains were closed, the swing was hidden away, but still had enough room around it to be semi-privately used, by one or two couples. When the curtain was open, activities on the swing could be erotic entertainment.

Pulling the curtain closed around the swing, Elena easily imagined herself on it. She'd be gripping the ropes, taking all comers, being spit-roasted, even fucked airtight. She loved the rocking motion, how it both helped with deep thrusting, but also could keep her orgasm on the edge, not letting her quite achieve completion, but delightfully stimulated. She imagined Jess fucking her. She'd bend over her while thrusting with a harnessed dildo, so Elena could suck on her nipples. Maybe while Eric fucked Jess from behind.

"She's not here yet, and I bet you already have her in that swing, taking your fingers and then your fist." Eric stepped down the stairs, backlit by a pool of light.

"Actually I hadn't been imagining that at all," Elena replied with a lift of her chin. "But thank you, now I am."

"C'mon, time to go upstairs. She just called to say she's on her way."

Elena looked down at her outfit. She'd chosen a green, blue, and black swirl-patterned "peasant" blouse. As she followed Eric back up the steps, she tugged on the scooped elastic neck so the blouse now sat off her shoulders. The arms were loose and gathered in with elastic at her biceps. She'd chosen tan capris a shade lighter than her own skin. Up on the main floor, she stepped into sandals, thin strips of tan leather crossed over a slight heel.

Eric had gone with what he called his "South Florida pirate" look. His shirt was white, loose on his upper body with long sleeves that gathered at his wrists. He'd left the buttons open well down his chest, golden hairs visible on exposed tanned skin. Eric's tan would never approach the deep tones of Elena's coloring, but they were a well-matched couple. Loose-style black pants and dark shoes completed his look.

These weren't costumes, but they were play clothes, things they bought specifically for when they were going out to the club or meeting up with others in the lifestyle for playtime.

Elena wondered what Jess had chosen to wear. She recalled the woman's hand-me-down work suit for their first date. Last week, Jess had worn a tight top and jeans. All good looks on her, but perhaps the blonde would like to buy some "play clothes." Elena decided to offer a clothes shopping trip for the two of them when Eric was working, as a fun "girls-only" date.

She was considering the logistics of a store dressing room when her thoughts were interrupted by the front doorbell. She laughed at herself. Eric was right; Elena was so excited for their date that she already had the woman naked in her mind, every way possible.

Eric had gone to the door, and she smiled as she listened to them talk.

"Glad you could make it," Eric said.

"Me too. Hector was a little weird as I left." Jess stepped inside, and Eric held open his arms in an invitation to hug, which Jess accepted.

"Hector's a little weird in general," Eric said. "But it's your day off." Elena noticed how Jess continued to rest her hand on Eric's chest, lightly stirring the hairs between the open neckline of the shirt. She smiled at the evidence of how comfortable Jess was around Eric.

"Gus insisted he wouldn't need my help. Apparently receipts were really not big last week." Jess shook her head. "Hector wanted to know where I'd be."

"What'd you say?" Elena asked.

"I told him the truth." The blonde smiled, and finally left Eric's side and moved to her. Elena held open her arms, and the blonde slid into her body for a hug and kiss. "I'm hanging out with friends," Jess said. "And we'd be working out."

Elena chuckled; Eric did too. "I like your chosen workout clothes," Elena said. "The orange really looks good on you."

"Thank you. I like your blouse, too," Jess added, brushing her fingertips along Elena's collarbones. Her skin tingled pleasantly from Jess's attention.

"So are you ready to swing?" Elena asked playfully.

"That's what I signed up for." Jess shifted the bag on her shoulder.

"You can put that in the living room, if you want."

"Actually, I thought I should contribute a few things to the cause," Jess said; her green eyes held an air of mischief. Elena's body tightened, and reflexively she squeezed Jess's arm, which made the blonde's smile widen.

Eric said, "Excellent! C'mon, and see what we've added." Disengaging from their hold, Elena took Jess's hand and led the way, following Eric down to the basement playroom.

Eric watched Jess move around the playroom. She first went to the riser they'd assembled last time, which now had a mattress, sheets, and Elena's ruffle. The pale pink sheets and deeper pink pillows were complemented by heavy red velvet curtains, currently pulled back along their railings to the four corner posts. The toe of Jess's boot caught on a box under the bed when she leaned forward to brush her hand on the sheet.

Eric enjoyed Jess's enthusiasm over the pair of costumes she withdrew: a princely styled cloak bordered with faux fur, and a shadow-thin fabric, which Elena had sewn onto a sturdy ring and further sewn in scattered petals. She modeled it with a giggle, placing it on her hair so the fabric draped down her hair, covering her shoulders and most of her back. "Love it," she declared.

Elena bit her lip, beautiful, and clearly smitten at the sight. "You look like a princess," she murmured. *Indeed*, Eric agreed—the blonde was almost fairytale pretty, especially with the fabric draping her golden hair.

"We can have a themed photo shoot," Eric said. "It's almost Halloween."

"That'd be fun," Jess said. After carefully folding away the costumes she had pulled out, Jess looked around. She noticed the maroon drape. "Another bed?" she asked.

"Not exactly." Elena shook her head. "Remember, I asked are you ready to swing?"

Jess walked over to the curtain and peeked inside. "Ooh," she said, and pulled the curtain open. "This is what you meant," she whispered.

"Ever used one?" Eric said.

"Never," Jess said. Her tone suggested that would be a soon corrected oversight. As she looked from Elena to him, the way her eyes darkened told Eric *I can't wait to try it out.* His cock grew hard from her evident enthusiasm, and he was grateful his pants were loose.

"I think it's time you got the full experience," Elena said. She moved against Jess, pressing her palms against the shirt, and then with a kiss and murmuring a request for permission, which was met with an affirmative, she started unbuttoning Jess's shirt and lowering her jeans to the floor.

"Eric," Jess called. "Would you put this somewhere?" He scooped up the purse from her hand and put it on the floor, leaning it against a wall.

"I think we'll need a small table," he said.

"Next time," Elena said, already pressing her mouth to Jess's exposed chest, and reaching behind to unclasp the woman's bra.

Jess tossed her head back and adjusted her grip on the swing's ropes. Eric and Elena stood on either side of her, their hands and mouths seeming to be everywhere on her body, sucking or tweaking a nipple one moment, then fingering her wetness the next. Elena kissed her, and Jess sucked on the woman's tongue dancing in her mouth. When she let the brunette's mouth go, she said, "I need you inside."

Elena's smile and "yes" turned Jess on even more. She reveled in this feeling of being completely wanted, of being the focus of the desires of two incredible people. Elena moved away after a parting kiss, and Eric's erection brushed Jess's shoulder. She moved a hand from the swing rope and grasped his cock. Pumping up and down, she massaged his shaft while his fingers stroked through her hair. Their eyes met over the short distance and she returned his smile.

Jess heard the sounds of latex stretching and knew Elena was putting on a glove. Eric's gaze met hers, and his mouth came down to hers at the same time Elena's lips found Jess's clit and one of her gloved fingers, wet with lube, slid into Jess. A tiny screwing motion and Jess felt her cunt opening up, softening, welcoming the finger, which soon became two.

Resisting the urge to be too loud right in Eric's face, Jess bit her lip and moaned and quivered. She rocked on the swing, trying to push herself onto Elena's fingers. The swing cooperated a little, and Elena's fingers slid more firmly inside, only to pull almost completely out when the swing retreated. Jess flexed her hands to release some tension. Elena's fingers returned on the next swing in, delightfully filling. Moving so the swing straps held open her legs more, Jess squeezed Eric's cock in her hand; he groaned against her ear, and precum dribbled over her thumb.

"God." Eric's voice rumbled across Jess's skin, lust roughening his tone. "You're gonna make me come. And I really, really don't want to." Jess chuckled; he occupied her mouth with another kiss. When he stepped back, she grasped his cock again, being a little more mindful this time.

Meanwhile, Elena's tongue and fingers continued to be intensely busy. Jess rocked and quaked, and she felt it wouldn't be long before she was covered in Eric's fluids and her own dripped down her ass and onto the floor.

Elena's tongue played Jess's clit like a clarinet, tonguing it like a reed and then licking up the length, alternating soft and hard strokes. Jess felt like her clit had become a little cock, and Elena's tongue was determined to lick every square millimeter. The woman's gloved fingers continued pressing and turning inside Jess, literally screwing her. Jess tried to focus momentarily and assess how many fingers the brunette was using on her, but the truth was, she didn't care. She only wanted the stretching, the clenching, the licking to continue, and drive her to orgasm. But when each moment arrived, when Jess thought she might finally be at that elusive peak, Elena shifted attention to her labia, or her vulva.

Finally, she spoke her only desire. "Please, make me come."

Eric's kisses moved from Jess's mouth to her nipples. His big, warm palm swirled in circles on her belly. Elena's fingers pumped until Jess felt knuckles rubbing against her. She let go of Eric's cock and used her arms to raise herself up to see.

At first all she saw between her thighs was Elena's dark head. Finally a small shift in position, and she saw the woman's hand corkscrewing.

"You want me to take your hand?" Jess asked. Elena had four fingers moving in and out easily. Her thumb tucked against the inside of the other four, and the knuckles at the base of Elena's fingers had been what she'd been feeling.

"You're very open. You want to try?" Elena asked in return. She widened her fingers, removed her thumb from Jess's clit. At the deep stroking, petting of Elena's fingers against the walls of her vagina, Jess's eyes rolled back in her head.

"Damn, that feels good," Jess breathed out. "Yeah, I think I could."

Elena nodded; Eric held Jess's shoulders, moving behind her and letting her lean on him, as well as rest all her weight on the swing. Her cunt remained wide when Elena removed her fingers to cover all of the glove in lube. Then cool lube was warmed by small strokes on Jess's labia.

Eric's hands wrapped around her chest and he played with her nipples. He kissed her throat under her ear and the tingles were delightful, but their gazes were both riveted to Jess's pussy, as Elena worked her hand, one finger at a time, inside.

With the swing's gentle motions and Elena's care and attention to turn and screw slowly, Jess was stretched and filled almost lazily. Soon they all were marveling at Elena's wrist outside Jess's pussy, no sign of her palm or fingers. Eric's fingers brushed her stretched pussy lips. He then kissed his wife, and finally her wrist; Jess shivered at the light contact from his mustache.

Then Elena moved her hand, curled it, actually, and the fullness caused Jess to gasp as an orgasm unexpectedly rocked her belly.

"That's beautiful," Elena said. "You're beautiful," she emphasized. Her hand turned again, and Jess felt every tiny movement. "I love the feel of you surrounding me like this." She placed a kiss to the side of Jess's clit, the skin stretched tautly around her wrist.

"Have you ever had Eric do this to you?" Jess marveled that she could talk. Every tiny shift of the swing, or Elena adjusting herself on her knees, was a tenfold-magnified movement inside her.

"We've tried. His hands are much larger than mine," Elena said. "I have fisted him, though."

"Really?" Jess cocked her eyebrow at Eric.

"Yes," he said. "Excellent tequila was involved."

Jess laughed; the motion gave her another orgasm around Elena's hand. "Oh, god, fuck, that's..." She exhaled steadily while Elena slowly withdrew. "Fuck," Jess lamented. "Now I feel empty."

"After a filling meal, we can come back down here for another round," Eric said. He held her up while Elena removed the swing's straps from around Jess's thighs.

Jess's legs shook when she first tried to put her weight on them. She tightened her kegels and felt the liquid of her own cum sliding onto her thighs. Elena returned from dropping the glove into the lined trash can and pressed their naked bodies together in a hug. The heated curves against her own gave Jess strength. "Ungh, god, this feels so good."

In the living room, Jess held Elena on her lap while they shared kisses. She was aware of the time and knew she had work the next day, but she was reluctant to leave. They had not returned to the basement, instead watching a movie while they talked and ate. She'd heard the full story of Elena fisting Eric in Mexico now.

When Eric came back from putting their dessert dishes in the kitchen, she saw him putting a leather bag on the end table before settling next to her on her other side.

"You ready to go again?" Jess asked.

"Just being prepared."

"You're very considerate. So many guys hate condoms."

He smiled. "Except with Elena, I haven't been bare with anyone in years. It's safe for everyone."

"Safer," Elena clarified. "Nothing's perfect." Elena then kissed her cheek. "Would you really want to wake up anxious in another week or so when your period's supposed to start, and wonder? I want you to come back again, feel safe here, feel free to experiment. Play," she added. "Condoms, gloves, and making clear what everyone wants, are just thoughtful cautions for ourselves and our partners, because we're adults and we care."

Jess was surprised at the vehement tone, and direct gaze from brown eyes. A small knot formed in her throat. She nodded. "Thank you."

"You let me fist you today, Jess," Elena said. "That was an amazing privilege. Don't ever think we take any of this for granted."

Eric nuzzled her right ear while Elena nibbled her left. A hand from each of them played with her nipples. She squirmed. The movement reminded her of how stretched she had been just a few hours ago. "I should probably go." She wanted to stay, wanted to push her body to the limits, experience more sex, more experimenting. The feeling that it might not happen again if she didn't take all she could now made her anxious.

"Still sore?" Elena asked, seemingly picking up on her anxiety.

"No. I want to stay," Jess said. "But I should go. It's late."

"There's always other nights," Eric said. He pushed off the couch and held out his hand. She took it and gathered her purse on the way to the door.

At the door, Eric kissed her. He murmured in her ear, "El would love it if you gave her a ride sometime."

"Where would she like to go?" She looked at the back of Elena's head, visible over the top of the couch.

"Not that sort of ride. You ever use a harness?" Eric asked.

"Oh. She wants me to wear one?" Jess asked. "You have a cock, and I know how good you are with it."

Eric laughed. "Thank you, Jess, but I'm not offended. Remember, Elena's had sex with other men, too."

"She wanted me to do that with her tonight," Jess realized.

"Yeah, she kind of imagined you'd take her on the swing."

"And then I..." Jess trailed off. "Elena," she said, "I'm sorry for changing the plans. You could have said something."

"I don't want to change what happened." Elena stood from the couch and joined them at the door. "Really, I'm okay." She shook her head at Eric. "I enjoyed tonight immensely. Just... come back soon, okay?" Elena pulled Jess into a hug.

Eric put his hand on Jess's back. She looked from one to the other. "I will," she agreed. "Thank you."

CHAPTER TEN

"WHERE'S ERIC?" Jess asked. She'd been invited over to the house before, but always to play with both of the Tanners. They were the couple; she played with both of them.

Elena sat next to Jess on the couch. "Eric's on a long flight schedule. Won't be back until Thursday."

Jess sipped her drink, ice water with lemon. Elena had pressed it into her hand almost as soon as she entered the door. "So, we would see each other on Friday, when you come to the club."

"I couldn't wait." Elena leaned forward and kissed Jess slowly, lingering. The drink was taken from her hand. When Elena pressed Jess's palm to her throat, Jess felt the woman's heart racing. Elena's palm on Jess's throat slipped slowly down her chest. Then a button popped.

"Wanted to see you," Elena murmured against Jess's mouth, opening in surprise.

Jess still couldn't find her voice, not while Elena was parting her shirt and pressing breathy kisses against the cool swells of her breasts, making her body shiver with the introduction of sudden heat.

Elena pressed her body against Jess's and rocked her thigh between Jess's legs.

"Oh," Jess gasped. "Is this all right... with Eric?"

Her hands were full of Elena, the woman already shrugging out of her sleeveless top and giving Jess access to her lacy dark blue bra.

Elena lifted Jess's hands, kissed each of the knuckles in tender turn. Then she cupped the palms to her bra. Jess's fingertips traced on the front clasp. She lifted her gaze until she found brown eyes.

"He told me to have fun," Elena said, stroking her hands down the rest of Jess's body, fingers stroking at the skin just above the waistband of her jeans. "I decided I wanted to have you."

Jess heard the snap-pop and felt her zipper sliding down. She felt the way the jeans loosened on her hips, but her mouth and her hands were occupied with Elena's kisses. Her gaze was filled with the sight of Elena moving on and over her body until she was naked.

Then Elena knelt between Jess's thighs, caressing and stroking Jess's pussy lips. Watching Elena's gaze devouring her made Jess's breath catch, the look was so hungry. Then the heated brown gaze lifted to find hers.

"Can I?" Elena asked.

Jess blinked. "What was the question?"

Elena laughed; Jess's heart flipped with the sound. "Can I have you?" Elena clarified. Her dark lips held an intense smile that reached through her eyes and seemed to hold Jess by the throat, tightening it. The husky accented words effectively seduced her. Jess was thoroughly on board with being seduced. She nodded.

Elena's fingers dipped and circled on Jess's inner thighs, close but not touching. "I want.... I need... to hear you," Elena said.

Jess swallowed, then cleared her throat and nodded. "Yes," she breathed.

Following the given permission, Elena lowered her head and flicked her tongue lightly across the hood covering Jess's clit. She gasped, but then sighed when Elena settled in with long strokes over all her folds. Each upsweep of the other woman's tongue ended with short, tight pulls on her clit with her full lips. The woman's hands continued massaging Jess's thighs, then draped them over Elena's shoulders. Elena's tongue plunged into her with determination.

Jess writhed and cried out through the lapping waves of pleasure. Elena chuckled against her flesh. Each time the sound vibrated into Jess's sex, making her clench her thighs against Elena's head.

Jess's fingers threaded into soft satin hair. The sensation grounded her at the same time two of Elena's fingers pressed inside, curled upward, and stroked Jess intimately. Elena sucked at Jess's folds while she pumped her fingers. Jess heard the sucking sounds from her muscles trying to grasp hold of Elena's fingers, and pulled her own thighs back, opening herself and looking down at the dark head between her thighs. "Deeper, more," she murmured when Elena met her eyes, nose buried in the light hairs on Jess's mound.

Elena smiled, and, shifting to add a third finger, continued to pump. Knowing her actions turned Jess on, Elena fluttered her tongue against Jess's clit where she could see the action. Then she lifted her head, replaced her tongue with her thumb, and said, "I want to watch you come, Jess." Jess swallowed as Elena stilled her hand, thumb resting just alongside her throbbing clit. Uncontrollably, a whimper passed her lips. "Will you?"

Stomach rolling, clenching and unclenching, on the edge, Jess bit her lip and nodded. Elena resumed her strokes. Jess's head fell back, even as her back arched and her hips rocked. Elena's touch was perfect, and Jess was on the edge of orgasm once again. She felt Elena's thumb leave her clit and she cried out in want.

Then Elena's thumb returned. A tiny tap, and Jess's orgasm rushed through her body. "Oh god, god, fu–El–*ehhh*-na!"

Jess turned her head blindly toward the body crawling atop hers. Lips sought and settled upon one another. Jess panted, Elena sucked each breath with another kiss, and her tongue danced in Jess's mouth.

Elena's hand gentled on Jess's belly. The kisses became more languid, and when Jess's eyes fluttered open, brown eyes were there to greet her. "Hey," Elena murmured, cupping Jess's cheek.

Leaning into the touch, Jess tightened her stomach muscles despite their quivering protest, and lifted her back off the couch cushions. She unbuttoned Elena's bra with one hand while kissing her and cupping the back of her head with the other.

Elena hummed in appreciation against Jess's lips when she pushed aside the bra and massaged and stroked Elena's breasts, pulling at the nipples. When the brunette rocked her hips against Jess's belly, Jess rearranged their positions on the couch, laying Elena's head and back against the cushions. She kissed her way down Elena's chest, onto Elena's tight belly muscles, swirling her tongue in Elena's belly button. Then she moved down further to the waistband of the other woman's tight denim short-shorts.

"My turn."

Popping the snap, Jess peeled off Elena's shorts, and rubbed the palm of her hand on the woman's mound through the lace-frilled dark blue underwear. She kissed the concave part of Elena's inner thigh, inhaling the arousal that had soaked the panties while Elena had been eating Jess so attentively. Wanting more, she sucked at the fabric, drawing the taste onto her tongue.

Then she pulled aside the fabric and went for the direct taste. Elena's hand moved to the back of Jess's head, holding her close. Jess lifted Elena's legs onto her shoulders, used both hands to spread the woman open, licking up and down each fold before fluttering her tongue directly into the center. Elena's fingers in Jess's hair were a guide—a tightened grip indicated a need for more, *right there*, loosening and stroking indicated enough, and *just right*.

Jess chuckled into Elena's clit as the woman's panting increased. She brought one finger from under her chin into Elena's core, stroking her way inside. Elena's hips thrusting in response almost dislodged Jess, but then she quickly grasped for Jess's shoulders and she was anchored again. She tugged, drawing Jess upward until their lips were together and she was settled between Elena's thighs, their mounds rocking together.

Elena's legs wrapped around Jess's and she rubbed herself against the ridge of Jess's pubic bone, moaning throatily and panting in Jess's ear. The slick flesh was hot, and Jess reached down between their bodies, holding herself up with her other hand, and set off Elena's orgasm with the barest direct touch to her clit.

Elena cried out Jess's name and wrapped her arms around her, pulling her down so her weight had to rest on Elena. She nuzzled into Jess's throat, almost purring like a cat.

"So, fun, huh?" Jess asked.

Elena palmed and tweaked Jess's nipple with an idleness that belied her next words.

"I have not yet begun to play." She chuckled. Jess joined her in laughter.

"You got plans for tonight?"

Eric looked over at Bryan, his copilot on this hop. "Gonna put my feet up and watch some cable."

"Well, if you get bored, I've been told there's gonna be a party in Margot's room tonight."

"Good to know." Eric nodded, but he was uninterested in partying tonight. He wanted to call Elena and ask her advice on the company's offer to switch him to a different flying schedule permanently. The actual number of flights would be smaller, but the new routes were all cross-country and down into South America.

Working time in the air would be longer per flight, but he'd earn overtime during every single one. That meant he'd bring in more money with less time spent away from home. Even better, he'd have three days off every four, instead of two days off after every five.

They did need his income, so he'd probably want to take the change in assignments, but Elena still needed to have some input. He might have to find some way to spend his additional time at home alone, rather than expect to keep Elena's schedule, or make her alter it. She might not want him underfoot while she was trying so hard to establish something independently.

Then again, he considered, El might be quite enthusiastic to have him around more. They could find more sexy time, or take touristy vacation "weekends" to other parts of the state. They could even spend quality time getting to know Jess.

His mind went back to Wednesday night. Even though he, Elena, and Jess had only met up twice for sex, Eric felt both times had been dominated by an awareness of a limited window of time. It certainly hadn't been "business"; the sex was amazing. But he had noticed how Jess and Elena acted like they wanted to do everything now. Both had a quick-passion intensity in their actions. Eric wondered, though, what could happen with some really open-ended leisure time, without a need to "pack it all in" over just a few hours. It was a lot to ask for—Jess worked nearly every night at the club, and started, apparently, early in the afternoons serving a business crowd. Elena had told him about the unexpected loss of her day off, too. Being a minimum-wage worker was a shitty position he remembered too well, and not at all fondly.

He broke from the memories as the airport started to appear on the horizon. Keying the radio, he tapped into the tower and communicated his details for a position in approach. Once he had received them, he acknowledged, "Ten-four, Tower." Eric adjusted the airplane's guidance and expertly set up the course change, verifying altitude with Bryan as he maintained his assigned heading.

He jerked upright, and his eyes darted to identify a dark, fast-moving object. "Fuck! What is *that*?" Whatever it was had sped directly across the airliner's path.

"Goddamn drone," Bryan cursed. Apparently, he had gotten a visual while Eric maintained flight control. "Flying black cats, damn unlucky things to cross our path."

"Nothing happened," Eric said firmly. And he was rather proud that his startle hadn't translated to any abrupt movements of the plane itself, since he had literally just switched from autopilot to begin manual approach and landing. He nosed the plane down onto the runway without a bounce. "Time to check this bird and get some shut-eye."

Elena uncurled from around Jess when her phone rang. "Hi," she said as she stepped into the bathroom.

"Hey, babe, sounds a little echoey, where are you?"

"I'm in the bathroom. Jess is asleep."

"So you did have her over," he said. "Are you having fun?"

"Yes, she wasn't sure at first, but I told her you said I should have her over."

"I'm glad. I should be home on time tomorrow. Do you think she'd enjoy a surprise pickup at the club?"

"You romancing our girl?" Elena teased.

"I think she hasn't had a lot of that. Some flowers, nice wine... more of my cooking," he added.

"More of your cock, you mean, stud," Elena teased.

"There's that, too," he laughed.

"Well, you need your sleep, flyboy. I'll see if she's up for seeing us again so soon."

"Okay."

"I'll text you after I send her back to the club."

"Thanks," Eric said when the young man manning the valet parking held the lobby door open for him. He examined the bouquet held in his left hand as he stepped through, considering again his impulse to pick it up. He thought about Elena's jibe that he was "romancing" Jess, and his reply that maybe the young woman was in need of that. He liked to think that he read people reasonably well. But how would she react?

"Eric?"

A plump, beautiful Mexican woman was walking out from the front desk when Eric turned at the call of his name. "Hi, Maya." He greeted Hector's wife warmly.

"I didn't know you and Elena had stayed last night," she said. "We could have had some fun."

He shook his head. "I just finished flying for the day and

thought I'd connect with... a friend."

"Staying here?"

"She works here. The new girl bartender?"

"Oh. Does Elena know you're seeing her?" Maya asked, sounding both surprised and curious.

"Yes, of course." Eric felt his usual after-work fatigue pulling at him and realized he needed to get a move on. "Point me to the staff rooms? I gotta go."

"The staff rooms are down the hall, behind the bar."

"Thank you," Eric said.

"Eric?" Maya's voice made him pause and turn back. "Next time you wanna come, let me know," she said.

Eric nodded. "Sure." He smiled and turned away.

He found his way to the staff rooms and frowned when he realized he didn't know Jess's room number.

He met an older man—gray scruffy beard and thin gray hair—stepping out of a room on the left side of the corridor. "Excuse me," he said.

"Yeah? This part of the hotel is staff only."

"I know. I'm looking for someone—Jess Davies?"

He narrowed his eyes at Eric, seeming to size him up. "She know you're looking for her?"

"It's a sort of surprise."

The man walked to the door directly opposite his and knocked on it.

When it opened, Jess stepped into the doorway. "Gus? You need something?"

"Someone's here to see you," he said.

"Thank you," Eric said to the man apparently named Gus. He turned to Jess and took note of the number on the wall by the door. "Hi, Jess."

"Eric, hi," Jess said, greeting Eric with a warm smile that included her eyes. She looked at Gus. "Thanks, Gus."

"Okay. Well, have a good day," he said to her. Eric didn't miss the side-eye from Gus, which strongly suggested that Eric should see that Jess did have a good day or Gus would have something to say about it.

When Gus was gone down the hall, for whatever had brought him out of his room in the first place, Eric smiled at Jess and held out the flowers. "For you," he said.

She took them. "Me? Why?"

"Consider it an invitation to join me and Elena at our home again? Today. If you're interested?"

She looked from the flowers to him. "I... well, um, you wanna come in for a minute?" She gestured at herself. "I'm not really ready to go anywhere."

Eric thought she looked quite good. Jess wore a pair of girl boxers, and a loose and long T-shirt that was partly caught in one side of the boxer's waistband. The way the T-shirt laid across her body let him know she was braless. "But you are interested in doing something?" he tried to clarify.

Jess looked at the flowers again and then stepped forward and kissed his lips, smiling into the kiss. "Elena tell you what we did while you were gone?" she asked, her breath brushing his lips.

"Yes," he replied.

"I really like the flowers," Jess offered as a response. "Come on in and help me find someplace to put them."

"Okay." Eric crossed the threshold, and Jess pushed the door shut behind him.

"I think I've got an empty soda bottle here somewhere," she said. "Have a seat while I look."

"If I sit down I might fall asleep," he admitted. "It's been a long flight pattern."

"From where?"

"Today was a two-stop hop from Logan, that's in Boston, to BWI in Baltimore. We also had to make a hub stop in Atlanta for folks transferring to westbound flights. I finally got back here about thirty minutes ago."

"It's only noon." Jess had found an empty ginger ale can, and Eric watched as she expertly wielded a pocket knife, cutting the first few inches off the top. She was unwrapping the flowers on the vanity counter when she asked him, "When did you start?"

"We left Logan at 1800 hours." When she blinked, he clarified, "6 p.m. last night." He leaned against the wall.

"Damn." She returned to his side. "Why'd you stop here?"

"I'd like to play some more with you," he said honestly, and met her green eyes searching his, laying his cards on the table.

"I'd like that too," Jess said.

"So come home with me?" Eric asked again. "You don't need to change on my account," he added.

She nodded, but added jean shorts over her girl boxers and grabbed her wallet. "I don't need much if we're just going to play."

He put his hand lightly on her back and followed her out of her room, before leading the way to his car parked out front.

Trying to figure out what to do when you're a guest in someone else's home was never a problem for Jess. She'd spent a childhood being fostered in a dozen different homes. To ingratiate herself with each new adult in her life, she would clean anything she could find, including bathrooms, tubs, and toilets. When she was older, she'd mowed lawns and watched younger children. The adults praised her initiative and her thoughtfulness, but they always sent her back.

She had cleaned up after their shared lunch. They'd talked for quite a while over the food, and Eric had looked brighter after eating. Maybe he wasn't as tired as he'd said.

After an initial "you don't have to do that" from Elena and then Eric, the couple left the kitchen. Jess heard the shower going and assumed the couple were reacquainting themselves after his extended absence.

She spread out the dish towel over the oven handle so it could dry. But now, looking around for something else to do, Jess came up empty.

Slowly, she walked out of the kitchen and glanced around at the open-plan home. The white leather seating of the living room angled around a faux fireplace, over which hung a wall-mounted flatscreen TV, where the three of them had previously watched a movie. She remembered everyone gradually removing clothing and stroking skin. Touching the leather couch again now as she sat down near one side, she recalled the comfortable feel of smooth white leather against her back while being pleasured.

She looked again toward the closed bedroom door and remembered Eric's proposal when he picked her up that morning from her room. He had invited Jess to spend the day again with him and Elena. But if Elena and Eric were having sex without her now, why was she here?

Then again, she didn't hear anything that suggested sex. Both Elena and Eric had been vigorous in their sexual encounters with Jess so far. Jess had plenty of sex where roommates weren't supposed to hear, and she'd bitten pillows to keep her own sounds muffled, or put a hand over her partner's mouth. But creaky bedsprings usually gave the activity away.

She shook her head. The Tanners didn't have creaky anything. They were well-off, and the way Eric talked, he liked keeping their things well maintained. Neither Elena or Eric were inhibited when it came to making sounds during sex. Eric wasn't a grunter; he liked to murmur how good Jess felt riding him, and he always spoke with her, asking if she wanted him to change angle, or move slower or faster. She liked the way she had learned to read his voice, hitches in his breath or catches between his words, and revel in her effects on him. Elena hummed when she was "coasting," as she called it. She was vocal in her need when Jess or Eric were pleasuring her. Elena, too, liked to "check in" with Jess. *Do you want more, less? Faster, slower?*

Jess was used to coarse language when having sex. Elena and Eric did use words like fuck, dick, pussy, and cunt, but sparingly. The choice words had never failed to occur near the moment her body was a breath away from an orgasm. They had definitely learned to read her as well.

Both Eric and Elena were, in a word, incredible. No wonder she kept returning for more. However, she was admittedly growing antsy.

"You're quiet."

Jess turned around on the couch to see Elena, still dressed in the same clothes as when she and Eric had arrived at the house.

"Thank you for doing the dishes," she continued.

"You're welcome," Jess said, and quickly stood. She studied Elena. Nothing about the woman's appearance suggested that she had showered, had sex, or even spent any time in bed with her husband.

"You look confused," Elena said as Jess approached. "If you wanted to relax and read, I have some bookshelves back here."

"Where's Eric?" Jess asked, trying to wrap her mind around the seemingly mixed signals.

"He's showered and taking his nap in the bedroom."

"Why aren't you with him?"

Elena now looked puzzled. "He's sleeping?" she replied. "I'm sorry I left you alone. But since you were doing the dishes, I went and worked a bit in my office."

"You have an office? But," Jess blurted, "I thought you were having sex." Jess's cheeks heated with her embarrassment as her filter succumbed to her growing confusion.

"Oh! Well, no," Elena said. She went on to explain, "Eric really does need a nap after a long flight. He waited so we could all eat together, but flying is exhausting. He might sleep all right for one night in a hotel and be fresh enough to fly, but he always sleeps better in our bed."

"But. I thought... when... he picked me up... invited me for more playtime." He had even brought a small bouquet of flowers, which now sat in an empty ginger ale can she'd snitched from the kitchen.

Glancing at her watch, Elena said, "It'll only be ninety minutes or so." She looked up and met Jess's gaze with a smirk. "We will have fun. When Eric wakes up, he's hard as a post."

CHAPTER ELEVEN

WHEN ELENA nudged open the door to the bedroom, Eric was stirring. He'd stripped down, as usual, and replaced all his uniform clothing with Jockey shorts and a loose T-shirt. He was starting to stretch from his burrowed position, rolling over onto his back to give his rising cock room to grow. Behind her left shoulder, Elena heard a hum.

She put her finger to Jess's lips and then waggled it toward the room, a silently offered *come on in*. Then she pushed the door wide. The motion drew Eric's gaze, his lips crinkling into a smile as he identified her first, and then Jess behind her. "Hey," he said, maneuvering to sit up against the pillows.

"Captain Tanner, are you feeling rested enough to fly a couple of hot women to the moon and back?" Elena teased as she moved around to the far side of the bed. When she leaned forward and put her knee on the bed, Jess did the same, following through on Elena's suggestions out in the living room.

Eric smiled up at her, and then looked to Jess. Then rolling fully onto his back, he lifted his arms and crossed his hands under the back of his head, flexing his pecs with a wink. "I'm rested. Just gotta have someone check out the mechanics." With that, he flexed his hips and the tent in his Jockeys grew.

Elena bent forward to kiss him. She also slipped her right hand across his belly and under the waistband of his underwear. Her fingers met Jess's, already pulling down the fabric and freeing his cock. When Jess wrapped her hand around him and massaged firmly root to tip, Eric's groan of pleasure filled Elena's mouth during their kiss.

Eric's mustache tickled her lips between their kisses, and Elena desired to have that sensation between her legs. She backed off the bed and reached behind to lower the zipper of her dress. As it slipped from her shoulders, she watched Jess's mouth move on Eric's cock, nipping up the hard ridge on the underside, then sucking the mushroom tip into her mouth through tightly rounded lips. The woman was simultaneously stripping out of her shorts and underwear, but each time she parted from Eric's cock, she would return to it with intensity.

After just a few moments, Eric started pushing his hips up from the bed, and tried to fuck Jess's mouth. Elena knew the other woman had discovered Eric's "hot button": tonguing the slit at the top of his penis. Her husband had admirable restraint, though. He was successfully holding back the urge to come immediately in Jess's mouth. He reached for Jess's shoulder.

"Whoa, whoa, Jess. Slow."

The blonde's face turned an adorable pink. "Sorry," she mumbled. She stopped her direct assault on Eric's cock and returned to the light nipping, but the intensity was still there, in the tension in her shoulders and hands as she held herself tautly in position over him.

"No. No," Eric said. His hand brushed the back of Jess's head before he broke her contact with his cock again by lifting her chin and steadily holding her gaze. He smiled. "It's okay."

Elena grasped Jess's hand resting at the root of Eric's penis, to keep her from retreating while she listened to Eric. He finally went on when he was sure he had Jess's full attention.

"No apologies are necessary. It feels good. Too good. I don't want to blow within the first five minutes of what promises to be a very good time," Eric said. "I'd like to spend some time flying at an easy altitude."

"What?" Jess's brow knitted in what Elena took to be confusion. Elena squeezed her fingers.

"We have all day." Eric threaded his fingers lightly through Jess's long hair. "I'd like you to sit on my face for a while," he said. "Please?"

Jess looked to Elena as if silently asking *Is he serious?* Elena nodded. "Go on."

Elena moved down to Eric's belly. She moved her hands soothingly the way she knew he liked over his hips and thighs. Under Eric's guiding hands, Jess moved up his body. She straddled his chest, then her knees went alongside his ears.

From her position, Elena had a perfect view of Jess's parting labia, and Eric's blue eyes as he looked his fill of the woman astride him. He helped Jess finish removing her T-shirt, and generously palmed her breasts.

"Yeah," he said, encouraging Jess. "Now, let me taste you."

From her position looking past Eric's erection, Elena saw every movement of Eric's tongue through Jess's labia. Jess's fluids painted a shine on Eric's chin. Eric's tongue pushed upward, deeply inside Jess, and Elena smiled when she heard Jess gasp. "Fuck. Do that again."

Elena inhaled deeply of Eric's musk and Jess's scent as both her bed partners' arousal increased. Eric's hums and Jess's breathy keening filled her ears. She rubbed her face on Eric's cock and raked her fingertips through the curling hairs at the root. The experience was a near-perfect sensory immersion, and Elena's own belly churned with need. She reached up and added the tactile memento of Jess's damp skin. The woman's back muscles flexed under Elena's fingertips.

Jess arched into Elena's touch on her back, her arousal rising even higher with the connection to the other woman and an awareness that Elena was somehow sharing in these incredible sensations. Her movement changed the angle of Eric's tongue pushing its way into her, and his nose bumped her clit. She gasped again and reached out to steady herself. Instinctively she clutched Eric's hair and heard him hiss—damn that felt good against her clit!

Wanting him to focus exactly there, she unclenched her fingers, and pushed down and in instead. She rocked her hips to find his tongue again. Her center of balance shifted, though, and abruptly she had to slap a hand into the shelf atop the headboard to keep from falling.

Behind her, Elena chuckled, and the light touch on her back became calming strokes.

"Slow down," Elena said. "Come here."

Jess turned her head to see Elena's brown eyes coming closer. The woman pressed her body against Jess's, hands roaming her skin.

Then lips kissed up a shoulder blade. Jess looked down as Elena's arms encircled her waist. Eric grinned up at Jess while his wife took control of Jess's pleasure. His hands steadily grasped her thighs.

Entranced by the darker skin of Elena's hands against her lighter-toned stomach, Jess watched as Elena moved one hand slowly up, raising tingles. The fingers paused, circled a nipple and then tweaked it, eliciting an involuntary gasp. Only a moment later, Jess realized where the other hand had gone as Elena's fingers parted Jess's folds and gently caressed the sides of Jess's clit. Bolts of pleasure went from her breast to her groin and circled back again. Jess let her head fall back onto Elena's shoulder.

Eric's mouth, and that tantalizing mustache, returned to Jess's center, while Elena held her open as if to invite Eric to go deeper—which he did. His tongue thrust, his lips tugged, and Jess felt sensation coalescing to this one place, her cunt, receiving such perfect attention.

Leaving Eric to plunder Jess on his own, Elena held Jess's chin and kissed her mouth. When their lips slipped apart, Jess realized that Elena was moving up and down. Curious, Jess lifted her head back and glanced down and around Elena's bouncing breasts. She was impaling herself on her husband's hard cock. Elena closed her eyes in her pleasure.

Lifting her soaked pussy from Eric's mouth, Jess turned around. For a moment she simply perched on her knees beside the couple to watch them.

Elena's body moved erratically, seeking the peak of pleasure. Taut thigh muscles pistoned the woman's center on and off her husband's cock. Her breasts jiggled with each move, and Jess couldn't resist cupping each in her palms. Elena's lips parted around a sound. "Ggggg."

Gently, Jess removed one hand from a breast and cupped Elena's cheek instead. When the brown gaze opened, Jess saw the dark pupils were dilated, turning Elena's eyes into an inky abyss. She pressed her lips to the woman's mouth, feeling warm and erratic breathing on her tongue.

Jess saw the moment the sensations finally pushed Elena over the edge into orgasm. The woman toppled forward, and both Jess and Eric's hands guided her down onto his chest.

While watching her own hand stroking Elena's back, Jess looked down and saw the woman's legs parted around Eric's still fully erect cock. It glistened with Elena's juices, but he obviously hadn't come.

"If you wanna ride, condoms, in the drawer," Eric said. Jess looked back and followed where he pointed, to Elena's bedside table.

Jess quickly sifted through the drawer contents and found a condom. Tearing it with her teeth, which earned her a grin from Eric as he continued to stroke Elena's back, Jess then licked Elena's juices from his shaft, staying away from the head this time. When she had sufficiently tongued him clean, she unrolled the condom. When her fingers reached the base, the back of her hand brushed Elena's folds, since the other woman still had her legs parted over Eric's lower belly.

Elena wriggled. Jess straddled Eric's thighs, and lifted Elena's to slip her own knees under as she slowly lowered herself onto Eric. Though she had experienced his cock before, this time he seemed thicker and harder somehow. Experimentally she adjusted, rocked, and felt the tip rub her deep inside. Eric made a low sound that Jess heard beyond her own. She told herself, *make it last.*

She stroked Elena's ass and lower back in an attempt to take her time. The brunette hummed in pleasure, too. Jess leaned forward; just before her lips pressed to Elena's spine, she met Eric's eyes. He was smiling. She felt the light touch of his hand to her shoulder, tangling a bit in the ends of her hair.

She suddenly realized that Eric held all of her and Elena's weight. "Is this okay?" she asked.

"I'm good," he said. "Go ahead and move."

So she did. It was a new experience. She'd never really interrupted herself, delayed an orgasm, or experienced a partner like Eric, who liked taking his time. She rose up slowly, feeling every inch of him rubbing her inside. She finally rose fully to her knees, just the tip of him inside her. Elena's legs were fully splayed, and she didn't resist a tiny swirl of a finger just inside the brunette's inner lips.

Slowly Jess lowered again onto Eric's erection. The tightness was delicious, and even the slight tension in her muscles she found intoxicating. She was only focused on sensation.

Delighting in the warm, soft skin under her palms and balancing with gentle pressure and circles on Elena's back, Jess rocked her hips. Then she squeezed her inner muscles on Eric while she rose up again. His drawn-out moan echoed hers.

This is an incredible fuck, she thought with self-satisfaction. She flexed inwardly again. Eric's inhalations and exhalations echoed hers while she kept moving to the mantra: *slow, slow.* She lowered again until she felt the hairs of his crotch against her clit. Beginning to feel the difference between excitement and urgency, she continued, and drew out both her pleasure and Eric's.

"So good," she murmured on her next descent.

When she met Eric's gaze again, she matched his grin. Then she saw Elena's lips curled in a smile against Eric's chest. Elena was studying her with deep brown eyes, crinkled at the corner. Maintaining eye contact, Jess brushed her fingertips on Elena's back, and slid them down her ass and then continued lower. She found and parted her soaked labia and curled one fingertip up inside. Elena wriggled, smiled wider, and hummed again.

Jess resumed moving up and down on Eric and paced her own pleasure with the sounds coming from Elena as she fingered her. She didn't realize until it was happening that she was orgasming. Elena's, Eric's, and her own sounds of pleasure filled her ears. She hadn't sped up and hadn't tensed. A wave of pleasure simply filled her up, and then crashed over her entire body.

His eyes screwed closed, Eric twitched inside Jess, and she felt his fingers fumbling against her belly. She wanted to lie forward, but she lifted off instead, and saw Eric was holding the condom in place. She gave his cock a last "thank you" squeeze with her muscles, and they shared a smile before she lifted herself completely off him.

She curled herself against Elena. The brunette slid off Eric and turned over, now snuggling into Jess as she sank into the cool sheets of the bed. She hadn't even realized how heated her body had gotten.

Eric sat up. "That was amazing," Jess said. Elena kissed her chest near her collarbone.

"Good," he replied, and leaned across Elena to kiss her, his lips nibbling and his mustache tickling. She giggled. He kissed her again, firmer. "There'll be food."

"I'm not hungry," Jess said, a little surprised that she wasn't feeling the usual hunger or exhaustion that followed sex.

"I'm sure you will be soon." Eric chuckled. "Elena's not done with you yet." He kissed Elena's cheek, and brushed Jess's shoulder as he moved from the bed. "You ladies enjoy yourselves. I'll clean up and be in the kitchen."

When Eric had disappeared inside the master bathroom, Elena rolled Jess onto her back and kissed and nipped around Jess's chest.

"So you're having a good time?" Elena asked. She was circling closer and closer to Jess's nipple, and Jess felt the tingling in her stomach that signaled she was aroused again.

"Yeah, I... when Eric asked me to slow down, I wondered why. But it... was better."

"More fun than you've had before?" Elena asked. She kissed up Jess's throat and under her jaw, raising more tingles. Then Elena was poised above Jess, her legs lifted from tiptoes and her elbows locked straight and holding her up. Air passed between their bodies and Jess shivered involuntarily, her hands lifting to Elena's hips.

When Jess tugged, Elena lowered herself gradually. Bits and parts of her slid against Jess while they deeply kissed. Jess was again caught in waves of sensations—tingles where Elena's fingers touched, throbbing that went deeper where their bodies pressed together, and the satin feel of lips moving on hers. There was the warm insistence of Elena's tongue beckoning her to give it chase when it retreated, and it was delicious. Elena hummed and sucked on Jess's tongue. The tingling in her stomach had turned to clenching, and that told Jess she was ready to go again. She detached herself from the pleasure of Elena's mouth and nipped at her salt-sweet jaw and throat.

Elena arched and shifted, straddling Jess. Jess felt the woman's wet center paint her skin as she moved against Jess's belly. Jess tightened her abdominal muscles, and with a partial crunch, brought herself up, arms wrapping around Elena's waist. She kissed Elena's breasts, and finally sucked one tip deep in her mouth.

Elena's arms went around her head, and Jess sucked on the one breast while Elena rocked her hips and brought herself to orgasm against the tight muscles of Jess's stomach. Almost immediately, Elena buried her face in Jess's hair and rocked herself to another orgasm, panting out a cry when she came.

Catching her breath, Elena whispered against Jess's hair, "I want you to fuck me. With the dildo. Will you?"

Jess grinned against the woman's breast and kissed it in brief parting. She leaned her head back, brushed Elena's dark hair back from her face, and said simply, "Show me what to do."

Elena felt the pleasure from Jess's response skitter over her skin, as if she had gotten a static shock. She scooted back, off Jess's legs, but returned for a quick kiss. Jess smiled; Elena felt giddy. She opened a dark wood box on top of the bedside table. Inside, on a bed of lint-free satin lay a thick silicone dong that curved into a fat bulb. She'd inspected it a couple days ago when she knew she wanted to have Jess use it on her, but it hadn't seen any action in some time.

Jess's inhalation made her look back over her shoulder to meet green eyes. "The bulb is for you," Elena explained. "It'll also give you better control for movement and depth." She reached into the drawer where Jess had been before, and retrieved a packet of lube, two sealed condoms, and the spandex harness.

She lubed the dong's end and then fitted it with a condom. She slid it through the cock-ring hole in the spandex. The condom stretched down the dong's entire length.

Jess stood up and reached for the spandex. "Just like underwear?" she asked.

"Yeah. Here." Elena handed over the second condom and the lube.

"Will you help me?" Jess asked.

"My pleasure." Elena delighted in this part. She got down on her knees and licked at Jess's center. With eager fingers, she dipped inside Jess and stroked the sides of her vagina, readying her for penetration again. Eric was big, but the bulb was fat and would be a different sensation. When Jess's legs quivered, Elena stopped. Jess watched with brightness in her green eyes as Elena added lube to the bulb end and unrolled the condom over it. She added a little more lube to the outside, and held out the sides of the harness pants so Jess could step in.

Elena guided the pants up the woman's legs until the bulb was pressed against Jess's open lips. She heard Jess inhale and exhale. Her fingers joined Elena's, and they slowly pushed the bulb in together. Elena enjoyed the view again as Jess's labia stretched and then closed around the narrow neck of the curved silicone. "How's it feel?" She moved it.

"Fuck. It's great." Jess's hands were on Elena's head, threading through her hair gently. "Fuck," Jess murmured as Elena moved it slightly again.

When Elena looked up, Jess's eyes were closed and she was swallowing, obviously adjusting to the sensations. "That's exactly what we'll do," Elena promised.

She stood, and with the dong pressing against her hip, Elena was wrapped up in Jess's arms and kissed thoroughly. When it started to turn hungry, Jess would pause, regroup, and slow things down. But Elena was ready for fierce possession.

"You don't have to go slow with me now," she told Jess, breathing against her throat before baring her teeth and pressing on Jess's jaw between them. She didn't actually bite, but the impression was the same, and Jess's response was immediate.

"On the bed," Jess said, her voice roughened by passion. Elena grinned and backed onto the bed, laying down. Her legs were off the sides, but Jess grasped Elena's legs around her knees and pulled.

"How much preparation do you need?" Jess asked. Her gaze was hungry on Elena's sex.

"Not much," Elena admitted. "I've imagined it a dozen different times."

"Hopefully I'll be half as good as you imagined," Jess laughed; Elena started to, but then Jess toyed with her clit, ending the laugh with a whimper. First wetting the dong's tip in Elena's own fluids, which fired lust through Elena, Jess finally started to push it in. Pussy throbbing in greeting, Elena's muscles automatically grasped and pulled. Jess moved slowly, though, Eric's thoughtfulness about making things last obviously still on her mind.

Looking up at Jess while she was penetrated, Elena enjoyed the sight. Blonde hair fell forward when Jess looked down, and her nostrils flared as she breathed. Her nipples were at attention as Jess experienced her own lust from the act they were sharing. When Jess stroked Elena's clit and caused Elena to gasp, Jess grinned and then did it again.

Jess didn't move the dong much, but when she did, the awkwardness of it was both a frustration and a turn-on. Elena felt incredibly moved. She'd had many experienced lovers in the past, and while Jess had admitted to having a lot of sex, it was endearing to think Elena might be Jess's first to explore in this way.

"Is this comfortable?" Jess asked. She adjusted her stance, and Elena saw in her face the moment the bulb notched up Jess's arousal. "Oh." She jerked her hips. The dong pushed abruptly deeper.

Elena grabbed for Jess's hips. "Yes. There," she urged. "Now fuck me."

Elena was soaking wet, and the noises of her juices squishing around the dong were intoxicating. Jess started shifting on her feet, before she caught on that she only needed to thrust and pull back slightly with her hips. Then Elena was being fucked properly.

Elena encouraged her new lover with words, with sounds, with gasps, and with moans. Jess's green eyes remained open and roved Elena's body. She moved her palms on Elena's stomach, which clenched. Then she stroked upward and pulled Elena's nipples with both hands. Elena felt her muscles insistently pulling on the dong, squeezing it, and she lifted her hips to screw herself onto it.

She locked her ankles around Jess's waist. Jess couldn't move back much, but she could still thrust. Elena felt the dong hit the top of her channel. She winced, but immediately the dong pulled back and rubbed the side. Almost unbelievably, Elena started to orgasm, and she grasped Jess's hand on her chest as an anchor.

It wasn't quick, more a series of pulses. Elena's sounds echoed that: short gasps mingled with high cries and low grunts.

Eric reentered the bedroom to hear the noises his wife made as she writhed and lifted, thoroughly enjoying herself. Jess was also vocal, but she was thoroughly intent on Elena, though he could tell when the dildo's bulb thwarted some of her control because she would jerk and bite her lip. He could see clearly how much she wanted to please Elena.

He walked up behind Jess and looked down at Elena's face, over Jess's shoulder. His wife had her eyes tightly shut, though occasionally she tried to open them, only to be sucked back under more sensations. Eric had watched her with other partners many times, but saw differences in the intimacy here between Elena and Jess. Their fingers laced on Elena's chest, and the tension ebbed and flowed between them.

He brushed his hand on Jess's back. She startled, then looked back over her shoulder. "May I hold you?" he asked softly. "You're doing wonderful things to her."

"Mm hmmm," Jess replied, and Eric smiled. He grasped Elena's ankles and separated them, helping Jess move them to her shoulders. This, he knew, would change the angle deeper and take Elena to the edge again.

At the same time as he pressed against Jess, hugging his body to her back, he heard Elena's gasps shift again to cries. He pressed his crotch against Jess's ass, which had the effect of pushing the dong deeper into his wife. "Follow the motion," he whispered against Jess's ear, then kissed her jaw. "We can fuck her together."

Jess learned quickly. When Eric pulled back his hips, her hips followed. When he pushed forward, she let his motion guide the dong back inside Elena. She held Elena's ankles against her shoulders as they repeated the motions several times. Elena was mewling her need to come.

With Jess's hands occupied holding Elena, Eric reached around and tweaked Jess's nipples, and her hips jumped against his. Elena growled, and Eric almost laughed. He kissed Jess's throat, asking, "You ready to have her come all over you?"

Jess opened her eyes and looked down. She continued thrusting, which impressed Eric with her stamina. She watched his hand trail down her belly, and then around Elena's thigh. He parted Elena's labia and scissored his fingers down the sides of her clit. Jess jerked, and he knew Elena's muscles had pulled at the dong. That was perfectly timed, though. Elena's juices flowed out over the dong. "There you go," he said. "Isn't Jess wonderful to you, El?"

His wife opened her eyes and finally saw him. Then she met Jess's gaze. She smiled, and the expression in her eyes was warm. "You have great control. I think you still need to come, though, don't you?"

"I... it feels great." Jess shifted. "Damn," she added.

"Now fuck me until *you* come, Jess." Elena wrapped her legs once again around Jess's hips.

Eric watched briefly from the bed as Jess resumed the rhythm he'd shown her. Elena returned to bliss, and, as Elena had told her, Jess rocked and twisted and pushed, obviously responding more to the bulb inside her as she indeed fucked Elena until she came. Eric almost laughed again when Elena had a second orgasm of her own, right behind Jess's.

"Oh, god," Jess murmured. "Damn. That was... mm, wow." She looked at Eric as she bent forward over Elena and braced herself on the bed. "My knees are shaking."

"Good. Come down here," Elena said. Jess collapsed. Eric's hand joined Elena's in making soothing strokes on Jess's back. The trio then shared multiple kisses in combination.

As Jess lowered her head to Elena's chest, Eric said, "I almost forgot. Dinner's ready."

Elena chuckled, Jess moaned something about being unable to move, and Eric did laugh this time.

CHAPTER TWELVE

ELENA EMERGED from the bathroom to find Eric and Jess still lying together on the bed, their blond heads close together. Curled on her side, Jess said something that Elena couldn't quite hear, but it made Eric laugh deeply. He rubbed Jess's shoulder and said, "I'll keep that in mind." Turning his head, Eric's gaze fell on Elena. He smiled. "You have an extra robe?" he asked.

"Of course." Elena went into the walk-in closet and emerged with one of her other robes. The gray robe's sides were bordered in rust red. She'd never found it flattering, but it had been a complimentary robe on a spa day she'd taken with Britt, on a day off between flights in and out of Cartagena.

Eric had already helped Jess remove the harness, which he took to the bathroom while Elena walked the robe to Jess. As their hands touched, Elena's gaze dropped and found the woman's crotch. Jess stood and pulled on the robe, lifting her arms. The motions moved her breasts and revealed her throat when she pulled her hair out from beneath the robe's collar. Witnessing Jess's absently seductive movements made Elena hungry for more intimate playtime. She stepped forward and put her hand on Jess's robe-covered waist and tied the belt. The blonde's smile widened. She brought her lips to Elena's and murmured, "Thank you."

"So? Dinner?" Eric's voice drew Elena's gaze away from Jess. She was already thinking that after dinner the three of them could return here or go to the basement playroom. She took Jess's hand. Eric led the way to the kitchen.

Eric went to the refrigerator and pulled out a bottle of wine. "Would you?" he asked Elena, handing it to her. "I'll bring out the dishes."

Jess walked alongside Elena. "I'll get the glasses if you tell me where?"

Elena went to the sideboard and removed a foil cutter and corkscrew. "There are glasses in the cabinet there," she said, pointing with a finger off the neck of the bottle to a cabinet on the wall between this space and the living room.

Jess presented the glasses by the time Elena had finished removing the wine's cork. Elena poured an equal measure of the wine, about three ounces, into all three glasses. Jess quickly distributed the glasses, and lifted hers, placed last, to swirl and look at the eddies. "Smells really nice," she said.

Swishing her wine under her own nose, Elena concurred. She started to take a small sip, but Eric's arrival with plates gave her pause. He moved around and left a plate at each place. "I hope it's all right that I served," Eric said.

Elena looked down at her plate and discovered the main dish was lightly sauced chicken. Catching a mildly spiced scent as she sat down, Elena thought it might be a mix of garlic, basil, and oregano. So, Italian chicken, she concluded, knowing most of her husband's quick go-to recipes. There was already a wooden bowl of tossed salad on the table. Also on each plate, Eric had placed small servings of stewed carrots. It was colorful and aromatic.

"It looks great," Jess said, reaching for her fork.

"A toast," Eric said, lifting his glass.

"Toast?" Jess quickly put down the fork, and she and Elena both lifted their glasses.

"To the best sex-filled day," Eric said. "With a beautiful brunette and a hot blonde."

Elena chuckled, and saw Jess smile and blush under Eric's grin. She clinked her glass to theirs in the middle of the table. "To a sex-filled day," she echoed.

"We haven't had one of these in a while," Elena said. "Not since layovers, when we both flew international."

"You said before you met while both working for the airline?"

"Yep," Eric said.

Elena cleared her palate with a sip of wine. "I was waitressing at an airport restaurant when I saw a flyer for flight attendants. I worked double shifts for almost two months to pay for training. I gave my two weeks' notice when I finished. I applied everywhere. Diligent liked that I spoke Spanish and put me on all their Central and South American flights."

"Why did you stop working?"

"After Eric and I married, things changed. I wasn't happy working passenger service. I tried to move to gate or ticketing. When that didn't pan out, Eric and I discussed me staying at home. It's tight occasionally. But I'm happier since I quit."

"But I thought you were in travel work?"

"I'm trying to start an adult travel and tour service," Elena said. "I miss traveling," she admitted.

"I haven't done much of anything except travel," Jess said. "And not even to exotic places—Portland, Phoenix, Paris." Jess paused, then clarified, "It's a town in Texas. I've also lived around Atlanta. I told you I've waitressed, stocked shelves. I even picked crops in Georgia. Just hanging out after work, I learned bartending skills, enough to pass muster while waitressing at a roadside restaurant when the lead bartender was swamped."

"How'd you end up this far south?" Elena asked.

"Originally I was headed for the Keys. I figured to get lost and find some peace and quiet. I'd heard one didn't need much to live, and that they kinda appreciate minimalists. But I broke down without a single dime to my name just off U.S. 1 here. The tow truck driver took me into the nearest place, the convention district, and dropped me there."

"Where you found your way to Caliente."

"I asked at several places. Caliente was the only place that didn't seem to care where I came from. Told me I could have work and a room to stay. I started as a waitress and delivered food in the bar and room service. I picked up one day behind Gus when he got swamped making drinks. Afterward, he quizzed me a shit-ton. Then he told them to make me assistant bartender or he'd quit."

"Gus sounds like a nice guy."

"He's the one who told me a bit about swinging," Jess said. "He said he and his wife were in the lifestyle, til she died."

"Surprised we've never met him," Elena said.

"How often do you pay attention to the bartender?" Jess said. "We're invisible most of the time. Order your drinks, tip us, move on."

"I certainly noticed you," Eric said.

"I wasn't working at the bar at the time," Jess reminded him. She shrugged. "I like the anonymity actually."

"Not a lot of friends?" Elena asked.

"More like none. When you don't stay in the same place for longer than a few months, it's kinda impossible. A lot of the people I crossed paths with over the years weren't exactly the keep-in-touch type."

"I hope you think we're friends," Elena said, and Jess nodded immediately. "What's the longest you've stayed anywhere?"

"Six months in a sharecropper's shack outside Atlanta. I went from picking crops, to packing boxes at a shipping center."

"What made you leave there?"

"Boyfriend troubles," Jess said. Her expression went dark. Elena wanted to ask for more detail, but realized it wouldn't be polite.

So she changed the subject. "Girlfriend troubles made me leave home," she said.

"Your mother didn't approve," Jess said. "You mentioned it."

"I didn't want constant criticism, so I moved away. Miami's far enough from New York," Elena said. "I immediately went to South Beach. Got into the scene there. Found my first job at a gay bar."

"How'd you end up at the airport?" Jess asked.

"Found a help wanted sign after seeing off a girlfriend to Columbia. South Carolina," she added with a smile.

Jess again washed dishes, insisting since Eric had cooked. This time, though, Elena and Eric hung around. Eric put on some music, dancing with Elena, and then taught Jess a few steps. It was nearly time for the club to open when Jess finally accepted she had to go. She didn't want to.

"Club opens at 7:00 p.m.," she said. "I had a really good time." She shook her head as she collected her clothing from the bedroom. Looking at the bed, she added, "Better than good. Great. Thank you."

Elena settled next to her on the bed while she dressed. Eric had stepped out to find his keys. "I'm... you're welcome. Anytime."

After pulling on her boots, Jess met Elena's gaze, and saw, with a flare of hope, the same reluctance to end things. She wanted to ask to see the brunette again but didn't want to assume.

"If... I... Eric and I came to the club, could we... see you?"

"If I'm not behind the bar," Jess said.

"Where will you be?" Elena asked in confusion.

Jess felt giddy relief. "No, nothing like..." She leaned close and found Elena's eyes. "If I'm not working, I'll be happy to see you."

"Yes?" Brown eyes were bright.

"Yeah." Jess smiled into Elena's kiss.

Eric glanced over to Jess frequently as he drove toward the club. She was quiet, and he noticed more than once she fidgeted with her hotel room key. "Jess?" Her fingers stopped moving and she looked over to him, eyes wide. "We're here," he finished. She gave a smile that was a quirk of her lips.

Getting out of the car and moving around to reach her door before she stepped out, Eric smiled at Jess. "So, we'll be able to see you again?"

"I'd like that."

Jess accepted his hug. "Us too." He stepped back and took her hand. "Come on, let's get you back to your room."

Eric tried the front door and found it still locked, a few minutes before open time. Jess pointed to a side entrance that staff and delivery drivers used to access the kitchen. That door was unlocked. Together they walked down the empty corridor. The lighting was low, but easy to navigate.

As they entered the staff hallway, Eric asked, "Who all lives onsite?" He was admittedly fascinated. He'd never really considered where the staff of a hotel or club lived.

"Hector and Maya, of course. A couple of the hotel maids, I think. Also Gus, whom you already met."

Jess stopped in front of her door. "Here I am." Eric watched her insert the key card and open the door.

He hesitated to follow her inside. "You remember everything? Didn't leave anything at the house?"

She shook her head. "Not much to forget." She looked around. "You... want to come in?"

He stepped in immediately at the invitation and looked around again. He'd been too tired to notice much earlier. He'd seen dozens of hotel rooms over the years of layovers. Jess's wasn't anything unique. But he scanned the space anyway, trying to see something of the young woman in the clutter.

There was almost nothing. A hairbrush, a few clips, a pen laid haphazardly over a used notepad. He looked from the dresser surface to the bathroom counter he could see along the back wall.

There were the flowers he'd given her at the beginning of the day, in their can vase. Then he turned and saw the bed.

"Single," he said, remembering how Jess had at first offered to host Elena and him here.

"Yeah, too small," she said.

"Elena and I can come by Friday and see you?"

"Yes," Jess said. "I close the bar at one, when everyone's in the rooms."

"Then maybe you can come home with us again?"

When he cupped his fingers underneath her chin, Jess lifted her gaze, and met his lips for a sweet kiss. "I'd like that," she agreed when she stepped back.

Stepping back out into the corridor, Eric turned and saw Jess leaning on the open door. He smiled at her and was warmed by her return smile. She closed the door to her room as he walked away.

Jess was hanging up some clothing to air out when she heard a knock on the door. Thinking Eric might be back, she quickly opened the door.

"Gus?" She met the gaze of the lead bartender, standing in the hallway.

"Hi, Jess. You good?"

"I saw Elena and her husband," Jess added. "The man you met this morning. He just dropped me off."

"A couple?"

"Yeah, I actually met him first, but Eric and Elena have been really nice to me."

"Just nice?" Jess sensed Gus was teasing her. "You were there yesterday, too." Jess nodded. "Might it be a bit better than nice?"

"A bit," she hedged, recalling how much sex they'd had.

"Good." Apparently thinking that was the last necessary word, Gus left Jess sitting on her bed. He let himself out, and she heard the door to his room across the hall open and then close. An hour later, they were both working side by side at the bar as the club music pumped around them.

CHAPTER THIRTEEN

ELENA SNAPPED her stockings into place with the garter clips and examined her appearance in the mirror. They were visiting Caliente tonight, but it was what would happen after the bar closed that had her most excited.

Elena held up two different bras to decide. The first was a lacy black pushup that showcased her nipples through open slots. The other was a shiny red strapless twist-n-stretch. Finally, Elena chose the classic black lace. She was reaching around her back to secure it in place when Eric stepped back into the room. She met his gaze in the mirror. His fingers smoothed over her shoulders and down to where they met her hands; he took over securing her bra. In many ways, it was like any other night they might be getting ready for swinging, but to Elena it felt different.

"Come on," he said. "Get into your dress. You stay naked much longer, and I'll keep you here for myself."

Elena chose a midnight blue domino dress. Fabric pieces had been sewn together at angles, and diamond-shaped openings liberally showed patches of her skin. The hemline of the dress was cocktail-length, but again the angles created by the fabric meant that her left thigh was mostly exposed, teasingly revealing her garter.

When dressed, she studied herself one final time in the mirror. Quickly tucking a misplaced curl of her dark brown hair behind her ear, Elena puckered her lips and reapplied lipstick. Finally, she nodded in satisfaction at the seductive picture she presented. Confidence flowing at last, she grabbed up her purse and met Eric at the front door.

The night was well underway when Jess finally settled into her work. She looked up at every motion out of the corner of her gaze, identifying patrons and making their requested drinks.

"Mai tai and scotch and soda, please."

Looking up, Jess automatically started to quote the price, only to meet Eric's blue eyes. Her voice jumped in the excitement she couldn't contain. "Eight—Eric!"

He smiled at her, and she drank in the sight of him. Tonight he wore dark blue pants and a white shirt that almost glowed under the bar's lighting. His matching blue tie sported a diamond-shaped gold tie tack.

"You look great," he said.

"You look wonderful," she replied. She couldn't resist looking past him for Elena while she prepared his drink order.

"She's here," he said. He took the mai tai she finished first. "Hoping to see you." He handed her a ten. "Will you have a break later?"

"Drink orders usually slow down when couples start heading to the playrooms."

Eric checked his watch. The idea of seeing him and Elena and talking to them again made Jess smile when he looked back up. "We'll still be here," he said.

"It's good to see you," she offered as he stepped away. No more could be said, when she was flagged down at the other end of the bar.

From a corner table, Elena watched as Eric talked with Jess. She wanted to get up and go over herself, but her emotions were riotous. Seeing Jess made her giddy—Jess looked beautiful—and anxious. Did she still want to see them? The contrast was dizzying. Finally she saw Eric look down at his watch and say something. When he turned around, Elena saw he had their drinks. She straightened in her seat, trying not to look like she had been watching.

"Your mai tai," Eric said as he sat down and passed her drink. "Jess still makes it exactly the way you like it."

She took a tiny sip of the mixed drink through the straw. Eric was right; it was perfect. "Thank you," she said.

Eric sipped his scotch and soda. "El," Eric said. She looked down at his hand covering hers, which had fisted on the table. "Jess will still be here at the end of the night."

"She's willing to go home again, with us?" Elena asked.

"Yeah," Eric said. "Drink, relax." He withdrew his hand.

Elena looked from Eric toward the bar. The blonde was turning. "She missed us," she said softly. *I missed her*, she added to herself.

Eric's smile was gentle and understanding. "Yeah, El. She did."

Eric finished his scotch and soda and asked a passing waitress for a refill order. Elena requested a water after her mai tai was gone. She was planning to be sober at the end of the night.

He didn't think Elena recognized it in herself yet, but he was pretty sure their playtimes with Jess would become more emotionally complex. She had turned down one of their regular playmate couples already tonight, in favor of simply looking around the bar space and drinking in Jess from a distance.

As Belle and Gavin walked away, Elena must have noticed Eric's surprise. "You can go with them, if you want."

He remembered that she had played separately with Jess while he was at work; before the blonde, they almost never played apart. Things were definitely shifting.

"I'll wait," he responded, and realized he really was okay with that. He was looking forward to Jess as much as Elena was.

They danced a little. But the club wasn't the same when you didn't come to play. Elena found herself slipping away to the bathroom and checking her makeup.

"El? You're still out here?"

She looked over to see Cris, a transwoman, touching up her makeup at the neighboring sink. "You and Eric are always headed back to the playrooms by this time."

"You and Caitlyn, too," Elena said, recalling the woman's wife fondly; they had married last year, and Eric and Elena had been on the short guest list.

"Not feeling it with anybody out there tonight. Might start looking elsewhere."

Elena agreed, "It's just not the same."

"Really? Never thought you and Eric might stop." Cris kissed

Elena's cheek as she passed to go out the door.

Elena studied her reflection. Where had that come from? Was she ready to give up clubbing?

When she returned to Eric, she asked, "Do you want to go home?" It was still at least an hour until Jess was off the clock. But if they continued to project boredom, they'd never find another couple to play here again. A bad vibe was like vinegar and drove away people who might approach them to play.

Eric had considered several times offering to host a house party, using his home's renovated basement for more than just his and Elena's private fun, but he hadn't been able to get a read on Elena's comfort level with that idea. She'd been so focused on other situations, it never seemed the appropriate time to talk about it.

"What about moving things to our place? Hosting a house party?"

She looked up from her fingernails, a sure sign of boredom. "What? When?"

"When do you think would be good?"

"It's November. Holiday season. I can't imagine people would be—"

"Folks really enjoy costumes and theme nights," Eric pushed, just a little. "Whaddya say?"

"Halloween's already past. Besides, who would we invite?"

"Let's just start with the frequent flyers. And no one gets a 'plus one.' We've got numbers already, so we'll call. Even if everyone accepts, that'd be, what? Twenty people?" While he and Elena had spent a number of years swinging, the people they liked to call up and *plan* to meet at the club were only a select few.

Elena leaned forward; for the first time, she seemed genuinely interested. "I've never prepared for a party that big," she said. "We'd need some help."

"Help with what?" Both Eric and Elena looked up to see Jess standing by their table, looking at them.

"I'm trying to convince Elena we should host a themed costume party at the house."

"Themed party?" Jess asked.

"Costumes encouraged," Eric explained.

"Halloween was last month," Jess said, but her gaze shifted to an expression of deep interest.

"I think people would enjoy it," Eric added. "We've got the costuming chest in the playroom, too," he said, adding a shrug as if it didn't matter to him. But he was definitely thinking how erotic it would be to have Elena—or Jess—riding him while everyone watched, and envied, just a little. He smirked.

Jess turned to Elena and said, "You should do it. Be the center of an orgy."

"You think so?" Elena asked. Eric didn't mistake the craving in his wife's expression. Her want for Jess was obvious. "Have you ever attended a house party? They're not like nights at the club. More intimate."

Jess shook her head. Eric watched the women's gazes searching each other. "No," Jess said finally. "But I want to spend more time with you... And Eric," she added, her gaze sweeping to include him briefly. "So, show me?"

Elena's eyes flashed, and Eric could almost read her mind. He remembered how the fantasy of publicly fucking Jess the first night, just after they'd met her, had sent Elena spiraling quickly into orgasm. They'd also just spent several hours, and filled a single day, with marathon sex.

"You only have sex with the people you want to," Elena felt necessary to add. Eric heard the roughness of her tone and knew she was thinking of ways to make sure people knew Jess was with them.

"Good," Jess said. "When is the party?"

Elena looked at Eric. "How about the ninth? That's a Saturday night. Popular."

"What about a daytime pool party instead? On Sunday the tenth?" Eric cast a glance toward Jess, knowing the younger woman worked Saturday nights.

"Broad daylight?" Elena asked.

Eric teased her, "I happen to like broads, especially brunettes and blondes... oh, and redheads, too."

Jess asked, "You don't mean we'd be having sex on the pool deck?"

"No, there's the playroom, but to the neighbors a backyard barbecue is totally normal," Eric said. After a moment thinking about the calendar, he added, "Oh, hey, especially if we go with the flow. The Monday after is Veterans Day."

Elena concluded, "I love it. Yes, let's do that." She looked up at Jess. "You could come over after work Saturday night, and wake up with us on Sunday. We can start the barbecue for around midafternoon."

Jess nodded. "I'd like that. Thank you for inviting me." She bent over and lightly kissed Eric's cheek, then Elena's. She left their table with a slight bounce to her steps.

Eric took Elena's hand under the table, feeling the tight fist she'd formed to restrain herself from reaching out after Jess.

"You really think we can throw a house party so quickly?" Elena asked.

"The playroom's ready for a grand opening."

"I don't want to overwhelm her. A half dozen couples," Elena said. After a pause, she added, "Max."

Though he knew what Elena meant, he decided to tease her and make her smile. "Max," he said, "could be one of a few choice singles." Max Pinone was a Hispanic single man Elena and he had played with before.

Elena shook her head. "You know what I meant."

"Yes," he said.

Jess returned to the bar. Gus looked up. The music was filling the room, but he seemed expectant. She wondered if he'd seen her with Elena and Eric. She lifted the spacer and moved behind the bar. "Hey," she greeted. "How are you doing?"

"People have been coming up. This is his last song of the first set. He'll be back after a water break. The crowd seems to like the music."

"You have a good ear," Jess agreed. "His style fits in here."

"I didn't think you were listening to him much," Gus said. "Those your friends?" he asked with a tip of his chin.

"Yeah. They've asked me to a pool and costume party at their house on Sunday the tenth." Between the conversation, Jess easily stepped back into taking and making drink orders.

"Isn't a Sunday kind of odd?" he asked. "Don't they work?"

"This is a day party." Jess made change at the till for someone paying their tab. "And Monday's Veterans Day. Lots of people have that off. I'll go over after work Saturday night."

"You're excited about this." Gus poured out one of the craft bottles into a glass and handed it across the bar.

"Yeah, it's a costume party and a pool barbecue with friends. What's not to like?"

She pushed another craft beer bottle toward a man in a blue polo shirt, then made a note on his tab over the register.

Flipping the light switch off, Jess took off her suit jacket as she walked out of the back of the kitchens.

"Still wanna come with?"

Eric stood by the entrance to the corridor of staff hotel rooms. Elena held his elbow, standing next to him.

Jess had almost forgotten the Tanners had invited her to go home with them after work tonight. She brightened, even as tired as she was.

"Can I entice you with a hot bath and a beautiful brunette?" Eric asked.

"I might fall asleep in the water," Jess said.

"Then we'll tuck you into bed, between us," Elena said.

"That'd be all right?" Jess asked.

"Yeah," Eric said.

In the car on the way to the Tanners' home, Jess lay in Elena's lap on the back seat; Elena smoothed her fingers through Jess's hair, having pulled it down from the clipped bun. The topic quickly moved to the forthcoming costume party.

"I can't wait," Elena said, and the eagerness of the other woman warmed Jess inside, making her heart thud audibly in her ears.

"Something military for the costume, right?" Jess asked.

"Right. Eric can loan you something."

"No, I think I have just the idea." Jess thought about where she might be able to score a simple set of fatigues, maybe an olive tank top and boxers. She remembered how much Elena had appreciated seeing Jess's muscled arms during the "tool time" photo shoot. "Should I bring anything?"

"Just you," Elena said, and her eager tone made Jess wish the party was sooner.

When the trio arrived at the Tanner home, as promised, a warm bath was drawn, and Jess, also as promised, fell asleep in it. Though, nestled in Elena's arms, she didn't drown.

Patted dry with fluffy towels, she was carried by Eric, naked, into the Tanners' bed. Eric and Elena crawled in on either side of her and kissed her cheeks good night.

Tying off a towel around her hips, Jess shook her blonde head, smiling wide toward the morning sun as her soaked hair slapped heavily against her back. Eric had suggested she use the pool while he worked on breakfast and Elena slept in. Swimming laps in the pool had been invigorating. She patted dry her hair with one hand as she entered the sliding glass doors and walked to the wide counter separating the living space from the spacious kitchen. She inhaled the aromas of bacon and eggs, and...

"Oh my god, apple pancakes!" She identified the smell at the same time she spotted Eric Tanner flipping them on the griddle.

The air-conditioning nipped at her mostly bare skin in the borrowed red string bikini. She leaned on her elbows on the counter across from sandy-blond Eric, grinning next to the stainless steel of his spatula.

He said, "We have every delight in this house."

She reached toward the skillet, her eyes meeting his. Both of them smirked as she sent her hand sideways to the wooden bowl of freshly rinsed grapes.

Popping a grape in her mouth, Jess eyed the beautiful pancakes he had just flipped on the skillet. They were perfectly golden brown. *God.* Jess immediately saw equally golden skin in her mind's eye. Her mouth watered with the desire to kiss it, touch it, taste it...

When she refocused, she found Eric's gaze still riveted to hers.

"If you don't linger too long," he said, drawing down the skillet heat, "you can wake her up."

Jess leaned further across the counter and caught Eric's lips in a quick kiss. It was, she realized, unnecessary, but it made this special to her. She was enjoying the warm delight of being welcomed so thoroughly. She certainly felt loved, as heat began to coalesce in her body. She chuckled and hurried to the bedroom.

The east-facing window here opened only onto the pool patio, so Jess pulled open one curtain. The morning's light swept across the king-sized bed and its remaining occupant.

"Elena," Jess called, letting her voice roll low and soft through the room as she approached the bed.

The Latina, partially under a sheet, wearing a spaghetti-strap silk negligee, stretched slowly, luxuriating in the laziness of their Sunday morning. Jess sat on the bed beside her, pulling back the sheet to gaze on lush curves.

"Morning?" Elena's voice barely managed the syllables, and Jess wriggled a little with delight. She skimmed her open palm over the satin skin of Elena's golden thigh.

"Yeah," Jess replied. Her fingers widened as she neared the warmth of Elena's center.

She eased her body against Elena's and claimed dark lips in a kiss that deepened slowly. Elena laughed low and folded her arms around the back of Jess's shoulders, before Jess pulled back. She nipped at her jaw. "You're learning all his tricks, dear."

"I'm learning what you like," Jess replied, pleased by the acknowledgement of her growing skills. She breathed along the tendon in Elena's throat, then trailed the tip of her tongue to the sensitive spot behind the woman's ear. A breast arched into her chest, the hard nipple evident even through the silk. Returning her mouth to Elena's, Jess moved two fingers in and out of the woman's center as they continued to trade open-mouthed kisses.

When Elena's inner muscles began squeezing her fingers, Jess lifted up. She parted her towel and inserted a thigh between Elena's. Elena bent her knee up against Jess's center. Jess rocked into the pressure of it, while adding rotation to her own fingers thrusting in and out.

Elena's body arched, nearing orgasm, and Jess could no longer reach her panting mouth. She pulled aside the silk negligee and latched on to a breast, plying her teeth on the engorged nipple. Elena gave a shortened cry. Fingers slid into her hair and gripped in rhythmic pleasure, as more of her release soaked Jess's fingers below. Jess grinned against the flesh in her mouth, eager for more cues to increase their mutual pleasure.

When Elena stopped pulling her hair and instead wrapped her arms around Jess's back, Jess knew the time of welcomed teasing was rapidly becoming a need for release. She added a third finger, and used her knee to add more pressure. Feeling her own wetness bathe Elena's thigh, Jess switched to chewing and sucking on the previously unattended breast. Another gasp and cry rewarded her attention to detail.

Elena grasped Jess's ass, fingers taut, digging into the cheeks. Jess now felt the caress of a third hand on the back of her thigh. She glanced back and saw Eric's smile and raised brow. Her cunt twitched with desire born of knowing what could be coming next. She lifted a little off Elena's thigh and briefly disengaged from the delectable kiss. Gazing deeply into dark brown eyes, Jess mirrored the woman's smile. Eric's hand slid to Jess's inner thigh.

She lowered her chest against Elena's, lifting her ass a little, and closed her eyes at the explosion of different sensations everywhere: her breasts pillowing against Elena's, the woman's hands, light and supple, now stroking her back. Elena's folds fluttering around her own fingers, while her own cunt welcomed Eric's touch, one finger curling inward, and another pressing deliciously against her clit. His lightly furred chest brushed against her back.

Lifting her upper body again, she welcomed his press against her back. Gazing down again, she saw Elena's dark eyes, pupils exploded by lust, watching them both. Eric's free hand cupped Jess's cheek and turned her face to his for a kiss. Elena's hands lifted to Jess's breasts, pulling aside the bikini top to pluck and squeeze Jess's nipples. Jolts of pleasure shot directly to her groin, soaking Eric's buried finger.

Eric's mouth swallowed Jess's moans. She curled two fingers inside Elena and sought out that spot while she rubbed her thumb alongside the woman's fully hardened clit.

When Eric's finger delved deeper, Jess heard Elena's cries join hers.

"Oh, fuck!" Jess gasped. Beneath her, Elena shuddered. Eric anchored her, so she didn't crush Elena as every one of her muscles shook.

She sagged, spent, muscles quaking in her thighs and stomach. Eric gently released her, half on and half off Elena, her head nearly in the headboard as she panted to calm her heart rate.

Elena nibbled Jess's throat, which caused dozens of little aftershocks. Jess groaned, and yet couldn't stop grinning goofily as Elena's chuckles warmed the skin directly over her thudding heart.

Jess felt Eric slide onto the bed and spoon against her back. Eric and Elena kissed past her shoulder, before Jess felt his mustache and lips brush against the back of her shoulder blade.

"So," he said into the sudden silence. "Anyone interested in my pancake breakfast?"

Elena chuckled and pulled Jess into her body. "Was that what you were sent in here to do?"

"Maybe," Jess murmured sheepishly against Elena's collarbone. She couldn't quite bring herself to feel guilty for getting off-track.

Eric and Elena laughed, which deepened Jess's pleasure. But then the couple rose, and Eric hefted Jess in his arms, while Elena led the way from the bedroom.

CHAPTER FOURTEEN

"WHAT TIME should things start?" Eric asked. "I know you told Jess, but she's going to be here most of the day. When do we want everyone else to arrive? I'm going to make the calls today."

"Do we want hors d'oeuvres before the barbecue?" Elena replied. She was on her laptop.

"Just the barbecue," he answered. The club never served dinner, and the action seldom moved to the playrooms before eleven. "What do you think about inviting people to arrive around one? Spend the afternoon around the pool. Take a dip. Have drinks, talk, a little music?"

"Do you think we should use the pool in an icebreaker activity?" Elena said, finally looking up. "Have all of them played with each other before?"

Eric shook his head. "I don't know about each other, but they've each played with us," he said.

"Yeah, but... shouldn't we make a point that everyone understands the rules?"

"They do, otherwise we wouldn't be inviting them, right?"

"The sites all recommend an icebreaker or a game, to get people comfortable."

"They're all experienced swingers, El."

"Not all of them," Elena said.

"Jess," Eric said, with clarity now about the source of Elena's anxiety. "We can go over the rules with her anytime. She's coming in the morning."

"I want her to have a good time," Elena said. "It's her first party."

"She will. We'll make sure of that." Eric went back to his original question. "What time should people arrive?"

"Between one and two. Everyone goes through to the deck first. I'll post the rules on the door to the playroom."

"Sounds good," Eric said. He reached for his cell phone. "Relax, El, this party's going to be great."

"Just make sure that everyone knows who else will be here."

"We'll introduce everyone on the deck as we bring them in," Eric said.

"The sites all recommend a game or something, to relax, get comfortable."

"El, everyone knows why they're here. Let 'em swim, eat, chat. It'll be good," he said, and stood.

Elena lifted her cheek to his kiss.

"I'll be outside making calls." He stepped out to the deck, immediately feeling the sun on his face. Miami's spring weather was blustery, but otherwise it looked to be a nice day. The weather apps all predicted minimal rain and temps in the eighties, which would continue through to the party date. He scanned his contact list and selected the first call to place. "Chana," he said when the call connected and a charming female voice answered. "Would you and Ren like to come to a party?"

Chana asked, "What party?"

"Barbecue, costumes, and swinging. Elena and I thought we'd have a house party. Barbecue, then fun in our recently finished playroom."

"So you finished that, finally?"

"We had a recent spark to finish. Are you interested? It'd be the tenth. Thought we'd go military theme."

"Sounds intriguing. You and El?"

"And a few others."

"Does sound like it could be fun. I need to talk to Ren. When will you need to know?"

"By Wednesday? I'll shoot out an email, too. With directions and stuff."

"Rules," she said.

"Of course," he answered. "So, will we see you and Ren?"

"Almost certainly," Chana said. "Our love to Elena."

"Same to Ren," he said.

Eric smiled at his success as he pressed the End Call button. Opening his note app, he put Chana and Ren's names as the first on a list: Guests. Back to the phone app, he scrolled through his contacts and found the number for their next potential play partners.

Jess looked down at her clothes one last time. It was nearly 4:00 a.m. She'd been as fast as possible, but she hadn't actually been able to get out of the bar until half past three. She hadn't taken down her hair from its twisted bun, just pulled off her work clothes and put on the fatigues she'd bought at the surplus store. She'd then driven to the Tanners, narrowly avoiding being stopped at two lights that went from yellow to red just as she was passing underneath them.

Removing the camouflage cap, Jess fluffed her fingers in her hair, only to remember and get them tangled in the bun, looking a complete wreck—if she hadn't already from the long work shift. With a sigh, she rang the doorbell. She looked at the door and noticed the peephole. Quickly, she moved so she could be seen clearly, and used the motion to try to untangle her long hair. Her clip sprang from her fingers to disappear somewhere in the bush alongside the front stoop. Debating whether to go find it, she shifted from foot to foot.

The front light clicked on; Jess blinked. The door opened. There was the barest pause as each woman regarded the other. Abruptly Elena grinned, reached out, wrapped her hand around Jess's wrist, and pulled Jess across the threshold into the house.

"Hey," Jess said, trapped between the foyer wall and brown eyes devouring her.

"Hi," full lips said just before they claimed her own.

If Jess had been tired, she felt none of that now. Elena's kiss was energizing, and she seemed to want to touch Jess everywhere at once. Fingers laced through her tangled hair, lips slipped to the exposed curve of Jess's throat. The woman's other hand pulled Jess's tank from the waistband of her pants.

"Careful, this is all I have for the party," Jess said, almost giddy as she gave her body over to Elena's explorations, right there, against the wall of the woman's home.

Elena helped her out of the fatigue jacket then straddled Jess's hips as she pushed the woman to the floor. Between murmurs of "hot uniform" and "so good," Elena unbelted Jess's fatigue pants, shoved them down her hips, and wriggled her fingers inside Jess while teasing her tongue over Jess's clit.

"Uh," Jess moaned, grasping fistfuls of Elena's hair. "Um, isn't Eric sleeping?" she whispered.

"Yes, I've been waiting for you to come." Elena's murmured words were deliberate, between kisses and licks on Jess's center. The woman's breath was teasing, hot, her tongue insistently pushing inside Jess's soaked cunt. Jess didn't think it was coincidence that she reached orgasm just as Elena finished her words.

Elena slid up and murmured, "So good to see you again." Jess tasted herself on Elena's lips while they kissed languidly. As more of Jess's senses returned, she realized the brunette wore only a thin nightgown. She rucked it up now and indulged her own fingers in the warm depths of the other woman's wet pussy.

Afterward, Elena helped Jess stand, and Jess collected the clothing items Elena had actually taken off. She was guided to the bedroom where she saw Eric asleep on the far side of the bed, facing away, the sheet tucked in over his body. The sounds of his light breathing reached Jess's ears. She looked at Elena curiously.

"Here," Elena whispered in answer to Jess's unspoken question. "Between us."

"Are you sure?" Jess asked, just as quietly. A squeeze to her hand and a slight tug said yes, Elena was sure.

Once she was only in boxers and tank top, Jess backed carefully onto the bed and held open the covers. With only a little fuss, all the while Jess sure the next move would awaken Eric, Elena and Jess were settled together, the brunette's head resting against Jess's shoulder, the rest of her body aligned to Jess's. Resting her chin against the top of Elena's head, Jess inhaled and exhaled the woman's unique scent, and let her consciousness fade away.

Elena studied the deck tables after she set down the last tray of toothpick-staked cheeses and meats on cracker thins. Pickles and olives were arranged on another tray. She'd also set out grapes and apple chunks, with caramel for dipping. A fruit and rum punch had been placed on a table with an ice bucket, and clear plastic cups just inside the sliding doors so they would be out of the direct afternoon sunlight.

Eric emerged from the basement. He smiled at her and flashed a thumbs-up, indicating he'd finished his task. While they had the toy chest, Elena had decided to get some small boxes. At first glance they looked like they should hold tissues, but lifting the lid revealed two sections. One side had sealed items—sanitary wipes, lube packets, dental dams, and condoms—and the other side had been lined with a plastic bag for quick disposal.

Eric's email had established that nakedness and sexual activities would be allowed only in the playroom. Necking and making out could happen on the deck and in the pool, but as soon as anyone wanted to be naked, they had to go inside.

The doorbell sounded. Casting her eyes to the ceiling, Elena inhaled and exhaled. And hoped.

She neared the front door and saw Eric greeting Max with a fist-bump. The dark-haired man had dressed as a Navy sailor. Behind Max, Elena saw Paola and Hernando Sanchez moving together up the walk. Hernando wore a khaki Army uniform, and Paola wore a green uniform cap and jacket over a green blouse and tight black skirt.

Elena smiled and accepted a kiss from Hernando, while hugging Max. Paola moved into Eric's arms. "We looked like a veterans' parade coming up the walk," Hernando said, "You're gonna get a rep as a patriotic son of a gun, Eric."

"Well, let's get naked and change that," Max said. He put an arm around Elena's waist, and the small group entered the house.

"There's drinks by the sliding doors, and the rest is on the deck," Eric said. "I'll fire up the grill in about an hour, after everyone's here."

Just then, Jess emerged from the bathroom. Everyone turned. Elena smiled when she saw the woman wore a tan tank top underneath a desert camo jacket, with its seemingly endless array of pockets. She wore camo shorts secured with a tan belt. The Velcro space for a rank and name was empty.

"Who's this?" Max asked, stepping away from Eric.

"This is Jess. She's..." Elena stopped herself when she realized she had been about to say "with us." Jess may have been over for the entire day, but she was another guest. "Another guest," Elena finished.

Max held out his hand. "Hello, Jess, I'm Max. Nice to meet you."

Paola and Hernando stepped forward then, too, and Jess was surrounded. The swingers had scented new blood. Eric and Elena exchanged frowns.

"Why don't we go onto the deck?" Eric said. "This way."

Elena led the group through the dining room. Max, Eric, and Hernando picked out bottled beers from the cooler as they passed through onto the deck. Jess took a flight-size mini wine bottle. Paola served herself a small cup of the punch.

Out at the deck, there were compliments.

"This is wonderful."

"You have nice privacy."

"What a lovely pool."

Eric and Elena had played at the club, but Eric thought, from the sound of things, that might change. If this went well today, perhaps they would host more parties. He wondered if that was disloyal to Hector and Maya.

When the doorbell rang again, Elena went to answer it. Chana and Rene Shoen had dressed up, too. Rene looked like he was straight out of some World War II French film. "It's my grandfather's uniform," he said. "I probably still smell a little like mothballs."

Elena chuckled, and inhaled deeply when she hugged him. "It looks good on you," she said when she took a step back.

Chana had obviously gone to a costume shop. When she removed her overcoat, her outfit was most easily classified as "sexy soldierette." She wore a pushup bra and tiny shorts, both in camouflage-patterned greens. She'd used shoe polish, almost like paint, in a variety of camo colors on a pair of black knee-high boots. "Sorry, I am not a 'combat boots' girl," Chana said. "It made my legs look too fat."

Everyone laughed. Elena took the overcoat and hung it in the front closet, then led the couple out to the deck. Max and the Sanchez's clustered with Eric and Jess, on a couple chaises and a deck box. Elena served Chana and Rene from the punch, since both declined the bottles in the cooler. She was about to make introductions, when the doorbell rang again. Eric stood and waved, signaling that he would get the door.

Max had already started to flirt with Chana, giving her a playful salute, when Eric returned with Caitlyn and Cris. Both wore complete Air Force dress uniforms. A quick glance showed their name tags both read C. Tinglass, so they'd married while in service, something Elena realized she had not known. She wondered if Cris had transitioned MTF before or after her discharge. While the military was coming along with LGBTQ rights, Elena knew it wasn't an easy place to be different. Cris and Caitlyn were both regular partners with her and Eric at the club, though they hadn't seen each other much in the last month. She hugged Cris and asked, "How are you?"

Bright brown eyes shone in a slender face with rounded pouty lips. "We've been playing the gay clubs," Cris said. "So glad to get Eric's call. Ready to spend a night drama-free."

Caitlyn rolled her eyes, leaned close, and kissed Elena's cheek before whispering in her ear, "She means she is ready to get fucked by your fella."

"Eric will be happy to hear that," Elena replied. "And you?"

"Anyone else here play with the ladies as well as you do?" Caitlyn asked. Elena blushed. She'd forgotten how easily Caitlyn expressed her pleasures.

As she went to answer, Elena paused. She looked around the deck, watching Max flirt with Paola, Chana letting Hernando and Eric inspect her uniform with caresses to her ass, stomach, and thighs. No, she realized, most of the women present were situationally bi. They were intimate with women, while also playing with their spouses, but only she would initiate solo sex with a woman. Well, her and Jess, she added. But she didn't want to draw Caitlyn's attention to Jess at the moment. "I guess."

"Will Eric mind if you spend time playing with us?" Caitlyn asked.

"No, of course not."

"Good." Caitlyn took her hand. "So, you ready to get this party started?"

Elena smiled and sat down; Caitlyn and Cris sat down either side of her. She looked across the deck to see Eric accepting punch from Paola as he started up the grill.

When some liquid dribbled down his front, Paola licked Eric's lips, and then licked the drips from his chin. Hernando was kissing Paola's neck.

"Seems introductions aren't really necessary," she said. Eric grinned at her. He'd been so sure that everyone would just find their way. She was relieved to see he was right. "But perhaps a tour, so you can decide how the rest of the party will go?"

"First," Max said, "a toast, to those who served in the military, past and present." He lifted his punch cup. He added, "I never served a day in uniform, but I'd be happy to help any woman out of hers tonight."

"To our military," Elena said, pointedly lifting the cup of punch toward Caitlyn and Cris, and to Eric, who waved the grill tongs in lieu of a glass. He was happy and in his element, and Elena felt her chest squeeze with acute joy.

The toast had been quick, the fruity rum punch sweet, and she was feeling good. She stood and grasped Cris's hand. "This way."

"You want to go downstairs?" Jess looked from the pool surface, where she had been staring as she let the music simply play through her while she sipped her third, maybe fourth, punch. "The others have mostly split."

Jess looked around to see he was correct. There had been a swarm of people up here, and she had talked with a few of them, but after a while she'd drifted to another cluster, made small talk, until finally she had just needed a moment off to the side.

Jess studied the dark, swarthy, thin-bodied man. Her brow creased as she tried to remember his name. They had been introduced.

"Max," he supplied. "And you're a friend of the Tanners?"

"Jess," she supplied.

"Yeah." He leaned back in his chair, the lights from the house behind her showing his entire form. "Only you don't seem to be their type."

"Their type?" Jess asked; she knew her brain was a little fuzzed by the alcohol, but the comment didn't make sense.

"They like to play."

"Mmm hmmm." She remembered their morning sex before being led to their dining room table and fed a breakfast feast. "They're wonderful."

"And you're staying here."

"Just since last night," Jess said. "I came over after work."

"Where do you work?"

"I tend bar at the Caliente."

"There you are."

Jess looked up to see Elena tying off a cotton robe's belt, as she leaned on the jamb of the sliding glass doors. "Hi," Jess said.

"Are you coming downstairs?" Elena asked.

"I was just watching the water," Jess said.

"There's much more interesting viewing downstairs," Elena said. She walked forward and reached out a hand toward Jess.

"Come on."

When their hands touched, Jess was surprised to hear Elena speak again. "Max?" To Jess it sounded very surprised, like the brunette had forgotten there was another person present.

"Hmm... Oh, yeah. Yeah." Max said, and he hurried away, leaving Jess and Elena on the deck alone for the moment. For the first time that day, Jess realized.

"Everyone's downstairs," Elena said. She moved her hands over Jess's jacket, and her hands slipped under, teasing touches up her waist and the sides of her breasts in the tank top. "I love your costume," she said.

"Thanks," Jess replied. "Gus pointed me to a surplus store."

"Aren't you hot wearing the jacket?"

"I think I can take it off now."

Deciding, Jess smiled as she stepped back, watching Elena look her over, the woman's expression openly admiring.

"I remembered how much you enjoyed the tool-time photographs," she said, slowly pulling it off her shoulders. "I'm GI all the way down to my boxers," Jess said. She looked at the floor. "Even found combat boots that weren't too big."

Elena licked her lips. "Come downstairs and meet the others?" she asked.

Jess said, "Lead the way," and followed Elena down the stairs to the basement.

Cris was sucking Eric's cock while Caitlyn rode Eric's face. He grasped two fistfuls of ass and lavishly licked Caitlyn's cunt. Abruptly Cris shifted tactics and licked at Eric's balls.

"Your wife's arrived with the new lady," Cris said.

Eric paused and looked toward the entry stairs. "Jess," Eric identified. The blonde wore just the fatigue pants now and a tank top. "Looks like she finally is gonna play."

She also looks very good, he thought.

"Someone else here would like to come." Caitlyn tapped his head. Eric chuckled and twirled his tongue on her clit. "That's better," she said, sighing happily. A moment later, she was rocking erratically and grabbing his hair. Cris unrolled a condom down Eric's cock.

A moment later, Caitlyn had pulled her hips away from Eric's mouth, and sank onto his shaft. He grasped her waist and sat up, holding her back against his chest. She kissed her wife, Cris, while her muscles squeezed him. It wasn't quite an overload to Eric's senses, the two women kissing and moaning with pleasure in front of him while his cock was being rhythmically pumped, but it was close, and he quickly reached orgasm.

Caitlyn lifted off him while he held the base of the condom tightly. Then he watched as Caitlyn and Cris rearranged into a sixty-nine on the mattress surface. He leaned back, removed the condom, and tossed it in the trash bin beside the bedding. Then he rested on one elbow and simply watched the couple enjoying each other.

Eric's senses picked up other noises, and, in a bid to identify them, his gaze swept around the playroom. The low murmuring voices he'd heard were Jess, Elena, and Max, standing together near the swing. Usually affable, Max looked a little annoyed. Elena put a hand on his chest and said something. Beside her, Jess pursed her lips and then stepped back. The blonde had taken off her fatigue pants and boots, and Elena's robe lay in a puddle at her feet. Max had a respectable hard-on showing. They seemed to be negotiating which one of them would be getting in the swing to be serviced by the other two.

Getting to his feet, Eric put on his boxers, then strolled casually toward the trio.

"Hey, Jess," Eric said, drawing her attention first.

When she looked at him, her widened pupils told him she was aroused. Her positioning, with Elena between her and Max, immediately told Eric the cause of her arousal was not Max. He reached out a hand, and she quickly took it.

"Glad you could make it," he said. She accepted the tug on her hand and stepped toward him. "Max," he said to his friend, "Jess has already had the pleasure of the swing. I'm sure she'd like to try something new."

"Are you joining us, Eric?" Jess asked.

"I can if you want," he said.

"How about tandem sex?" Max suggested. "You and Elena, and me and Jess?"

Jess bit her lip; Eric suggested, "How about Elena and you, and Jess takes me?" Jess's relief shined in her eyes. "We can use the weightlifting bench and face each other." He knew Jess enjoyed watching Elena.

Max looked at the bench. "Sure, okay," he said. He sat quickly and straddled the bench, briefly stroking his cock until it was pointed upward. Quickly he smoothed a condom down its hard length.

Eric sat down on the opposite end of the bench, facing Max. He wasn't going to be hard immediately, so he kissed Jess's neck as she straddled the bench in front of him. Without drawing a great deal of attention to things, he helped her move onto his legs and settle on his thighs, just in front of his cock. She looked back at him, her expression slightly puzzled. He kissed her. His fingers tugged a bit on her pulled-up hair and she reached up, untangling a long twisting pin from within the mass. Her hair fell loose. He buried his face in it and sighed.

Lifting his eyes, he saw Elena and Max both watching him and Jess. Elena had straddled Max and was moving herself onto his cock. Max settled one hand on Elena's waist, and the other moved up to play with her nipples. The tendons in her throat stood out as she lifted her chin and leaned her head back. Max bared his teeth in a mock bite on Elena's shoulder. The two of them moaned.

Eric's hands mirrored Max's, one on Jess's hip and the other up higher, circling her nipples. Jess inhaled and exhaled sharply, and her hips twitched as she reacted to all the sensations. He wished for a moment that he'd thought to put a hand under her and slide his fingers into her. He'd experienced the tight clench of her muscles on him before. In lieu of that he communicated his joy of touching her. He slid his lips along her shoulder and traced the shell of her ear with his tongue. His fingertips danced around her nipples.

Finally, he decided to give them both what they wanted: him inside of her. With his other hand, Eric reached between her thighs and slid a finger between her labia. His cock twitched, wanting to join in the fun. Jess's hand fumbled down to his thigh and then behind her back and grabbed his cock. She groaned when she found him.

So did he. When he focused again, he saw Elena moving rapidly up and down on Max; the man was groaning and gritting his teeth. Elena's eyes however were riveted to Jess.

Bent forward, Elena planted her hands on Max's knees, and then Jess's. Max grasped Elena's hips, and he was rising and pushing up into her while she sought out Jess's breast; the one Eric was not playing with disappeared between her lips.

Jess keened, and her hand squeezed Eric's cock hard enough that he hissed. She released him. Instead her hand went to Elena's head, holding it in place.

Elena must have been milking Max quite intensely, because the man was hunched at the shoulders and thrusting erratically.

Watching his wife hungrily sucking Jess's breast, and the ecstasy on her face, Eric felt come drip from his cockhead even though he was far from hard. Then Jess came undone in his arms, and a soft cry accompanied her orgasm. Eric's drips became a dribble; his balls pulled into his body and pushed more come up his soft shaft. Elena's head rested on Jess's breast while she caught her breath, and Jess stroked her fingers through Elena's hair.

Max held the base of the condom but didn't move. Finally he lifted his head and his gaze intersected Eric's. There was dismay there, but something else as well. Eric realized it was jealousy when he saw the other man looking at Jess. They both watched Elena lift herself off Max and slide tighter into Jess's embrace.

CHAPTER FIFTEEN

THE FIRST thing Jess realized was that she had not had actual sex. She joined Elena and Eric at their sex party, and she didn't have sex. The digital clock on the microwave announced it was 1:02 a.m., and she sat sipping a cup of hot tea at the breakfast bar of the Tanners' kitchen.

Jess heard Elena's voice in the foyer, saying good night to the last departing couple. She'd been pulling on her fatigue pants when Elena introduced the wife, Chana, sitting down next to her to put on flat shoes. Chana had long straight dark hair, and smiled at Jess, the corners of her gray eyes crinkling. So Jess had said "hi," and that, it seemed, was enough. Chana had gotten back to her feet and kissed Elena on both cheeks. Then her husband, Rene, walked up with Eric. The two men were smiling and shook hands. Chana bussed a kiss against Eric's right cheek then tucked her hand around her husband's arm, and the two walked upstairs.

Eric and Elena had followed the couple, and Jess had followed up the steps behind them. The playroom scent faded behind her as she closed the door at the top of the stairs.

She sipped again at the tea, enjoying the warmth of it moving down her throat. She wasn't normally a tea drinker, but somehow it had felt more appropriate to say "tea" rather than "coffee" when Elena offered her the choice. She wanted soothing, not stimulating. For reasons she was still unpacking, her mind was spinning.

She'd attended a sex party, enjoyed some conversation, then briefly held herself outside of it. Finally she joined others in a room explicitly designated for sex. She'd seen Max's cock; he'd been proudly displaying it from the moment Elena brought them downstairs. But she hadn't wanted to experience it for herself on the swing as he had suggested.

She'd been uncomfortable until Eric held her in his arms and stroked her while they watched Max fucking Elena. She'd loved watching Elena's body move, and the sounds had been arousing. She'd started to feel aroused again herself and grabbed for Eric's cock, though at the time she wasn't sure what she wanted to do with him.

Then Elena had leaned forward, kissed her, and caressed her face. She had held Elena after the woman orgasmed on Max's cock.

Eric had gotten stiffer against her back, and she'd felt his precum dribbling on her skin when Elena came. But he'd not penetrated her, and, surprising to her, she had enjoyed the simple pleasure of being between the couple, feeling both their warmth, surrounded by the scents of sex and musky sweat.

Footsteps entered the kitchen, and Jess looked up. Eric now stood beside her, and Elena moved toward the counter with the coffee maker. His hand covered Jess's. "How are you?" he asked.

"Fine," she replied.

"You're quiet," Elena said; she sipped at her coffee.

"Processing," Jess said.

"It was your first party," Eric said. "Not everything you expected?"

She wondered what to say; she'd experienced so much, and at the same time, it had been so different. "I guess I didn't really understand what to expect," she said finally. "It felt different."

"Different's good, though, right?" Elena asked. "There's so much to explore. So many sensations to experience. I always find it exhilarating."

Elena glowed with proof of her words. Her face was as animated by her enthusiasm as her voice. Jess's chest filled with a warm feeling, seeing the brunette this way. She glanced at Eric when his fingers moved on hers, and saw that he, too, watched Elena. His blue eyes crinkled at the corners and his expression looked the same as she felt: Elena's pleasure was somehow hers, too.

Jess nodded her head and sipped her tea, her eyes resting on Elena drinking her coffee. Eric's hand moved from hers and then onto her shoulder. She looked away from Elena and met his gaze.

"It's late. Why don't you sleep here again?" Eric suggested.

Elena added, "Stay until Eric goes to work?"

Looking at the smiles on both Tanners' faces, Jess's decision was easy. "Sure."

Remembering how good it felt the night before to curl up with Jess in bed, Elena took the blonde's hand, and felt both energized and calmed by the contact. It felt addictive being wrapped in the blonde's arms. Elena remembered, too, how she had sought out contact with Jess even when Max was fucking her.

In the master bedroom, Eric quickly stripped down to his boxers. Elena turned from putting her robe up on the hook behind the bathroom door to find Jess standing quietly in the middle of the space, still wearing the tan tank top and the GI-issue boxers. Her hair, which Eric had enticed down earlier, curled around her shoulders. Somehow her eyes were even greener in the low lamplight.

Elena took the younger woman's hand again. Pressing forward into Jess's sturdy body, she walked the blonde backward until knees buckled against the bedframe and Jess sat down hard on the mattress. She could see questions forming in Jess's eyes.

Sliding onto the bed and spreading her knees to each side of Jess's hips, Elena let her own gaze swivel between green orbs. Elena pressed her lips to Jess's and urged her, "Lie back." She lifted her head to check Jess's response and be sure she was comfortable.

Jess's smile was small, still endearingly surprised, Elena thought, by how much she was desired. Elena stroked her fingers across Jess's collarbone and further down, to the skin visible where the tank top had rucked up above Jess's waist. Jess's gaze remained locked with hers.

Eric cupped Jess's shoulders, making the blonde look above herself toward him. He kissed her nose.

Though the action was innocent, even sweet, Elena's belly filled with lust—fast, thick, and demanding. "No sex," she said aloud, a reminder to herself. "Just sleep."

She caught Eric's smirk out of the corner of her eye. Following a steadying inhale, Elena exhaled slowly, and then fluidly lowered her body against Jess's, partly on top of the other woman and partly along her side.

"If you say so," Jess said. "Though maybe another round of

wakeup sex?"

"Maybe this time we can wake you up," Elena agreed.

The other woman's arms embraced her. Rough and slender fingertips traced randomly on Elena's neck, under her hair, then down one arm toward her hand.

Responding to the silent request, Elena bent her arm and moved her fingers to entwine with Jess's. Head pillowed against the other woman's breast, Elena felt Jess's center warm her thigh. She adjusted, moving more of her weight to the bedding, and felt Jess squeeze lightly around her shoulders.

"You comfortable?" she asked Jess.

"'M good," Jess said. Elena smiled against the breast under her cheek.

"'M glad." She echoed Jess's sleepy response, feeling a light chuckle bubbling up in her throat. She raised her eyes and saw Eric's hand on Jess's shoulder.

Eric and Jess abruptly shifted and moved. When Elena saw Eric's eyes closing in Jess's hair, she realized that he had pressed his own body along Jess's back. His hand fished down Jess's legs and onto Elena's thigh.

"Covers," he said when Elena's questioning gaze met his.

"Warm enough without 'em," Jess mumbled. "You guys are better than any hotel heater."

Eric grinned and pulled the sheet up over the three of them anyway. He kissed Jess's cheek before laying back down again. "Well, that's got to be the best endorsement of group sleeping I've ever heard."

Elena silently agreed and felt a wide smile shaping her lips. She closed her eyes and snuggled even closer to Jess. Finally she let sleep claim her.

As dawn broke through the window above the bed, Jess felt two mouths tugging at her breasts, and her fingers were tangled in both dark and dirty-blond hair, two heads that she tried to guide and hold close. Her tank top had been pushed up and bunched under her arms, baring her breasts to her bedmates' hungers. The sensations were varied and skyrocketing her arousal because of their maddeningly attentive randomness. Bites and licks intermingled with sucks. Squeezes on the small masses were followed with sucking, before teeth chewed ravenously.

She cried out with unintelligible pleasure. One mouth became gentle, lingering, caressing, soft. Arching her back, her arousal loud and demanding, Jess pulled at strands of hair, aware dimly of the differing textures, but only wanting to convey her need: *more, more.*

It seemed that Elena and Eric were determined to fulfill Jess's growing desire to be completely consumed.

Their mouths were never still, and their pleasure was as vocal as her own. Elena's and Eric's hands were everywhere on her. One large and one small hand moved on Jess's waist, both warm and seeking, stroking, caressing. Sound vibrated against her breast, asking if she wanted more. Jess immediately pushed on the heads in her hands. "Fuck, yes," she breathed.

One warm large hand remained on her belly, slipping beneath the waistband of her boxers and sifting through the hairs on her sex. Fingers from the other, smaller hand moved to her calf and then thigh, and then inner thigh, the touches akin to tiny notes of promise.

Jess writhed, pushed, whimpered. Elena chewed her nipple, and finally, her fingers toyed with Jess's pussy lips. But it was only a brief touch before retreat. Elena stroked again on Jess's inner thigh while she sucked on Jess's nipple.

"G-uh." Jess breathed out slow, wanting more, but at the same time not wanting the sensations to cease. Her body pulsed with need.

Eric's mouth moved from Jess's breast to her collarbone, to her jaw, to her ear. His fingers, still tangled in the hairs over her sex, moved nearer to her clit. She felt her center swell with soaking wet heat. Then she felt a finger, Elena's finger, circle low on her sex. The tiniest penetration, stroking, Elena wet her fingers in Jess's own fluids. Jess's belly constricted, her cunt pulsed.

One finger became two. Elena's fingers pushed inward, turned, twisted, curled, retreated. Elena played Jess's body like a guitar. Sounds Jess couldn't recall making before poured from her throat, pulled from the deepest parts of her.

It wasn't until she felt Elena's mouth on her sex that Jess realized the other woman had moved between her legs; Eric's mouth had seamlessly replaced the sensations on her breast. His fingers circled her clit while Elena teased and tongue-fucked her. So that was how they would avoid bumping heads this time. Jess started to chuckle, only to be cut off by her own orgasm.

She couldn't remember starting, and she couldn't fathom stopping. "Oh, mmm, nnnng." The rhythm of her sounds was entirely guided by Elena's and Eric's flawless playing of her body.

"You feel incredible, coming around my fingers."

Elena's words were the first sensible sounds Jess processed through the chaotic sensations. Eric's hand once again stroked soothingly on her belly. Elena's lips and tongue, now broadly flat, moved over her mound. Three fingers slipped away; she missed their deep caress immediately and whimpered.

"Again?" Elena asked. Her face slipped into view, leaving kisses behind on Jess's skin. The brunette was smiling, and her chin shined with the moisture she'd buried her face in moments earlier.

"You've worn me out," Jess said. She brushed her fingers through the ends of Elena's locks. "I do like it," she added with a laugh. "But maybe after something to eat?"

"I've just eaten," Elena replied cheekily.

Eric laughed, which drew Jess to turn her head to see him. While Jess was entangled with Elena, Eric had sat up and put his feet off the far side of the bed. "Neither man nor woman can live by sex alone," he intoned.

"Maybe not, but it'd be fun to try," Elena said, her shiny smile becoming a smirk, and she winked at Jess. That had to be the cutest expression Jess had ever seen. The woman easily combined traits of a seductress with the playfulness of a kitten. The phrase "sex kitten" seemed oddly appropriate as Elena straddled Jess's waist, holding her in bed, and moved her hands over Jess's stomach. "What do you think, Jess?"

Jess was saved from answering verbally when her stomach rumbled. The reaction of all three of them was comical. Jess turned red-faced; Eric's mouth opened, then shut again; Elena's eyebrows vanished up into her hairline.

"Right. Food." Elena left the bed, stood, and held out her hand. Taking it, Jess slipped off the sheets, tank top still rucked up and boxers askew. "You make a very enticing soldier," Elena said, and her appreciation was clear.

Elena's gaze devoured Jess, sex-hungry thoughts plain in sparkling brown, but the woman's surveys always finished with Jess's eyes, removing any objectification. Jess smoothed down her top and adjusted her boxers. "Thank you," she said.

CHAPTER SIXTEEN

ERIC STEPPED out of the driver's side and met Elena at the trunk. She had already pulled his flight bag onto the curb. "Thank you," he said. Instead of taking the keys from his hand, her face was obscured by her hair falling forward. He followed her gaze down and saw her hand gripping the handle of his bag; he put his empty hand next to hers, stretching his last two fingers over hers. "You miss flying," he said.

She looked up immediately, and protested, "I don't." He raised an eyebrow at her, their "be honest" signal. She started again. "Okay. I don't miss working flights. I miss experiencing new places."

Ah. He said reasonably, "Fly standby. We could see Toronto together." The Canadian city was one they hadn't seen together yet. As a result of the temptation, Elena's eyes did briefly light up.

However, she shook her head. "No, I'll plan our dinner for Turkey Day. You'll be home?"

Eric nodded. His new work schedule, just two weeks old, started with a Miami-Toronto direct, with an overnight stay in the Canadian city. To assist with the seasonal uptick in the northeast corridor, he was hopscotching Diligent Air flights up and down the east coast. His final flight assignment this week would land at MIA around noon on Thursday, Thanksgiving Day. Then he had three and a half days off with Elena before flying out again next Monday.

Elena hugged him; he kissed her and finally pressed the car keys into her palm. He offered a second option. "Go see Jess."

Elena's lips twitched, which meant she really wanted to, but had reasoned back out of it. "She's working."

"Just hang out for a morning or afternoon. It'd make you both smile." He took his bag in hand. She wrapped her arms around his neck, clinging in a way she hadn't in a while. "The bar's on your way home." He left the suggestion in her ear and pulled away.

He was reading deep thought behind brown eyes when a security guard spoke behind him. "Ma'am, sir. You need to move your vehicle."

Eric showed his crew ID. The guard moved on, but their time for goodbye was done. Elena slid behind the wheel and drove away.

Stopped at an intersection, Elena saw a huge clock on the bank on the corner. It showed 7:42 a.m. on a Monday morning, and she was surrounded by commuters headed to work. She thought about Eric's suggestion to visit Jess.

She's probably still sleeping, Elena thought. The thought of Jess sleeping brought to mind the memory of the morning after the party.

The curtains, though drawn closed, were brightened with the morning sun fully risen. Elena had stirred at the sound and feel of warm breaths on her head. Gradually aware, she flexed her hands and feet, making bare skin contact with Jess's abdomen and ankles. She had inhaled the scent of the woman, and, despite the vigorous and plentiful sex only a few hours earlier, Elena had filled with lust. She had restrained herself and asked first, nuzzling into the sleeping woman's face with kisses. However, she'd been beyond ecstatic, burying her tongue in Jess's sex when the woman blinked her eyes open and gave a gravelly "Yes."

She and the blonde were sexually well matched. In fact, Elena had tried the "just hang out and shop" idea with Jess before. They didn't make it out the door, and almost had their first sex in the woman's hotel room. They were only stopped because Jess was summoned to work.

It was surprising to feel so intensely about a sexual playmate. She enjoyed sensual foreplay and simple chatting with casual touches. With Jess, she felt hungry and needy for the fullest physical contact.

She pulled into a space at the front of the hotel and strode quickly inside. She passed a young man exiting. Briefly she admired the tight workout shorts and bare chest. His muscles flexed as he paused, stretched, and adjusted the cell phone securely strapped to his upper arm. She turned away when he lifted his head, not interested in flirting with him.

"Elena?" Turning at the voice, Elena found Hector looking at her in surprise from behind the hotel's check-in desk.

"Hector," she replied. "*Hola.*"

"Haven't seen you or Eric around much."

"He's on a new flight schedule," Elena said. It wasn't the sole reason they had stopped frequenting the club, but she didn't see that he needed a full explanation. Between only getting to see Jess when she wasn't working, and finishing their own playroom, Elena wasn't sure she wanted to return to the Caliente.

"Pass my love to Maya," she finished, before walking toward the door.

Movement down a corridor drew her attention before she reached the front. A more direct glance identified blonde hair. She turned down the corridor.

She hadn't spotted the blonde head again, but at a corridor junction she found a door leading out to the parking lot. To her right, another corridor led to the inner areas of the hotel and club. The door ahead led to the darkened bar. It had been nearly a month, but already the layout was unclear in her head, despite the fact she and Eric had met many couples in the bar before they moved through the corridors to the other areas.

"Elena, what are you doing here?"

Turning from the dark bar, Elena turned to find Jess in shorts and a T-shirt, some sort of napkin-wrapped food in her right hand. "Hi," she said.

"Hi," Jess replied. "Nothing's open right now."

"That's all right." Elena shook her head. "I just stopped by after dropping Eric off at the airport."

"Oh?"

"His new assignment takes him to Canada. He'll be back Thursday, though."

"All the way to Canada, huh?"

"Yeah, it's only the second week, but he's enjoying exploring a bit of a new city," Elena said.

"Have you ever been?"

She shook her head. "No. He suggested I fly standby sometime and see it."

"Why don't you?"

"I didn't have an overnight bag."

Jess chuckled. "You should've just gone for it. Missing an adventure for lack of underwear?"

Elena blushed. "He suggested I come see you."

"So, is that why you're here?" Jess leaned one shoulder against the wall, her posture relaxed. Her gaze seized Elena over the food as she took a bite.

Reluctantly breaking the gaze, Elena took in all of Jess's figure, head to toe. She licked her lips. "Would you like to hang out?" she asked abruptly, forcing her mind away from images of Jess naked and splayed before her on a bed, any bed, though the one that featured in the snapshot moment was her king-size one at home.

"The bar opens at eleven."

"Could we go out, get coffee?" Elena suggested. "My treat."

"I'd like that," Jess accepted.

"Great. I'm parked out front." She turned, going a few steps to open the door leading out. When she looked back, Jess was balling up the napkin in her hand, her cheeks puffed with the final bite of her breakfast.

A few chews, then the blonde swallowed and walked toward her. She tossed the napkin in a trash receptacle in the corner by the door. "I should get my stuff," Jess said.

Elena shook her head. "No need. Like I said, my treat." She reached back and took Jess's hand in hers. Calm slid into her chest as the other woman's fingers laced with hers. "Let's go."

Elena drove them to a coffee bar. Stepping out of the car, Jess looked up at the wrought iron grillwork on some stately bank building. She almost questioned the location, seeing a bank ATM and a lobby entrance first. But then her sweep of the property found an A-frame signboard on the sidewalk. *Coffees Lindas* was located around the north side of the building.

"I thought you might like to see where I first worked," Elena said.

Jess recalled that Elena said she'd started in Miami as a waitress. Jess was surprised. She'd thought they were just going to a Starbucks. Even a DD would've been a treat, since she had learned long ago to drink the swill served in pop-shop gas stations. The brunette took her hand and led the way along the sidewalk next to fencing that enclosed open-air patio seating. Everything felt definitely like a high-class date.

There was even a maître d' standing at a wooden service podium. "Two for coffee," Elena said.

"Yes, ma'am. The coffee bar is in the back," he said, leaving them to make their own way.

Elena explained as she led Jess through the restaurant to a smaller second space. "The restaurant opens with brunch service at 10:00 a.m. every day. Until then, the coffee bar is accessible through the patio entrance," As she entered through the archway, she added, "There were many mornings it was just me, the grinder, and a foggy predawn filled with a trickle of bleary-eyed customers."

They passed between small clusters of leather and cloth armchairs and tables. Some were high-back, some had footstools, and others looked like antiques. It was eclectic, like a bunch of tiny living room sets had been taken from a Rooms To Go. Jess spotted the patio entrance, the morning light through it catching her eye, before she saw the coffee bar to the right of it.

A woman with long dark hair and a streak of red it in that matched her lipstick was making change for a customer in a business suit. They chatted and smiled, and the customer finally stepped away with his coffee. Elena stepped forward. "What do you like?" Elena asked Jess. "They have beans from everywhere."

"I have no idea," Jess said. "Coffee's coffee. I know there's Columbian."

"There's Columbian, yes, but also Peruvian, Brazilian, Costa Rican. That's just South and Central America. There are dozens of varieties from Africa, the Mediterranean, Asia, Europe."

"What do you like?" Jess asked, deciding that was probably the safest response. She felt suddenly out of her depth.

"This morning I'm feeling Sumatran," Elena said, turning back to the counter. "It's full-bodied, but smooth."

"Okay," Jess said.

"Two Sumatrans, please, Ruth," Elena said. Jess noticed the woman wasn't wearing a tag, a definite sign of Elena's familiarity with the establishment and staff.

"Of course."

"Is Nami here?" Elena asked while Ruth was grinding and setting up the brew in a press.

Ruth's reply was quick. "Not this morning, maybe afternoon. Her arthritis was acting up."

"Is that happening more often lately?" Elena asked. "I haven't been by in a while."

"Yeah," Ruth replied. All the while she was continuing to efficiently prepare their cups. "She won't admit it, but she's definitely having more bad days than good."

As Jess took her coffee from Elena and followed Elena out to the patio, she asked, "Is Nami the owner?"

"Yep, she's Nigerian, brought over by her parents when she was four. Ruth was her son's wife."

"Was?"

"Gopal died in Iraq a few years ago."

"Ruth's a widow?" The woman had seemed as young as Jess.

"Yes. She and Kai live with Nami."

"Kai?" Jess was beginning to get overwhelmed by all the new names.

"Kai is Ruth and Gopal's son, Nami's grandson. He'd be almost... seven now." Jess shook her head and sighed. "What?" Elena asked.

"You've got so much *history* here. I've lived in a lot of places, but I can count on one hand the number of people I got to know, or who really got to know me." Jess hesitated, sipping at her coffee after speaking. "I didn't get to know most people beyond their name."

"Why did you move around so much?"

"Foster system, at first. Then, when that ended, I move around searching for work. High school GEDs don't get you much these days in the way of permanent jobs." She had no idea what really made her keep talking, but she babbled on. "If cash goes missing from the till, I'm the first to blame since I've got a petty-theft record. I'll just drive until I'm out of gas, then find some sort of work."

She looked up at Elena, wincing when she saw the woman was looking down at her coffee. "I'm a great storyteller, huh?" Jess tried to toss it off, but she always felt this was why it was hard to stay someplace—telling her story always made her remember how shitty it sounded. No one wanted to befriend a loser. "Look, relax, I made the whole story up. I'm really a rich heiress, traveling incognito." She forced a laugh.

"No, you're not." Elena's voice sent shivers down Jess's spine. It was cutting, sharp, angry. "Jess, I appreciate you're not used to people listening, but I am listening. I'm not put off by your past." The brunette looked up and gestured at the coffee bar. "I think maybe that's why I brought you here. To share mine, so you'll feel comfortable sharing more of yours."

"Elena, I..." Jess trailed off. "Really, my life's been a mess. At times, I wish I was someone else, so the things I've seen and done could be someone else's story."

"But they *are* your experiences." Elena reached across the table and grasped Jess's hand. "I'm sure you know they've made you who you are."

"Who am I?" Jess scoffed. "A bartender, renting a hotel room by the week. I barely own more than the clothes on my back. Don't even have my own car anymore."

"Then change that," Elena said. "Do something about it."

"Like what?"

"Go back to school. The community college—"

"With what money?" Jess said. "Even for the flight attendant program you saved for two months while working. I eat at the hotel kitchen, and leftovers off people's plates at the bar. I have maybe *two dollars* left after paying my rent each week. Tips can give me some extra, but all I had was last spent on the clothes for your party." Elena winced when Jess's thoughtless statement landed. Jess rushed to add, "Don't... I didn't mean to say..." She was silenced in the face of Elena's glare.

"You meant to say 'shut up', because my experience is too different." Elena nodded. "Eric does tell me I get too involved at times." She started to her feet. "I'll take you back to the bar."

"Elena." Jess hurriedly followed. She finally reached out for Elena's hand. "Please stop. I'm an asshat. I let my mouth run away with shit far too often."

"It's not shit if it's really how you feel," Elena said. She had stopped on the sidewalk just outside the patio seating, but she was looking down.

Jess leaned against the ironwork, arms hugging herself. "I don't really feel that you should 'shut up'," she said carefully. "You're amazing. And I get that you feel you started with nothing."

"I did."

"I have even less. No savings, no place, no family, no..." When Elena raised her eyebrow, having obviously sensed what was coming, Jess corrected midsentence. "Okay, a *couple* of friends. But honestly, I'm more used to solving my own problems."

"Okay." Elena, too, leaned against the ironwork, and looked over at Jess. "Here's the thing—what you've told me of your history suggests you don't solve your problems, you give up and leave."

Jess dropped her head, shame-faced. Elena was right.

"I don't want you to leave." Jess lifted her head as Elena's words penetrated. She was meeting the woman's earnest expression when Elena finished, "I want to know you're here, that I can keep being with you."

"I'm right here."

"For how long? You've admitted your employment and living situation isn't getting you anywhere."

Jess wanted to say they'd keep having sex as long as the brunette wanted; it was so good. Playing with Eric and Elena had made Jess feel more alive than she had in a very long time. She got the feeling Elena wasn't talking about that, not really. "I told you I loved the party," she said. "And I really didn't mind getting the fatigues."

"I don't want to just see you at parties," Elena said emphatically. "God, Jess, when we woke up together the next morning... I loved it."

"I'd love to do that again, too," Jess said in easy agreement. "So let's plan a date for Eric, you, and me to get together. My next day off—"

"Are you free Thursday?" Elena asked suddenly. "Friday?"

"Those are usually both busy days at the bar," Jess answered.

"But it's Thanksgiving," Elena said. "I know Hector closes the club. He and Maya go see family in Baja."

Jess blinked; she hadn't realized that. Still, she shook her head. "It's not like Gus has anyplace to be, so he'll probably open up for others in the same situation."

"That can't mean there'd be a lot of people, right? Just ask."

After a moment, Jess nodded. "All right."

When Elena got Jess back to the bar, Gus was moving around stock in the back. Anxiously, Elena tapped her foot on the frame of a stool while Jess went behind the bar to talk with him.

Blocking out the handful of patrons behind her in the bar, Elena heard nothing beyond the rattle of glasses and bottles, which made her anxious. There were, however, also no raised voices. She fiddled with a cardboard coaster in her fingers to distract her thoughts.

"You want to take Jess for Thanksgiving?"

Elena fumbled the coaster and looked up into the face of an older man with an overly seasoned tan. His prominent jowls and unshaved gray stubble would have been rakishly attractive a long time ago. His eyes bored into hers. Instead of answering, she said, "Jess tells me you're her friend. So am I."

"More'n that?"

"Maybe," Elena said. "I just would love to have her over for the holiday. But she wants to help you if you're open."

He harrumphed. Elena wasn't sure how to take that, and she jumped when he said, "We ain't opening."

Jess was coming forward with a large tray of clean glasses. "What?"

"I said we ain't gonna open for Thanksgiving, or the day after. Whatchamacallit? Black Friday?" He moved away from Elena and nodded to a man waving a bill. "Whatcha want?"

"Bud," the man said. Gus flipped over a clean glass and tucked it under the tap. When it was full, he handed the glass across the bar, taking the bill in exchange.

Elena watched Jess stare at him. "Why not?" the blonde asked him. "Where are you going?"

"I got plans," he said.

"You never told me about any family," Jess said. "Just Genevieve."

"There's family we choose, too," Gus said. Elena watched Jess; the blonde's expression held deep care for the older man, but also surprise. Gus added, "Thanksgiving's about family, so that's that. We'll close midnight Wednesday, and open again noon Saturday. I'll go see my family and you see yours."

He looked toward Elena as he finished, and she turned to see Jess looking at her as well. She tore her thoughts away from Jess and met Gus's gaze. His expression suggested whatever she would say would be gruffly turned aside. So she only nodded. "May I have a water with lime?" she asked.

"Jess, customer request," Gus said, and he stepped away.

Jess scooped some ice into a tall glass, moved quickly to the filtered-water tap, and then pressed a wedge of lime onto the rim, some of the tart juice mingling with the water. "Here you go."

"Thank you."

The woman's pleasure was plainly visible when Elena found Jess's gaze. "Thank *you*," Jess said thickly.

Elena nodded. "I'll pick you up early Thursday. Say, seven?"

"What are you making for Thanksgiving?" Jess asked.

Elena sipped her water, thinking about how she wanted to

spend the two days with Jess and Eric. Images of conversation, laughter, eating, kissing, and cuddling, as well as sex, filled her mind. Quietly, she said, "Memories."

Jess swallowed. Her lips parted like she wanted to say something. Then she closed her mouth, shook her head, and gave a small, shy smile. "Mmm."

Elena's stomach tightened at Jess's inarticulate sound of pleasure. "Mmm hmm," she agreed.

CHAPTER SEVENTEEN

"A WHOLE bird seemed like too much," Elena said as she moved around the kitchen, preparing brunch for herself and Jess. "When I realized how much less time would be involved, the turkey rolls sounded even better."

Turning around as she finished speaking, Elena saw Jess had poured two glasses of apple juice and now stood sentinel by the coffee maker, watching as it finished dripping.

"I can't recall having a big turkey on the table anywhere growing up. So it's not part of any tradition for me," Jess said. "Though I do like cranberry sauce and stuffing." Jess laughed at something. "There was almost always cranberry sauce left, but stuffing was a different story."

Elena bit her lip briefly, pleased that their rough patch earlier in the week seemed to have smoothed over. Jess was definitely less defensive and more open. Elena held tightly to each precious nugget of information, committing it to memory. However, she had to be careful and just listen, rather than start problem-solving.

"If you didn't have a turkey, how was the stuffing cooked?"

"In a casserole, from a box," Jess said easily. "Oh, wait." She smacked her palm lightly on the countertop. "I do remember a turkey. It didn't make it to the table, though."

"It didn't? Why not?"

"I got my hand stuck inside the turkey waiting to go in the

oven. The stuffing had been prepped and put inside. I thought I was so smart. I figured to get some stuffing before any of it made it out to the table."

"Really?" Elena took a cup of coffee as Jess finished pouring it, then led the way to the dining table. She thought about the size of the typical turkey cavity, compared to a small girl's hand. "How'd you get stuck, though?"

"I wouldn't let go of the fistful of stuffing in my hand. I screamed for the turkey to let go. My foster mother came running and started yelling when she saw what I was doing. I yanked, hoping to run away from trouble. My hand came free finally with a little prize stuffing, but the turkey and its pan smashed on the floor."

"Oh no!" Elena laughed. "How old were you?"

"Five or six?"

Elena pictured Jess as a young girl, hair probably in braids, holding a fistful of stuffing and staring wide-eyed at the turkey. "You must have been adorable."

"The mother didn't think so. She swatted my butt with a metal spatula, and I had to stand through dinner."

"No!" Elena couldn't imagine disciplining a child like that.

"I went back to a group home before Christmas that year." Jess attempted nonchalance and shrugged her shoulders. Orange marmalade on her toast tumbled off and dribbled down her crisp white shirt. Jess's attempt to clean it up smeared the stain. "Ugh."

Elena's gaze fell to the woman's chest. She leaned across the small distance and licked the woman's fingers clean. Jess throatily hummed at the contact. Elena's mind turned from cooking to... eating. She tilted her chin up and found Jess looking down, pupils widening. "Take it off."

"I just shouldn't wear white anymore," Jess said, and there was a note of teasing behind her words.

"Come on." Elena stood and took Jess's hand. When their fingers were laced together, she pulled the blonde to the bedroom. Elena went into her closet and found a robe. "Here."

Emerging, she saw Jess had pulled open her blouse. The fabric hung to either side of the other woman's breasts, and her nipples were tautly visible within her bra.

Jess's smile invited Elena forward. Palms sliding around the woman's waist and underneath the shirt, Elena kneaded deliciously warm skin and firm muscle. She lowered her head and nibbled across the tops of Jess's breasts. Finally she cupped one in a palm, flicking the nub and pulling down the bra to trace its shape with her teeth. Pleased moans filled her ears, and Jess's fingers dug with wanton desperation into Elena's hair. She continued to graze the nipple with her teeth. Sudden and hard, she sucked the tip. Hips jerked, and Jess gasped.

"I'm glad you don't have too much cooking to do," Jess murmured, her fingers sliding into Elena's hair. Elena moved with her onto the bed. Gentle fingers lifted her gaze to meet green. "I've been thinking about nothing but time with you since I left on Monday."

"Same." Elena kissed the fingers that brushed her lips, and then kissed the mouth that pressed to hers. She submitted to the hands pulling at her own blouse, but insistently pressed her lips along Jess's collarbone and up her throat to nibble the strong pulse under Jess's ear.

An almost bruising grip seized her arms and she gasped; fingers spread wide, loosening immediately. "Sorry," was murmured above her, and hands turned to gentle strokes.

Elena hummed into an ear, feeling the air moving against her now bare back. She balanced on one hand, then the other, letting Jess strip away her blouse, before the other woman unzipped the side of her skirt. Elena helped shimmy the fabric away down her own legs.

Her knee pressed between Jess's thighs, Elena rose up and looked her fill of the woman's body splayed beneath hers. Lowering again, she pushed bra straps from shoulders and kissed skin. Jess sat up and unhooked her own bra while Elena did the same.

Once they both were bare, they slid together in a feast of sensations. Jess's nipples pushed into Elena's breasts. The musk of their mutual arousal filled Elena's nose. She shifted to inhale more deeply and their nipples bumped together. Their gasps lingered in her ears. She initiated a deep kiss, pressing her tongue into Jess's mouth. A tantalizing mix of coffee and apples whet her sexual appetite for more.

"I want to taste you," she told Jess between kisses.

"Same here," Jess replied.

"Mutual?" Elena asked, sliding to the side. Jess's hands grasped at her. "I'm not going away, just turning around," she said. Jess didn't need any more coaxing. Her hands went between Elena's thighs and helped them both to reorganize.

Jess turned on her side, spreading Elena's legs to straddle her head while the brunette's fingers parted Jess's thighs. Their movements similar, Jess spread Elena's labia and stroked glistening folds, her taste buds already pinging in anticipation of the other woman's flavor. Brushing at the woman's clitoral hood with the side of her thumb, Jess gathered a little of the moisture. Elena's taste was always so smooth, like cocoa cream. She dipped her thumb and enjoyed the fluttering of Elena's center around the tip. Tracing the heated flesh with her fingers, Jess coaxed her lover's center open, then plied the woman's sex with her tongue.

Elena eagerly tongued Jess's sex. Occasionally one or the other jumped at a particularly sensitive touch, but it was often followed by chuckles of joy at causing the other to be "clumsy."

When Jess felt her body beginning to peak, she slowed her touches, hoping Elena would also. The other woman replaced her tongue with her fingers. The pressure, just right, sent Jess spiraling. She grabbed Elena's ass, pulled the woman's pussy tight against her mouth, and gasped her orgasm into Elena's flesh, which in turn tumbled the brunette over the precipice into her own orgasm.

"Oh *fuuuuuuuck*," Elena breathed. Moving her hips she ground her pussy against Jess's probing tongue. Jess lapped up the dripping fluid and licked quivering flesh. Elena's thighs squeezed against Jess's ears and she barely heard the "uhn, uhn, uhhh," as the woman came a second time.

"Thanksgiving dinner was so delicious you started without me?"

Elena's face lifted from where it had started to rest on Jess's thigh. Jess peeked around Elena's leg to find Eric standing in the bedroom doorway. The man's teasing smile was unmistakable. "Hi," he said when he met Jess's gaze.

"Elena brought me in to change clothes."

"Really?" Eric said. "Seems you're wearing your birthday suit."

"That's the best holiday clothes," Elena said. She added, "You're overdressed."

Jess added, "I can help fix that." Needing no further invitation, Eric threw off his overcoat, and his captain's hat landed with it somewhere by the door. He was loosening his tie when he reached the side of the bed. Jess took one hand from Elena's back and reached out, deftly separating his belt between her nimble fingers.

He sat next to them and removed his shoes and pants. "I just finished a four-hour flight," he said. "The wrong parts of me are stiff."

Elena moved into his lap and lifted his face to meet hers for a kiss. "Massage, then?" she asked him. He hummed an agreeable response.

Jess took Elena's nod to her as a request and moved behind Eric's shoulders. She finished removing his tie and Elena unbuttoned his shirt. Husband and wife kissed as Elena's fingers moved through the hairs on his chest.

When Eric turned his head away from Elena's kiss and the brunette's mouth had moved to Eric's nipples, Jess welcomed Eric with a kiss of her own and her hands settled on his shoulders, smoothing over and then digging into his tightened muscles. His groan of relief spurred her to continue.

Eric leaned back, his upper body supported by Jess while the woman massaged his shoulders. He'd enjoyed professional massages before. While the younger woman's hands were unskilled, the intensity in her face while she worked told him how much she wanted to bring him relief, and so it did.

He inhaled and exhaled, filling his lungs with the scents of the women and their previous sexual activity. He reached an arm around Elena's back and hugged her to him, moving his palm down her ass and parting her labia from behind. She kissed his neck and slowly moved on his fingertip.

Lifting his head to find Jess, he smiled when their gazes met. "Jess," he said simply.

She intensified her massage of his shoulders until he lifted his other arm, cupped his hand behind her head and encouraged her into a gentle kiss.

Now that he had her attention, Eric maneuvered away from Jess's legs and delightful hands. Then he laid back against the bed pillows. Elena straddled one thigh and continued to fuck herself on his finger, now two, inside her tight wet heat. He patted his other thigh. Jess looked questioning.

"I have two hands," he said.

Jess laughed and moved to spread her legs over his. He slid his hand down Jess's back and enjoyed her response to his touches. Parting her fleshier cheeks, Eric pressed his fingers inward and found Jess wet and warm.

The women tangled their fingers together in the middle of Eric's chest. He had to move very little while they thrust themselves on his fingers. Erotic moans and tightening fingers encouraged both

Jess and Elena to ride until there was no holding back the waves.

Afterward, Eric was still tired, but he was reluctant to sleep. Instead hands roamed and explored one another with soft touches. When Eric's fingers smoothed over a spot under her left breast, Jess jerked and snorted out a giggle.

"Ah, that's interesting," he murmured. "What other spots could I find if we spend all three days exploring you," he said, nuzzling her hair as he switched to stroking the length of it.

Jess looked up from her cuddling position. "You're home for three days?"

"It's his new schedule," Elena said from her position against his right side. "He flies four days and takes off three."

"That must be nice."

"I haven't done it long, but so far, yeah, I'm enjoying it." Eric smoothed his hands over each woman's back and pressed a kiss to each pair of lips, making it clear that this homecoming activity was partly why. "The crew went all over the city Monday night. Canadian Thanksgiving was a while back, so holiday deals are already posted in stores, and the city's all decked out for Christmas." He shrugged. "I took lots of photos that would make nice backdrops." He looked again between the women in his arms, then teased, "Maybe I can get a sexy elf and Mrs. Claus to spread their cheeks... I mean, cheer, for my camera."

Elena chuckled. "You have a Claus costume in the sex chest," she reminded him.

"You or Jess could wear that and nothing else," Eric said.

"Sounds fun," Jess said. Eric recalled how much enjoyment she had shown during the last photo shoot. Many of the pictures were now in his folder of favorites. He began thinking how golden her hair would look curling under the white fluff edging on a Santa's cap.

Elena grasped Jess's hand. "Since you don't have to go back until Saturday," she said, "I think we can find time to do it."

"You're not working?" Eric asked, looking toward Jess, who was getting out of the bed.

Jess shook her head. "Gus declared the bar closed both Thursday and Friday." She disappeared behind the master bathroom door.

He turned to Elena. "I have a better idea than dealing with Black Friday crowds."

"And what would that be?" she replied; her smirk suggested she was already guessing where his mind had gone.

"We should spend the day in bed fucking like rabbits."

She kissed him. "Sounds fun."

"Mmm hmm." Eric reached out, grasped Jess's hand as the blonde returned. He tugged, bringing her back to the bed as he sat upright. Dropping his legs off the side of the bed, he encouraged her to come between them. He looked up from their joined hands and met her gaze.

"When Elena told me she wanted to invite you for Thanksgiving, I agreed it was a great idea." He looked back at Elena, who had moved up behind his shoulder and also looked up at Jess. He met Jess's gaze once more. "Knowing you have more than just today off is even better. This is a holiday for family and friends."

Jess's eyes lit up. "Really?"

He nodded. After a beat watching the green-eyed gaze move from him to Elena and back, Eric cleared his throat. "So, is there actual food, or were you ladies too busy muff diving to cook?"

Jess pulled him to his feet. Elena tucked herself under his other arm, and the trio left the bedroom for the kitchen.

It felt surreal to Jess. Here she was, sitting at a dining table in a house instead of a charity hall for a meal, celebrating Thanksgiving. She sipped wine and nibbled on a turkey roll, her second. The most incredible, thankful thing, though, was Eric and Elena sitting at the same table looking at her over their own wineglasses, discussing the minutiae of their lives like she was family.

Eric had already related having fun shopping in Toronto, though he wouldn't tell Elena what he'd bought. "Have you heard anything on your inquiries?" he asked.

"I did, finally, get an email back from a club in Costa Rica," Elena said. "They liked the brochure. They sent back updated pictures of the grounds and new booking rates, slightly better than the ones we had when we last went. So there's something of a good deal."

"Sounds promising," Eric said. "Should we visit again, just us, before leading a group?"

"A group?" Jess asked. "What sort of group?"

Elena answered, "An adult tour group. Manteca's is a swingers' club in Costa Rica. There are several other resorts in the country, but this one answered my emails."

"Wow."

"The new business is letting me combine everything I love," Elena said. "Event planning, international travel. And sex," she added with a smirk, and took another bite of her baked sweet potato.

"Isn't foreign travel dangerous?" Jess asked. "In the news, it sounds like Americans aren't really well liked."

Eric answered her. "American money is always welcome. Exchange rates can be unfavorable, though?" He glanced at Elena, an unspoken question in his tone.

Elena shook her head. "If some economic policy shifts too much, particularly against Latin America or Latinos, that might change, but the exchange rate is good—about 560 colones to the dollar." She spoke the currency's name with a strong Latin accent. "Room rates are about half that of an American three- or four-star hotel. Even better, Manteca's is all-inclusive."

"It does sound good," Eric said. "We should probably do a full week."

"That would give me time to explore the nearby sights in person and decide what off-premises activities to add as excursions."

"When would you go?" Jess asked, feeling nervous.

"The best times to go are late January and February," Elena said. "Holiday rates drop back to off-season levels."

Brown eyes alight with excitement, Elena smiled widely; Jess smiled for her. Hiding behind her wineglass, she wondered why her smile felt forced, why she felt conflicted.

"More wine?" Eric asked.

She looked over and found Eric studying her, his blue eyes warm. "What?"

"Your empty glass." He indicated with a hand.

"Oh." Sheepishly she put it down.

Eric pulled the wine bottle out of the ice bucket on the sideboard. Once her glass was refilled, he returned it to her. "There."

"Thank you." His smile relaxed her.

"What sort of interest have you gotten?" Eric continued the topic with Elena.

"I'd like to roll out the idea during our holiday party," Elena replied.

"We'll have another house party. Same guest list?"

"I'm still trying to decide on a date," Elena said. "Your days off are now regular. But Friday and Saturday are too busy for Jess," she said, looking at Jess.

"What's my schedule matter?" Jess said.

"You can't take off all the busiest days at your job and hope to keep it," Elena said.

The words and sentiment were simply expressed, but they hit Jess powerfully. She swallowed. "It's your party," she replied, not sure why that mattered so much to point out but needing to do so.

"Yes," Elena replied. Her hand found Jess's on the table. "And I want you there."

"You want to sell folks on a sexy trip. It's not like I could afford to go. We'll get together after you've made all those sales," Jess said.

Elena frowned, but nodded.

Elena insisted on clearing the dishes and told Eric and Jess to "do something with yourselves." She'd be along in a few minutes.

With her hands in soapy water, working out a crusted bit of green beans from the casserole dish, she thought about the conversation over dinner. She did want to go overseas, travel, and lead an adult tour; the dream business she had been planning for almost a year was nearing fruition.

However, even while she and Eric had been planning the trip, she had seen Jess across the table. A voice in her head morosely said, *you couldn't see Jess for a week.* That had prompted her quick acceptance of Eric's idea for another house party, only to be stymied for a good date because of work schedules. Then there had been Jess's outright admission that she wouldn't come because the primary activity would be a sales pitch she couldn't get involved in anyway.

But she is here now. Elena smiled and put the last cooking dish in the drainer, added detergent to the dishwasher, and set the cycle to run. Drying her hands even as she crossed through the living room, Elena tossed the towel onto a small lamp table before stepping through the basement doorway.

Elena hesitated at the top of the stairs when she heard Jess's voice. "Do you think she'll like it?"

Eric's response was a barely audible sound, and curiosity moved Elena down the stairs. By the time she reached the bottom and could see Jess and Eric crouched together by the sex chest, the clicks of her shoes had alerted them to her presence. Two smiling faces looked up at her.

"What will I like?" she asked.

Jess stood quickly. "Eric says you like roleplaying."

"Yes," Elena said.

"We roleplayed my first time here," Jess said. "For Eric's photo shoot."

"We did." Elena recalled it all clearly, memories replaying: the leather belt on Jess's naked skin; strong muscles in relief in her arms; finally, Jess's body writhing under the vibrator until she came.

"But it wasn't roleplay, not really," Jess considered. "Eric turned off the camera, and we didn't create a dialogue. I want to do another one."

Elena looked at Eric, who only smiled, not willing to give away anything. Jess was meant to take the lead. "What do you have in mind?"

"It's Thanksgiving," Jess replied. "There are a lot of traditions beyond turkey and stuffing." Elena smiled and immediately recalled Jess's story of being a young girl trying to get stuffing and instead being caught with the turkey.

Jess continued, "I asked Eric why he wasn't watching football today." Elena frowned.

"I told her I prefer sex sweat to sport sweat," Eric supplied.

Reaching into the toy chest, Jess revealed pom-poms, a twirling baton with fat rubber ends, and a "sexy cheer" costume Elena had worn to a swingers' Halloween party a few years ago. "He said he dressed as a soccer player when you last wore this."

Elena clearly remembered that night. "The football pads were too small on Eric." She knew she sounded disappointed. Back then, she had tried not to. And after a bit, it hadn't mattered much; she might not have been fucked by a "football player", but that night she had been enjoyably DPd between Thor and The Hulk.

"Do you still want to fuck the star football player in high school?" Jess asked. Elena nodded. Jess looked at Eric and her expression spoke: *I told you.* She turned back to Elena. "Would you still like to?"

"You?" Elena asked.

"Yeah." Jess's green eyes flashed with desire.

"Yes," Elena accepted.

Eric smiled and pulled out the pads from the toy chest.

CHAPTER EIGHTEEN

FUCKING MY *actual high school quarterback couldn't possibly have been better than this*, Elena thought. She leaned into Jess's shoulder, with the other woman's arm wrapped around her. They sat together on the couch with Eric just stepping back from adjusting the television and camera connector. On the living room television screen, the image resolved tracking and finally showed her and Jess straddling the workout bench in the playroom. Elena wore her cheer costume. Jess wore the harnessed dildo, and the football shoulder pads had been laced securely over her shoulders.

While Eric had set up his camera and lighting, she and Jess had talked about what the basic scenario would be: congratulating a win, or consoling a loss. Elena had chosen the win scenario, a cheerleader congratulating the quarterback. She'd told Jess how her high school's team had losing seasons every year she'd attended. The school had done better in basketball, but Elena had always preferred the beefier builds and tighter pants of the boys on the football team over the lanky, tall basketball players.

Onscreen in Eric's video, the scenario had begun. Jess was saying "thank you" for the support, and Elena was hugging the blonde, nipping her ear and tugging her ponytail. Elena squirmed on Jess's lap and voiced a wish she could "really show my appreciation." She rubbed her breasts into the pads and her nipples stood to attention from the friction.

The blonde hugged her back and pushed the harnessed cock into Elena's belly. Lifting Elena, Jess massaged her ass with both hands and then rubbed the dildo head between Elena's barely covered pussy lips. "Give me the prize," she said in a gruff, trying-to-sound-male voice.

Elena had laughed, and they'd kissed. She'd gone to her knees on the floor and deep-throated the toy cock. Jess had played up the scene and thrown her head back with grunts and "fuck yeahs." Both hands went to the back of Elena's head, and she jerked her hips up and down. Elena pulled back and examined the dildo as if admiring her handiwork, then she licked underneath the harness and sucked Jess's pussy lips into her mouth. Out of sight of the camera, she had put lube into her palm. When she next lifted her hands into view, she closed her fist and thoroughly coated the dildo until it glistened.

When she started to straddle the bench, to lower herself onto the upraised dildo, Jess had stopped her and placed her hands onto Elena's thighs, and then between her legs. Lubed fingers then twisted inside Elena. She hadn't realized at the time how easily Jess went from three fingers to four when Elena had demanded, "More!"

She'd felt deliciously full, and then fuller still when the dildo joined the fingers. "God that was intense," she said, even now reliving the dizzying euphoria of a nearly continuous string of orgasms.

"You were soaking, my love," Eric replied. She glanced toward him where he'd settled into the corner of the couch cushions.

Jess gave an embarrassed chuckle. "I was just hoping it wouldn't slip into your ass. You were moving up and down so far, the dildo kept coming out. I didn't want to miss."

Elena laughed. "Well, you can do that all the time, Jess. It felt perfect."

"I think the fucking should be Eric next time. I was salivating, and frustrated every time I couldn't quite catch a nipple in my mouth."

"Oh, god." Elena sighed happily. "The few times you caught one in your teeth, it felt like I was going to come out of my skin. Felt electric."

"Any more ideas for the holiday photo album?" Jess asked.

Elena laughed. "Eric did suggest Santa and the elves."

"Mrs. Claus actually," Eric corrected.

Jess suggested, "What if Mrs. Claus and Santa tested out a few of the naughtier toys with their helpful elf?"

"Ooh," Elena said, "I like that idea."

From the chest in the basement, Eric and Elena retrieved a Santa hat with attached wig and beard, a white-fringed red Santa coat, a red and green jumpsuit with matching pants comprising of one red leg and one green leg, and an elf hat with jingling bells attached to the tip. Elena helped Jess pin the hat to her hair.

Elena transformed into a sexy Mrs. Claus with a red dress; however, the real sex appeal, Jess thought, was the brunette's brown eyes winking at her from behind "granny" glasses. Eric had holly-green boxers displaying surfing Santas on underneath the Santa coat. Once he put on the hat, the attached wig and beard hid almost all of his face.

Santa and Mrs. Claus then went through "show and tell" and selected several naughty toys from the toy chest. Enthusiastic Elf Jess approved nipple clips and nubbed finger sheaths. Eric demonstrated anal beads with Elena. The brunette came, quivering and sweating, while he licked her clit and gave a fast tug to remove the beads. Enthralled by the other woman's orgasm, Jess agreed to a set of anal beads.

Soon she had been lubed with a finger and the beads were pressed in one at a time, four in all on a small string. She took a few steps, acclimating to the feel of the balls inside. The vibrations when the balls rubbed against each other were arousing.

That had been only the beginning of a sensory-laden sex session.

Jess's knees almost buckled when Elena helped her fasten into place a belt with an included clitoral stimulator. Eric had palmed the remote control. She gaped up at him, trying for an indignant expression, but failed miserably, laughing instead because "fuck that was incredible!"

Still he gently stroked her back while she lay on her stomach on the playroom's platform mattress recovering. Elena kissed the "gorgeous globes" of her ass and occasionally tugged on the anal string, a reminder of the beads' presence.

When the brunette moved up, Jess twined her tongue with Elena's in lazy kisses, and Eric used a nubbed condom on his cock to slowly fuck her. Occasionally his cock rubbed just right against the back of her channel and jostled the beads in her rear. Frequent tiny orgasms rippled through her belly and she sighed.

Elena rolled Jess onto her back and unclipped the elf's jumper top. Then she lavished Jess's nipples with attention while straddling her belly. Jess writhed more when she felt tugging on the anal beads, and an orgasm started spiraling up through her belly.

She grabbed Elena's hips and tried to ground herself, but then her hard nipples were caught in the clips. "Oh fuck." Electric-like pulses sped between her nipples and her ass. The chain between the clamps and the string between the beads were both being tugged, and the explosive sensations collided in her pussy, which throbbed around Eric's cock. "So, god... uh, uhn, ggg."

Coherent thought fled. When she opened her eyes she found Eric had pulled out and bared his cock near her head. Grasping it, she guided it to her mouth, and tasted his cum when it slid onto her tongue. While she licked Eric's cock and smiled up into his face, she could feel Elena tugging the anal beads free and licking at her pussy. The clitoral stimulator started vibrating, and Jess's pussy clenched and flexed some more. It felt like she gushed all over Elena's eager tongue. She moaned her pleasure aloud around Eric's cock.

His cock twitched, and he pulled out of her mouth. Body still swimming through an orgasmic sea, Jess levered up on her elbows and almost demanded he put it back. Then she saw he was hurriedly pulling on another condom.

"Time for a little Claus on Claus action," she said. Elena continued to lick and suck at Jess's pussy while Eric rubbed his wife's lower back and grasped her upraised ass. Finally, he thrust into Elena from behind. Jess enjoyed watching the man's shoulders and chest muscles flexing when Eric moved.

"He feels so fucking good, doesn't he?" she encouraged Elena. The woman hummed into her wet pussy and stirred Jess toward another orgasm. She stroked her fingers through Elena's damp hair.

The playroom filled with grunts and groans and moans of pleasure. Jess felt the clitoral stimulator judder. She was succumbing to the tidal pull of yet another orgasm when she heard Eric and Elena achieve their own fulfillment. Eric pulled out of Elena, kissed her hip and lowered onto his back beside Jess. Elena slid her body up over Jess's and removed the nipple clamps. The release of pressure was almost orgasmic in itself, and Jess gasped into Eric's mouth pressed to hers, while Elena tenderly kissed her nipples.

Finally, Elena's head rested on Jess's shoulder, and Jess's blood had stopped roaring in her ears, so she could hear her companions' steady breathing. She watched Eric kiss Elena's cheek and curl against her back.

He met her gaze with a delighted smile. "Mrs. Claus and I appreciate being able to so thoroughly test our toys, Elf Jess."

"I'm happy to help," Jess said. "I'll definitely *come*, *anytime* you want more help," she added with emphasis.

"You're such a good *naughty* elf." Elena pressed a tiny kiss between Jess's breasts.

"Thank you, Mrs. Claus," Jess replied, lifting away the "granny" glasses and kissing Elena's nose. "Damn, those glasses are sexy."

"Do I hear a teacher-student fantasy?" Eric's question made Jess blush, a clear sign he'd found one of the blonde's secret desires. Elena filed away the information.

Jess was tying her damp hair in a ponytail when she emerged from the master bedroom and joined Eric in the living room. "Hey," he said. She sat down next to him.

It was Saturday morning, and the three of them had shared the big bed again the previous night. Jess had slipped out, then awakened them both with a tray full of coffees and cinnamon rolls. The coffees had been prepared exactly as they each preferred, showing the blonde's thoughtfulness.

"You about ready to go?" he asked when she remained quiet, appearing to watch the program he had pulled up on Netflix.

"No," she said. She was fully dressed—including her shoes—in her "work" clothes, dark slacks and white shirt. "Well, I'm dressed," she amended. "I'm not ready for things to end." She tucked her leg up and held her ankle while she turned to him. "Depressing how long it might be until I get to see you again."

"This ol' thing?" he snorted, gesturing deprecatingly to himself.

She shook her head and laughed. "You and Elena are hot. Stunning. It's almost unbelievable that you would flirt with me, much less invite me to have sex with you. To keep having sex with you. We spend hours naked, laughing, without a care in the world beyond the next pleasure." She sighed and rubbed her face. "Then I leave, and it's like the world goes from loud and joyous full color to... gray." Jess looked down at her hands. "I didn't realize how little I had in life before you two started to fill it up with so much."

Eric took her hands off her face. "You added color to mine, too, Jess. And Elena's. Never doubt that." He could see that serious thoughts continued behind the woman's green eyes, but she nodded. He ruminated, "Lots of color, huh? How do you feel about edible paints?"

"Something to look forward to?"

Eric looked up to see Elena entering the living room.

Jess stood. "That sounds like fun," she said. She turned back to Eric. "Time to go. You be safe when you go up there," she said.

"I will." He stood and wrapped his arms around her shoulders. "How 'bout I visit the bar next Thursday when I get back in town?"

Elena smiled at him and her gaze drifted down, her expression adoring, onto Jess squeezing into his body. "Would you like to meet up this coming week?" she asked Jess.

"I'm opening the bar every day at noon."

"Get together for coffee some morning?" Eric suggested helpfully. Jess frowned. When Elena frowned too, Eric said, "You'll think of something."

Elena fell thoughtfully still then abruptly turned to Jess. "Have you ever done running?"

"When someone was chasing me."

"I meant jogging? I can look for paths in your area." Elena eagerly suggested, "Thursday? About nine?"

Jess looked full of hope and full of worry, which gave her an adorably confused expression. He caught her hand, and when she looked toward him, he smiled. "Okay," she answered Elena, whose smile was relieved.

CHAPTER NINETEEN

THE RUNNING path Elena found for them was a patch of green that threaded around and between many of the convention hotels. A placard at the entrance proclaimed the collection of running, biking, and walking paths a project of the Miami Tourism Council. When the parking attendant had asked which hotel they were staying at, Jess flashed her hotel cardkey from the Caliente. That allowed them to waive the twelve-dollar parking fee, which, Elena guessed, was a subtle way to discourage locals.

Elena was getting out of the car, having swapped her slip-ons for socks and running shoes, when her gaze found Jess again. Jess stood at an instructional board reading the rules: share the path, no littering, no feeding animals, dogs leashed at all times. The rules were useful, but, Elena thought, Jess was where her gaze wanted to stay.

The blonde had put her hair up again in a ponytail, the ends a curly profusion. Standing as she was, with her hands on the waistband of her blue shorts, bare arms dappled by sunlight through the nearby trees, Jess's casual physical beauty took Elena's breath away.

Jess was so different from other women Elena had met in the lifestyle. Her face was frequently makeup free. She didn't seem to own a dress or a skirt, instead wearing jeans or shorts every time Elena had met her. She looked down the blonde's legs and found white socks and canvas sneakers. In contrast, Elena wore high-arch-support padded leather cross-trainers. Jess was right. They were from very different worlds.

Elena wanted to deny it. She'd been a barrio girl growing up; surrounded by families on food stamps, and received public aid. She had gone to school, then to the big city and worked for an apartment, and, finally, achieved a full-time job with benefits. She had worked hard to reach middle-class status. Certainly it was possible for anyone.

"Which way?" Jess said, turning toward Elena as she approached.

"We need to stretch first," Elena replied. "There's a bench we can use over here." She took Jess's hand.

At the bench, they completed several leg and back stretches, with Jess copying Elena for each one. Once Elena felt herself loose enough, she studied the patterns of runners, cyclists, and walkers. "How about going left? The path seems to go around the water and circle back to here," she said.

"I'll follow you," Jess said.

Despite her words, Jess mostly ran alongside Elena and carefully copied her running strides. When Elena felt her body settle into the pace, she was able to clear her mind of everything but her and Jess and the late November morning. It was breezy but warm, probably mid-seventies, which was typical of Miami in late fall. She not only felt but also heard the wind through the clanging flagpoles in the hotel courtyards. There were migratory geese flying in and landing all around the water, and native cranes and cormorants, as well as turtles and frogs on the shoreline. Despite being essentially in the middle of the city, there was a slice of pastoral peacefulness here.

As those sights and sounds became commonplace white noise, Elena was drawn to the sounds of her running companion. Jess didn't seem to labor to breathe, and her strides were even. She didn't drag her feet on the ground, and she seemed to be comfortably moving her arms along her sides while she ran. Many first-time joggers either moved their arms too forcefully or tried not to move them at all. Both situations would reduce stamina, and could cause back, neck, and shoulder pain.

Elena noticed Jess's ponytail was swinging hard side to side. "Stop," she said, slowing gradually. "We should fix your hair. I'm afraid the constant swing will start hurting your neck."

"How?"

"You're starting to hold your head still, and that will just make your neck ache."

"So, I should tie it off low?"

"Yeah, but a bun would work, too." She led Jess to a bench and they sat down together.

"I have another hair tie," Jess said, pulling it from her shorts pocket, "but no pins or clips."

"All right, so lower the ponytail. Let's see if that improves things."

After helping Jess adjust her hairstyle, which Elena enjoyed for the sheer pleasure of running her fingers through the blonde's soft locks, they resumed running.

"Did you always run?" Jess asked. "Like, the track team at school?"

"I was on the cheer squad, no time for other sports."

"But you have all this technique," Jess said.

"I learned to run—safely—while working for the airline. I couldn't pack much on overnights. Running, as long as you have good shoes, can be pretty much done anywhere, any time of day or night, which meant I could be assured of keeping up a routine, even if I had a weird flight schedule."

"Did you?"

"What?"

"Often have a weird flight schedule?"

"I was assigned to a lot of flights to provide Spanish language support. Doing safety checks in Spanish. Helping Spanish-speaking passengers. It reassured passengers that we had an actual Spanish speaker aboard instead of a recording. They could ask questions. Passengers surveyed said they saw it as a sign the airline could be more responsive."

"So, what went wrong? It sounds like you were valued."

"By the passengers I helped. For many crew and white passengers, I was the 'Spanish one'." Hit by a wave of remembered problems, Elena became distracted and stumbled in her stride. She was falling toward the ground before she realized what was happening.

Jess reached out to try to catch her, but the awkward grab instead sent both of them tumbling to the ground.

Wincing, Elena felt the pavement scraping her elbows and knees. "Damn," she cursed before she rolled herself around and sat up.

Next to her, Jess struggled to sit up. "Ow, mmmf." The blonde smothered a curse as she attempted to remove pavement bits from where they'd dug into her knees. "Sorry."

Elena shrugged it off. "I got distracted. Thank you for the grab. I would've taken a header instead of just falling on my ass."

"Are you okay?" Jess asked. She picked at a sluggishly bleeding cut in her right knee.

"We should find some antiseptic and clean up. That cut on your knee could get badly infected."

"I'll be fine," Jess insisted. "You've got a cut on your leg here." When the other woman touched near the spot, Elena hissed. "I guess it's bad?" Jess asked.

Looking at it, Elena growled. Her adrenaline had hidden it, but she saw and felt the deep cut now, stinging and aching. When she tried to move her leg to stand, she felt a muscle protest in her calf. "Damn."

"What?" Jess had gotten to her feet. The cut on her knee had dripped but seemed to be stopping.

"I twisted something." Jess leaned forward. Elena saw the wince as she pulled to help Elena to her feet. "You're not doing better. Maybe this wasn't such a great idea."

"I liked it," Jess said. "Except for all the distractions."

"I know why I was distracted, but what caught your attention?" Elena wanted to know

"You." Jess's smile was bashful and captivating, and her green eyes sparkled with craving.

Elena couldn't have stopped herself from responding to that craving if she had wanted to—which she didn't. She surged forward and pressed her lips to Jess's and wrapped her arms around the other woman. Jess returned the hug, and the passion of Elena's kisses was returned. Their lips slipped together and apart again, chasing and causing moans, which spurred more craving. Her weight shifted, and she gasped at her twisted calf.

Jess pulled back from their kiss, steadying Elena with her hands on her arms. "Okay?"

Endorphins rolling through her body, Elena chuckled. "Better than okay."

Jess laughed, shifted Elena's weight and turned her around. "Let's go back to my room."

"Mmm hmm," Elena murmured while she envisioned making

out with the blonde on her bed.

During their stumble-walk back to the car, Elena felt the aches and stings from her fall return as the endorphins and adrenaline fled. It left her shaking and chilled. "Would you drive?" she asked Jess, handing her the keys.

Jess nodded, and helped Elena sit down in the passenger seat before moving around to the driver's side. Elena watched how carefully Jess examined the console, steering wheel, and the signal and light levers before putting the key in the ignition.

Jess had Elena sit on the toilet seat in her small bathroom while she sat cross-legged on the floor and doctored the other woman's cuts and scrapes. She winced sympathetically at each hiss Elena made as the antiseptic did its work.

Placing an elastic bandage over the cut, she finally looked up into Elena's face. "Time to check the calf," she said.

Elena tried to pull her leg from Jess's grip in protest. "No, I'm—" Jess moved her hand closer to the bruise that had formed. Elena caught her breath and tried again. "Pretty sure it's okay, just twisted. I—oh, uh. Shit." Jess held on to Elena's ankle firmly as she prodded around the bruise.

"Sorry," Jess said. "It's a deep bruise, and it's still purpling. You should elevate it and I'll get ice from the machine at the end of the hall." She stood and kissed the corner of Elena's eye where a tear had squeezed through. "Keep it elevated and watch for swelling." Lastly, she offered Elena two generic ibuprofen.

Jess helped Elena to stand and balance on one foot, then supported her out of the bathroom and onto the bed. She moved pillows, and soon Elena was comfortably propped against the headboard with her lower leg elevated on a couple pillows.

"My bed's not as comfortable as yours, I know," Jess said, "but I have to go to open the bar with Gus. At my first break, I'll drive you home."

"But then how will you get back here to work?"

Jess frowned, having not really thought about that. It would take far too long to find a bus to catch back. She protested, "You'll be stuck here."

"I'll get up in a couple hours and drive myself home. Or," the brunette added with a grin, "I'll sleep, rest up, and stick around. Offer some more enjoyable exercises when you're done working tonight."

Jess settled to the bed and gently balanced her weight against Elena's upper leg while leaning close to search the brown gaze. "You're really someone special to me, you know?"

Elena cupped her face, and the two shared a kiss. When she gently pushed Jess back, the brunette said, "You too, Jess."

Jess didn't want to leave. She wanted to curl up with Elena, take care of her, trade kisses all day.

"Go on, get to work. The sooner started, the sooner done, right?" Elena said.

"Yeah," Jess said. "I'll come check on you, okay?"

"I'd like that," Elena replied.

Jess hurriedly tended her own minor scrapes and cleaned her knee before applying a bandage and dressing for work. Once finished, she returned to the bed to find the brunette had slid down and closed her eyes. Tenderly she brushed the woman's hair from her forehead and placed a small kiss on her dark skin before leaving the room.

Striding off the plane to use the airport lounge facilities during a brief layover, Eric turned on his cell phone. As he entered the lounge, his phone dinged several times with text messages. He glanced at the phone's screen to catch the last text message just as it was retreating. Without bothering to read the messages, he snapped out, "Hey, Siri, call Elena."

His only thought? Elena seldom messaged or called unless she knew he was on the ground.

Sitting on a couch, he put the phone to his ear, waiting for the connection to open.

"Eric? Hi."

"Yeah, I'm laid over in Rochester. Saw your text. What's up?"

"You didn't read them, then," Elena said. She sounded upbeat. He was mystified.

"No, I... you don't usually message me for anything," he finished. "So, did something happen?"

"I texted." She paused then started again. "I fell while running this morning," she said. "But I'm okay. Jess caught me."

"So you did find something you could do together." He smiled. "That doesn't sound too bad. You're all right?"

"Jess drove us back to her room, cleaned and bandaged me up. Currently she's at the bar, and I'm in her bed with my leg elevated."

"You need that?"

Elena gave a wry laugh. "Well, she has sure hands and a calm touch." Eric snorted with amusement. Elena continued, and he heard the reluctance in her tone. "I'll make myself leave soon. I want to slip into the bar and say a quick goodbye."

"You want to check up on her," Eric corrected.

He could almost envision the shrug of her shoulders to make less of her feelings. Elena's words were quiet. "She insists she can take care of herself."

"It is all right to want to take care of her too, El," Eric said. He waited in the silence, certain he knew the thoughts Elena wrestled with.

She finally spoke. "It is?" She was silent for several seconds, and, only because he sensed she was still forming her thoughts, he waited. Finally, Elena spoke again.

"Her hotel room here is a hole."

He'd seen it. Definitely simple, but he had seen worse. "It's not that bad."

"Paying for it drains away every dollar she earns. That's no way to get ahead."

"El, how Jess lives is her business."

"Still... couldn't we *offer* to put her up for a while?"

"*We* could." Eric suspected, though, that Elena would do most of the talking.

"Don't you want to be able to see her more often?" Elena asked.

"Her moving in with us isn't necessary for that."

"I'll wait until you get home," Elena conceded.

"Just don't be too hopeful. Jess likes her independence."

"Eric," Elena said, and if it sounded a little like she was filled with urgency, Eric tried to understand. "I love you."

"I love you, too, Elena. Give my love to Jess when you see her."

CHAPTER TWENTY

JESS TAPPED her foot to the music, using a soft rag to polish the service counter's surface.

"Drink?" She turned to the sound of a male voice that wasn't speaking to her. A dark-haired man stood a few feet away wearing a crisp white shirt, green-and-red tie, and sprig of mistletoe pinned to his jacket pocket. The woman next to him, to whom he had been speaking, wore a festive Christmas-red cocktail dress, a green stripe accenting the line of the dress off one shoulder and down to the waist, ending in a large bow on her hip. Jess shook her head, making the bell on the end of her elf cap jangle.

"Oh, hey, yeah. We'd like a couple champagnes," he said, lifting up a billfold and extracting bills he then stuffed in the huge jar next to the beer pulls.

"Certainly," she said, lifting two plastic champagne flutes from the stacks under the counter. On the counter as they watched, she filled each three-quarters full, per policy. "Here you are." He smiled at her, a little lingering smirk that told her if he didn't have a date... She purposely turned to the woman. "You let me know if you want another," she said.

The woman, with a short Dorothy Hamill-styled cut and freckles across her nose and cheeks, blushed almost as red as her hair at the attention. Jess smiled. The man slipped his arm around his date, put her drink in her hand and steered them both back out to the dancing space on the far side of the tables.

Couples and groups were mingling, rising or sitting, nibbling at the complimentary chips, pretzels, and dips, awaiting the company president's arrival for the celebratory cake cutting. Company parties were all the same, and after Jess's tenth one this month, all squeezed in between her shifts at Caliente, she was weary of the entire routine. When booze flowed, propriety seemed to fly out of everyone's head by midnight, like some fairy-godmother's spell had worn off.

"White wines, please." Jess looked up abruptly from watching a portly man she'd bet three weeks' pay was the company president, finally arrive at the rented ballroom's entry.

"Eric?" Jess smiled, wishing she wasn't behind the counter and could greet him properly. He put two five-dollar bills in her jar. "I'd give 'em to you and Elena on the house," Jess said, passing over two glasses of a white.

"You took the indie gigs to make money. Can't keep giving away free drinks to all the pretty boys"—he leaned in—"or girls." He winked. She laughed, the bell on her cap jingling again. He flipped it out of their faces, which were now only a few inches apart.

"Is Elena here?" she asked, looking around behind him.

"Of course she is. This is the Diligent company party."

"That was tonight? This party?" Jess shook her head, jangling the bell discordantly along with her thoughts. "How did I not realize that?"

"I'm not surprised. You've been working every night since the month started."

She looked him over. "You just making an appearance before heading over to the club?" He was in a brown sports jacket, wide-collared shirt, chest hairs just visible at the neck. It was a little more like his club clothes than a company holiday party.

"Nope, going directly home as soon as the boss cuts the cake and I cut a couple rugs with my lady per regs." His smile was wry. Eric hated the politicking, preferring to fly his planes, and avoid the games. But he planned to get a promotion to management in the airline someday. That couldn't happen if he didn't press the flesh from time to time, talk up the timetables, and share in the route gossip that made others aware he was knowledgeable about the company, not just some cockpit flyboy.

"Tanner?" Jess pulled back when the male voice behind Eric made him stand up straight and wince before making his expression "holiday bright" and turning around.

"Livingston, I presume?" Jess turned away so no one paid attention to her chuckle at Eric's joke, but was also pleased it had the desired effect on the portly man from airline management, evident when she heard him laugh and slap Eric on the shoulder.

"You flyboys love those adventures."

"Jake." Eric ventured the personal level sooner rather than later, extending his hand, which the man shook. "Happy holidays to you and your wife," he said.

"And you and yours," Jake replied. "Ellen, wasn't she?"

"Elena." Jess watched Eric bite his lip.

"She used to work for us, didn't she?"

"Yes."

"Good for you, plucking the little lady out of the working world," Jake said.

Jess silently bristled on Elena's behalf. The woman had enjoyed working, and now she put her skills to use on starting her own business. Eric said nothing, though, silence being the better part of valor when it came to some of the sexist views of upper management.

Exchanging a look with Jess over the man's balding head, Eric put his arm around the boss' shoulders and steered him toward a cluster of other pilots.

Eric was good to shut it down before Elena returned to his side. She wouldn't let sexist stuff stand.

Jess went back to work, pulling the tap for another man who stepped forward and requested a beer. During the exchange of money for the glass, he reached out and jangled the bell on her cap with a fingertip and a leer. She resisted rolling her eyes until he had walked away, thankfully without verbally propositioning her. *Another thing to keep Elena far away from*, Jess thought.

Then she saw her emerging from the restroom corridor. Elena was stunning, but that was nothing new for the Latina, not really. Tonight, though, Jess thought she had outdone herself. The dress was forest green, sequins flickering in the ballroom's swirling lighting. It came up to a narrow strip of fabric over her right shoulder, showing off a great deal of her shoulders and chest, and the fall of the dress perfectly hugged her from breast to hips. She held a matching clutch in her left hand as she swept into the room, finding Eric with a quick swivel of her head. She smiled up at him when she tucked her arm into his, and he kissed her before introducing her to the men and women in the small circle.

"D'you know how to make cherry bombs?"

Jess inhaled and exhaled, reluctantly taking her eyes from arguably the handsomest couple in the room. She smiled brightly at the customer. "Anything you like. Is that what you want?"

"Yeah," he said. His eyes roamed the room while she mixed.

Finally when she had dropped in the maraschino cherries, watching them fizz in the drink's depths, she drew his attention back. "Here you are."

He studied the tumbler glass and then downed the drink in one gulp. He slapped the glass back on the counter. Jess jumped. "Another."

"Pay for that one first," she said.

His eyes were rimmed with red when he looked back at her. She looked around the room where his eyes had been riveted while she was mixing and saw the source of his emotions. A bubbly redhead was pulling provocatively at the tie of a Superman-type, all beefy arms barely stuffed into a navy-blue suit. The man in front of her by comparison was a Clark Kent: bookish, a little knock-eyed behind wire-rim glasses. Obviously his date had found someone else to spend her time with.

"She's not worth it," she told "Clark." "So, forget about her."

"Would you date me?" he asked.

"That's a kinda tricky question," Jess replied, replacing his now empty cherry bomb with straight up lime soda with a single cherry. "I'm currently... occupied." She glanced over to see Eric taking Elena's hand and leading her to the dance floor.

As they swung together into the beat of an upbeat rendition of "Rockin' Round the Christmas Tree," she smiled. Elena stepped high as she spun out of Eric's embrace, and then dipped back as he caught her across his left arm and pulled her back in. She rolled upright, pressing her body to his, and Jess felt her body tighten knowing exactly how good both Eric and Elena's body's felt pressed against her.

"That's what I want someday," Clark said. "Eric and Elena are gonna be old and gray together somewhere and still kicking it up."

Jess nodded, now suffering a bit of holiday blues—damn Clark. She began buffing the counter, a silent "go away" to Clark.

He seemed to take the hint and, lifting his lime soda in a half salute, turned and walked away.

Biting her lip, Jess continued to buff the glasses and countertop while she surreptitiously watched Eric and Elena dancing. There were other couples on the dance floor, but Clark was right, the Tanners were the only two who really looked to be enjoying each other more than the music.

Elena kissed Eric and stepped away from the table with their empty glasses. She'd seen Jess at the bar and watched man after man approach her, most walking away easily and quickly with their drink orders, but others lingering, trying to chat up the pretty bartender. After she and Eric had come off the dance floor, a promise on their lips to just finish their drinks next and go, she had seen Jess again, and the blonde wore only a fake smile. Elena had seen the expression a few times, when Jess was feeling particularly orphan-like.

Watching Jess as she approached the bar, Elena listened to the discordant cadence of the bell on the elf cap. She smiled wryly at Jess's obvious attempt to cheer herself. "Hard day at the workshop?" Elena asked softly, drawing Jess's gaze to her.

"Hey." Jess's greeting was wan, and the fake smile had yet to fall.

Elena looked around behind her, then leaned forward across the counter. She didn't immediately pass over the glasses in her hands, though Jess moved to take them. Keeping her voice low, she asked, "Are you having a lot of trouble from drunks tonight?"

"No, no. It's good. I'm fine. Making good tips."

Elena grasped Jess's fingers from the glass and held them. Jess looked afraid now. "You look a little like the lost girl again," she said gently. "You sure you're all right?"

Jess's smile faded and she looked away. "I gotta get back to work."

"What happened, Jess?"

"Eric said you were heading home. Why are you still here?"

"Because we're enjoying the music and the company," Elena said, wishing she could pull Jess to a table and really talk to her. "When do you finish here?"

"Last call is 1:00 a.m."

"So, we'll see you about two?"

"I can't come by tonight."

A man walked up as Elena was trying to figure out what to say. "Bourbon, neat."

Jess turned to him, her gaze leaving Elena bereft. "That'll be two dollars," she told him.

Elena drifted away, puzzling over Jess's behavior.

Eric cupped her elbows and kissed her forehead. "Everything all right?" he murmured against her skin.

"Something's wrong with Jess."

"You wanna stick around?"

"I know we normally leave early, but..." Elena looked over at a forcefully bubbly Jess pouring champagne for a couple. Her laughter was just a little too loud, a little too long, and it pained Elena's heart to hear it. "She needs us to stay," she finished.

"Bar's closed," Jess said without looking up from the industrial sink where she was cleaning out the shaker glasses and other implements from her bartending kit.

"I was just hoping to have a drink off the bartender."

Jess jolted upright and saw Elena leaning on the doorway. "Hey," she greeted wanly. Elena stepped forward, cupped her cheeks—her hands held glass or Jess would have done the same—and kissed Jess sweetly on the lips.

Jess bit her lip. "I thought you and Eric were gonna leave."

"We decided to make sure you got home safe."

Jess dipped her gaze away. "I'm fine." She lifted her hand to cover the one Elena had put on her cheek. "Thanks."

"You're not fine. Something happened earlier tonight, and your sparkle fled. What happened?"

"Just got to thinking," Jess said. She went back to cleaning her equipment.

"About what?"

"About what I'm doing."

"You're working a lot, so I thought the goal is to make some money?" Elena pointed at the kit. "You bought that, an investment."

"I'm still gonna just be a bartender," Jess said. "Maybe I should move on."

"Move on?" Elena pulled back, and Jess wanted to avoid the searching look, but the hand grasping hers was strong. "Jess..." Her voice trailed off as she reached for Jess's cheek, holding her chin firmly and making her meet her eyes. "Why would you go away now when things are starting to go so well?"

"I don't want to be a bartender, listening to drunk men's sob stories, when I feel just as alone as they do," Jess blurted. Then she covered her face, and to her complete disgust, burst into tears.

"Whoa, whoa. Hold on." Elena removed the towel from Jess's hands and laced their fingers together, pulling them up to Jess's shoulders, where she firmly gripped as she pressed her body into Jess's. Jess let her push them against the wall, eyes rolling back as she absorbed the addictive feel of Elena's curves aligned to hers. Elena's lips kissed her eyelids and then brushed featherlight down Jess's cheeks to her throat, sucking intermittently between kisses. Jess's moans grew with the arousal swirling in her belly. Jess's hands moved uncertainly, both trying to cling to the other woman and pull herself away. After watching them tonight, she felt she had no right to any of it.

Keeping one set of fingers twined with Jess's, Elena released one hand. "Go on," she murmured into another claimed kiss.

"El..." Jess's breath fled as she helplessly pulled Elena tightly against her, lips absorbing the satin feel of Elena's mouth, hand caressing the solidity of Elena's body. She gasped, and then Elena's tongue pushed between her lips. "Oh god," she breathed, her knees weakening. If not for Elena half holding her up, Jess was sure she would have collapsed on the floor.

They ended up there anyway. Elena slowly guided Jess down the wall, straddling Jess's hips as her legs splayed before her. Elena cupped Jess's face and kissed, and kissed, and kissed her again. She guided Jess's arms around her back and down to cup her ass under the skirt of her dress, before returning her hands to Jess's face and cradling it tenderly, resuming kissing.

Against her palms, Jess felt the heat of Elena's center close to her fingers and whimpered. Elena wore garters, her underwear barely a scrap of silk covering her center. Jess's mouth went dry. She croaked, "Elena."

Elena parted Jess's peppermint-striped shirt, tugging the tail out of the holly-green pants. Pinning Jess's arms beneath her thighs, Elena pushed the top off her shoulders, trapping her arms to her sides as she bared her breasts, heaving in a green bra. Jess started to speak, but Elena's mouth cut off the sound.

"Jess," she said when she let her breathe again. Her palm rested over Jess's pounding heart. "I'm here."

"Why aren't you with Eric?" Jess asked.

Elena looked up away from Jess, and Jess heard the door to the kitchen open. She squirmed to see, to get to her feet, freeing her hands from beneath Elena's body. Elena held her to the floor.

"Hey," Elena said.

"Everything all right in here?" Eric stood over them, concern and worry tugging away his smile. Jess pressed herself into Elena's chest. Elena hugged her.

"Eric, I..."

"I was a little worried about you... both," Eric said. He crouched down and rested a palm on Jess's ankle. "Long night?" he asked, looking directly into Jess's eyes.

"I..." Jess couldn't explain.

"Too many long nights, I think," Elena said. "I think you need a night off." She brushed the long wisps of hair escaping out of Jess's braid from her face. "We'll go out, do something special, the three of us."

Eric reached out and pulled both Jess and Elena to their feet. "We're all out right now," he said.

"She's feeling lonely," Elena explained.

"Ah, dense male here. Gotcha." He nuzzled Jess's throat. Elena pressed against Jess's back, the three of them making something of a sandwich, with Jess in the middle. Eric kissed Jess and brushed her nose with his; it was something he rarely did, but the gesture immediately made Jess feel lighter. "Tonight's kind of gone, but do you trust me?"

Elena cupped Jess's hand against Eric's chest. Jess looked to her and saw her nod. "Yeah," she answered him, thinking back to the time he had first approached her to join him and Elena after clubbing. His charm was irresistible.

"Then clean up here. Are you off work tomorrow?" He looked thoughtful when she nodded. "Okay. Let's go home. When the sun goes down tomorrow, we will put these fears of yours to rest, Jess." He wrapped his arm around her back and kissed her temple. She closed her eyes and let her body rest briefly against his.

CHAPTER TWENTY-ONE

STEPPING INTO the 1920s-modeled supper club, Jess unbuttoned the long coat she had borrowed from Elena and smoothed her also borrowed lavender cocktail-length dress. The brunette had been so happy to throw open her wardrobe for Jess to dress for the trio's date that Jess had felt like it was Christmas morning not only for her, but Elena as well. Her long hair was pinned back to one side with a matching wide clip.

They all checked their coats, and Eric put the claim slips in his briar-green suit's inside breast pocket. Elena put her hand on Jess's upper arm and slid her other arm around Jess's elbow. Eric took Jess's other side, his arm encircling her back, hand skimming her ass before settling on her hip. She looked up at him; he lowered his face to hers and tickled her lips with his mustache, which he knew she loved.

"Hungry?" he asked.

"She's always hungry," Elena said, lips against Jess's throat as she spoke. Jess heard the light laughter in the other woman's voice. When Elena eased back, Jess turned to see brown eyes twinkling at her. Hunger did indeed pull at her belly, though not exactly for food.

The maître d' spoke with Eric and was told of their reservation. "Right this way, *mes amis*," he said. "We have arranged dining for you in the loft this evening."

Jess looked up at the words, seeing a second level that looked remarkably like theater boxes—balconies hidden by rich drapery—just before they were led up a narrow staircase. The dining alcoves were private, yet each faced a narrow corridor. Cream-colored upholstered benches encircled oval tables set with crystal and linen cloths. Jess received nods from couples at various stages in their dining.

"Here we are," the maître d' said, finally stopping before an empty table. He plucked the reservation card from the front and pocketed it in his dark suit. "May I suggest an aperitif?"

Eric looked to Jess and Elena, taking their nods as permission. "Three Brandy Alexanders."

"Very good, sir." The maître d' dipped his head and withdrew. Jess and Elena slid into the seating, Eric going to the other end so that Jess was in the center, with him and Elena on either side. She found the long draping tablecloth shortened on this side, so that their legs fit unencumbered beneath, and side by side.

Eric tapped his finger on the tabletop. "They turn the tables and open the balconies when there's a show on the stage. This is a converted theater."

"I'm beginning to see that," Jess said, steepling her hands and looking around at their surroundings. "The place is gorgeous."

Elena pressed against her left side, a hand drifting into the hair at her nape and the other settling warmly on Jess's exposed thigh. Warm breath hummed in her ear as she said, "So are you." Jess closed her eyes and absorbed the sensation of soft lips brushing the taut tendon behind her jaw.

Eric leaned in, his mustache tickling the other side of Jess's throat. His breath was warm, and his words teasing as he admonished Elena. "I think we ought to let the woman eat before we ravish her. She'll need her strength." His hand met Elena's on Jess's lap, and both of them slid their fingers under the edge of her dress, the heat from their touches to the inside of her thighs nearly immolating her with desire on the spot.

Jess exhaled, shakily reached out a hand in each direction, and cupped a cheek as Eric and Elena both pressed their lips firmly to her throat. They hadn't even reached the appetizers and Jess was ready to be done with dinner and move on to the next course, which she hoped sincerely involved getting skin to skin and thoroughly sweaty with both Elena and Eric. "So, what's on tap for the evening?" Her voice, unsurprisingly, was breathless.

"Dining, dancing," Eric began. He grinned at Jess. Elena's hand drifted up his chest, grasping his tie, loosening it a little.

"And more dining," Elena added into Jess's ear with a voice draped with delight and conspiracy.

Jess opened her eyes to find a waiter setting down three long-stemmed wide bowl glasses, moving one at a time in front of Elena, then herself, and finally Eric. She lifted the glass, studying the contents critically as Elena nuzzled her throat. She sniffed, catching the mix of nutmeg and creme de cacao just under the rich tones of a top-shelf brandy. She nodded to the waiter and he withdrew. Taking a sip, she turned to Eric. "I approve."

He laughed and kissed her, his tongue tasting the light froth dusting her lips. "Only one I've had better was mixed by you," he said as their lips parted.

She smiled and sipped again. Elena cupped her chin and drew her face around to kiss and taste the drink on her mouth. "Mmmm," Elena hummed. "Perfect mix."

Jess nuzzled Elena's cheek as the woman pulled away, and watched as she sipped on her cocktail. Soft foam gathered on her upper lip, and Jess leaned in when the glass moved away. This kiss was sweet, succulent. Eric's hand came up to her mid back, thumb moving in gentle circles. Elena sucked on Jess's tongue, making desire pool suddenly in Jess's belly. She felt the heat in her cheeks as she eased back, pressing into Eric's chest. He held her hips, his fingers across her belly making her tingle, at the same time Elena's hand once again found her thigh.

Elena's eyes were dark pools of desire as they found Jess's through the dim lighting. "Makes me think about chocolate sundaes."

"Sounds like dessert has been planned," Eric said meaningfully. "Dinner thoughts?"

Jess sat forward, hands braced on the seatback and Eric's pants-clad thigh. "What's on the menu?"

Another voice spoke up. "Tonight's dish is a choice between pineapple-glazed grilled chicken or red-wine beef tips." Looking up, Jess found their waiter patiently standing before the table, hands behind his back. "Which would you prefer?"

Eric kissed Jess's temple, and answered, "I'll have the beef tips."

Elena and Jess chose the pineapple-glazed chicken. The waiter withdrew. Jess puzzled aloud, "The waitstaff seems unfazed."

Eric said, "This is rumored to have been popular with the

Miami mob for a long time. Discretion became their business."

"Mobsters? And it's now a dinner club?"

"Among other things," Elena said. "Basically a no-judgment zone."

Jess nodded and lifted her drink to her lips. Feeling Elena's hand moving softly on one thigh and Eric's resting on the other, Jess absorbed the ambience she couldn't see but could hear beyond their booth. Instrumental music created a soft background, along with the sounds of china, silverware, and glasses clinking in the hands of neighboring diners.

She had never experienced anything as ritzy as this place. When she had been with Craig they'd never been able to afford it. After jail, she'd kept to simple sustenance. She looked left and then right, at Eric and then Elena, thinking how much they had opened her eyes to possibilities. On the streets, learning to survive since she was sixteen, Jess thought she had life figured out. At least the part that it was always going to be a struggle, always going to be trying to kick a person like her in the teeth. But Eric and Elena had come from difficult upbringings, too, and yet here they were in some of the most sumptuous surroundings Jess had ever seen. Totally being themselves, and being accepted for themselves.

"Thank you," she said. A hand squeezed on each leg, acknowledging her words.

The food when it arrived was delicious, leaving a warm satisfaction in Jess's stomach, neither too much nor too little food. At one point she had commented on the aromas coming from Eric's beef tips and he'd presented her with a bite. Offering him a taste of hers was a natural reply. He kissed her afterward. She turned to offer Elena a bite as well. Since they had the same entree the gesture was unmistakable: share and share alike.

Elena smiled into the bite and then lingered into the kiss, leaving Jess chuckling. "Trying to outdo Eric?" she said.

"Friendly competition," Elena replied, pressing in for another quick taste of Jess's lips.

Jess looked down to see her meal was finished. She sipped at the accompanying wine, a dry white, clearing her palate and considering the evening already a success.

"It's not over," Eric said. "We're both going to take you on the dance floor next."

Jess smiled and felt a quickening pulse at the double entendre, which she was sure now was completely intentional.

"There's a space set aside up here," Eric said. "Very private."

Elena dipped her hand between Jess's legs under the table. "However, if you would prefer, we can stay right here for privacy."

They'd had sex in front of other people before, but this was seriously more public than an orgy at a private home.

"Dancing is first." Jess sipped the last of her wine and dabbed at her mouth with her napkin.

"You've got the keys for where and how fast we go tonight, Jess," Elena promised.

Eric slid out from the table and held out his hand. When Jess took it, he guided her to her feet. While she adjusted her dress, he pulled Elena up, and Jess watched as the brunette molded her body to Eric's and the couple briefly lost themselves in kisses that visibly weakened Elena's knees, and vicariously pooled arousal in Jess's belly once more.

Eric's voice was roughened by his own need when he spoke. "So. Ladies, shall we?" He held his elbows out toward each of them.

The waiter just outside their alcove exchanged nods with Eric and moved toward the top of the stairs, while Eric led Elena and Jess in the other direction. They found a heavily draped archway. Beyond, Jess could hear music and the swish and stomp of shoes. Eric held aside the drape, guiding both women forward through a door he keyed open. "Here we are," he said.

The space was heavily draped, naturally sound dampening. The dance space was roomy, and Jess noticed only half a dozen other people present. Four moved on the dance floor in various configurations, partnering and unpartnering to the beats of the music.

Small, low couches lined the wall, spaced by small tables with single drawers. On one of the couches sat two people, a Latino man with silver hair and dressed in a pinstriped suit, and a woman sat on his lap, her back against his front. His hands held across her chest as she rocked with her head thrown back. Her feet, arched high in four-inch heels, tapped on the floorboards. Jess recognized the rear-entry positioning and smiled at the open display.

The current song ended, and Jess looked around in the brief silence to see Eric straightening up from the digital jukebox. He waved Jess to the center of the room where he put his arm around both her and Elena just as the music started.

Jess smiled as the upbeat dance tune began. She stepped into the beat, turning and twisting. Soon she was laughing with abandon. Rolling her hands over each other, she slid back on her heels and tossed her hips. Eric turned to face both her and Elena, and Jess angled so that they were three points on a triangle. Elena's face was high with color and, by the third song, bore a shine of perspiration.

The three moved to the center of their little triangle, dancing in close, foreheads resting together as they moved their feet, and looking from one to another's eyes. Jess aimed a kiss for Elena's lips, only for it to land on the woman's nose. She laughed and started to back up.

"Get back here." Elena wrapped up Jess in her arms and kissed her back properly as Jess felt Eric swivel his hips into her rear.

Jess rolled her hips into Eric's hands and spun Elena around, pulling the woman's hips back into hers, coaxing the hips to grind into her pelvis. The trio danced forward in a train, laughing as they moved to the closing beats of the tune.

Holding Jess's gaze over her shoulder, Elena ground her rear meaningfully into Jess's pelvis. "Eric gets his turn first," she murmured. "Then I want to make love with you." Elena punctuated her statement with a hand under Jess's chin and pulled their mouths together for a determined kiss.

Elena slipped away from Jess's hands trying to hold on to the lithe body. Jess watched her settle demurely on a couch, ankles linked and knees together to the left.

Jess turned into Eric's arms as the new song started. He lifted one of her hands to his chest and his other held her hips. Resting his head against the side of hers, he murmured the lyrics into her ear, and she more than willingly softened into his hold. His hand moved warmly up and down her back before cupping her rear. She wiggled her ass, inviting more of his touch. His hand left hers on his chest, only to stroke that one down and pull her body into his hardening erection. Her response was to grind forward into it.

His fingers moved under her dress, between her thighs, and beneath her underwear. She felt the tip of one slide in her wetness, and nuzzled into his chest as the broad finger inched inside. Her center twitched around the digit, and Eric lifted her with both his hands under her ass. His strength made her feel protected and cherished as he held her and spun her. They kissed, mouths lingering together, and she enjoyed the soft brush of his mustache against her nose.

Her knees settled to either side of his thighs as he lowered them to a couch. She ground into the tent of his erection. She unzipped his trousers and separated the panel of his underwear. She fished a condom from the pocket where he always kept them and rolled it over tip to base. Setting down onto his cock in this tight position made her feel full instantly. Every tiny twitch magnified the sensations. She closed her eyes, rocking her hips and cupping her arms around his neck. She opened her eyes at a touch to her back and found Elena sitting beside Eric. The look on the woman's face was enthralled, tender and loving. Jess pressed into the palm Elena cupped to her cheek, and then turned and kissed the fingers as she rode Eric's cock.

Jess's heart thumped to the beat of the music and her center pulled at Eric's cock. The combined actions finally pushed her over into a gentle release. He kissed her throat while her mind drifted.

She still felt energized beneath the calm, and signaled this to Elena by pulling the woman's face up to hers and deeply claiming her mouth, pushing her tongue past lips opening more than willingly.

"Next dance is mine," Elena affirmed, nibbling back at Jess's lips. Jess followed Elena upward when the woman made to move off the couch. Their palms slid together, each pulling back on the other, bringing them both upright in the middle of the floor. Jess glanced toward Eric, seeing him adjust himself discreetly and signal to a passing waiter. After a moment's consultation, the waiter scurried to the jukebox and entered something. Turning back to Elena, Jess cupped the woman's face in her hands. Then she knew what Eric had done as the first notes of the song began: "I Can See Clearly Now."

Elena pulled Jess into her and the two began swaying to the music.

Feeling clear and settled, Jess lifted Elena's head, tracing her fingertips under the woman's jaw, looking deeply into the brown gazing lovingly back. When they kissed, tongues caressing, Elena's hands cupped Jess's face, fingers sliding into her hair. The motions of Elena's fingers sent sensual shivers into Jess's groin, and she moaned softly into their next kiss. Elena now held control. As the song's final notes faded, Elena stroked down Jess's front, separating their bodies until she pushed squarely on the woman's shoulders, setting her off-balance and backward onto a couch. Elena quickly straddled Jess, grinding down on her as Jess settled hands on the writing woman's hips. Their kisses grew in intensity until Elena pulled herself away, pressing a lingering finger to the lips in parting. "Such sweetness," the brunette murmured. "But you have something even sweeter awaiting, don't you?"

Grinding down so Jess could make no mistake what she meant, Elena gradually moved down Jess's front, palming and pressing breasts and nipples before pulling at one through the fabric of her dress. Jess's hands helplessly went into Elena's hair, the fine strands tickling her fingertips. Her forearms were suddenly resting on her own thighs. Elena had lowered herself completely to the floor between Jess's knees. She looked around to see Eric standing at the jukebox with what looked like a glass of ice water. Otherwise the room had been emptied. Roberta Flack's "First Time Ever I Saw Your Face" started playing. Jess held Elena's gaze as the woman broke into a slow, devilish smile, and her fingertips began circling on Jess's ankles in time to the music.

Jess's head rolled back as those same satin fingertips traced their way up the inside of her legs to her thighs, disappearing beneath the hem of her dress. She felt the tip of a warm, wet tongue following the path of fingers and hummed appreciatively as she stroked Elena's hair, then murmured, "Elena, yes," over and over to let the woman know her attention was eagerly desired. At the first touch of that pushy little muscle between her labia, Jess felt her entire lower body convulse toward a single point. She gasped and clutched at Elena's hair, causing the other woman to pull back. "Sorry," Jess gasped.

Elena chuckled and, in truth, undeterred, returned her lips and tongue to Jess's center, the minor irritation of her cotton underpants being bunched aside quickly forgotten in the rush of pleasure. Elena's gifted touch ratcheted Jess's passion higher and higher until she couldn't contain the pleasure and it pulsed and flowed through her. Elena sucked and licked until Jess could only twitch and murmur to let her up.

Rising and helping Jess smooth her dress, Elena then cupped Jess's cheek, her thumb brushing away tears drying on Jess's skin. Kissing Jess sweetly, Elena settled onto Jess's lap, placing Jess's hand between her thighs. She whimpered when Jess's fingers found her, warm, wet, and welcoming. "Jess."

Elena's clit was hard and tender to the touch, making Elena gasp at the slightest provocation. It was obvious to Jess that Elena had spent most of the evening aroused, simply because of spending their time together. Jess kissed her, swallowing Elena's breathy pants as she slid two fingers past the rigid nerves and curled inside, feeling Elena's walls throb and soften, pulling her in deeper. She twisted her fingers and Elena clutched at her neck, rocking her hips, and found release quickly.

She kissed Elena's forehead, then felt a big hand on her shoulder before Eric's lips pressed to her forehead and he settled to the cushion next to her.

"Thank you," she said, brushing her fingers through the sweat-dampened ends of Elena's hair.

"You're welcome," Eric said, and his fingers brushed through her hair as he kissed her temple again.

Elena smiled at them both, brushing first Eric's cheek then Jess's. "You've become part of us," she said. "Eric and I talked it over. We want you to move in."

Lara Zielinsky is a bisexual married woman and a mom living in Florida with her family. She's been writing since she could hold a pencil. She grew up reading since books were always around when friends weren't plentiful. When these stories weren't reflecting the things she thought about, she started writing her own. Her criteria for a good story idea is one that has not done already.

"We Three" is Lara's third published novel. Find links to her other books at

supposedcrimes.com/collections/types?q=Lara%20Zielinsky

To connect socially, you'll find Lara's author pages on Amazon, Goodreads, and Facebook. Tweet to her at twitter.com/lczielinsky. Follow her blog at

larazielinsky.blogspot.com.

Turning Point

It's Hollywood. Actresses hate getting passed over for roles and cold shoulders are common. Petty sniping is part of the fabric of the place, but it takes two to fight. Actress Cassidy Hyland is throwing a birthday party for her son which she hopes will spark a truce with her cold co-star Brenna Lanigan. Instead the encounter becomes the first step of a journey neither woman ever imagined her heart could take: to love another woman. *Turning Point* explores the struggle of these women caught between what is safe and sure, and what the heart truly wants even if it doesn't understand.

Brenna is "just over the hill" by Hollywood standards. She's 41, with two teenage sons, and a second husband back in her Midwest hometown. She has spent from age 18 onward working in theaters, movies, and television, living out roles that other people write.

Cassidy is relatively new to the industry. At 32, she came to California after majoring in Literature and Drama in college. She did a little modeling, got small parts, had a child, and escaped her abusive marriage when she landed on "Time Trails."

2007 Winner Lesbian Fiction Reader's Choice Awards:
Favorite Lesbian Romance Book

2008 Golden Crown Literary Society Finalist for Lesbian Debut Author